Rea

Never

"Lain entertains with this romantic reimagining of Peter Pan set in present-day New York City."

—Publishers Weekly

"Another smash from a talented author that leaves you believing in the magic of the world."

—The Novel Approach

Knight of Ocean Avenue

"Billy and Shaz make a phenomenal couple, always building each other up and having fun together, even when facing brutally difficult circumstances. They really make it work!"

—RT Book Reviews

"This story was an absolutely enchanting journey.... I can HIGHLY RECOMMEND Knight of Ocean Avenue."

—Gay Book Reviews.

High Balls

"Like all of the books penned by this author, there is a delicious combination of spice and romance, leavened by humor and warm fuzzy moments."

—Night Owl Reviews

"An intriguing storyline, a dose of mystery, and some family-time bonding all makes for a wonderful novel from Tara Lain."

—Top 2 Bottom Reviews

By TARA LAIN

Hearts and Flour
Return of the Chauffeur's Son

ALOYSIUS TALES
Spell Cat
Brush with Catastrophe
Cataclysmic Shift

BALLS TO THE WALL
Volley Balls
Fire Balls
Beach Balls
FAST Balls
High Balls
Snow Balls
Bleu Balls

COWBOYS DON'T
Cowboys Don't Come Out
Cowboys Don't Ride Unicorns

DREAMSPUN BEYOND
#15 – Rome and Jules

DREAMSPUN DESIRES
#5 – Taylor Maid

LONG PASS CHRONICLES
Outing the Quarterback
Canning the Center
Tackling the Tight End

Published by DREAMSPINNER PRESS
www.dreamspinnerpress.com

By Tara Lain (Con't)

LOVE IN LAGUNA
Knight of Ocean Avenue
Knave of Broken Hearts
Prince of the Playhouse
Lord of a Thousand Steps
Fool of Main Beach

MIDDLEMARK MYSTERIES
The Case of the Sexy Shakespearean

PENNYMAKER TALES
Sinders and Ash
Driven Snow
Beauty, Inc.
Never

TALES OF THE HARKER PACK
The Pack or the Panther
Wolf in Gucci Loafers
Winter's Wolf

PRINT ANTHOLOGIES
Balls to the Wall – Volley Balls and Fire Balls
Balls to the Wall – Beach Balls and FAST Balls
The Pack or the Panther & Wolf in Gucci Loafers
Sinders and Ash and Beauty, Inc.

Published by DREAMSPINNER PRESS
www.dreamspinnerpress.com

TARA LAIN

THE CASE OF THE SEXY SHAKESPEAREAN

DREAMSPINNER
PRESS

Published by
DREAMSPINNER PRESS

5032 Capital Circle SW, Suite 2, PMB# 279,
Tallahassee, FL 32305-7886 USA
www.dreamspinnerpress.com

The Case of the Sexy Shakespearean
© 2018 Tara Lain.

Cover Art
© 2018 Kanaxa.
Cover content is for illustrative purposes only and any person depicted
on the cover is a model.

Mass Market Paperback ISBN: 978-1-64108-015-6
Trade Paperback ISBN: 978-1-64080-454-8
Digital ISBN: 978-1-64080-486-9
Library of Congress Control Number: 2017916617
Mass Market Paperback published July 2018
v. 1.0

Printed in the United States of America
∞
This paper meets the requirements of
ANSI/NISO Z39.48-1992 (Permanence of Paper).

To my mom, may she rest in peace, who adored
mysteries, and to KC Burn, who inspired me to want
to write a cozy.

ACKNOWLEDGMENTS

MY THANKS to Lynn and Elizabeth for always looking out for me and the stories I can tell.

CHAPTER ONE

THE MUSIC flowed through him like wine—like freedom—and Ramon threw his head back, letting the swish of hair against his shoulders tickle him as he danced. One of his partners, a big muscular stud with tattoos on his neck, leaned over and kissed Ramon's cheek. Strutting away, Ramon just laughed. *We all love our illusions, and I'm his.*

Not to be outdone, the pretty blonde girl who had also leaped onto the floor to dougie with Ramon shook her pert chest against his back. Bless her heart, she'd misjudged her target, but he gave her a butt bump in return, and she giggled.

The music crashed to an end, and Ramon swept a bow at both partners. They both looked like they'd enjoy a second act of some kind, but he tipped an imaginary hat and walked back to the bar, where that handsome dude with the silver hair had promised to save Ramon's seat. Ramon didn't get out much. Only rarely did he feel comfortable enough to go out and meet the public. He needed all the good reactions he could soak up, like fuel to keep him going until the next time.

Sure enough, there sat Silver Fox at the bar, gazing at him with open admiration while draping a very expensively clad leg over the empty barstool. Ramon gave him a grin. "For me?"

Silver Fox chuckled soft and low. "If not, I've almost lost my leg at the knee three times for nothing." He gracefully removed his appendage, and Ramon slid onto the seat, grabbing the icy craft beer the bartender had left in his absence. He wrinkled his nose. *Yuk, it's yeasty.* He flicked the hair from his eyes with a toss of his head and pushed the glass toward the bear of a bartender. "This is caca, darling. Bring me a glass of champagne instead, please." He turned on his barstool toward the crowd, where a wall of people had formed between him and the dance floor, all of them clapping and whistling like they were watching WWF with oiled fighters.

A young guy with dark, slightly wild eyes separated from the crowd and stepped toward him, staring at the floor. *Kind of cute. Kind of not.* The guy glanced up through heavily mascaraed lashes. "Excuse me. Are you by any chance Ramon Rondell?"

Ramon frowned and looked around warily, then tried to return to pleasant face as fast as possible. "Where did you get that information?"

"Uh, I saw you come in and asked the guy at the door who you were. He said your name was Rondell. I was kind of hoping. I'm a huge fan." He shrugged and extended a napkin and a pen. "May I have your autograph?"

"What if I'm not Ramon?"

The kid grinned. "You're so gorgeous, I don't even care."

Ramon glanced at him. *Caught. What can it hurt?* He laughed and scrawled his name across the flimsy paper.

The guy gazed at the signature like he'd been given an original copy of *Tom Sawyer*. "I'm such an admirer."

"I'm happy to hear it." He started to turn back to his beer.

"Are you going to write a book on the real identity of Jack the Ripper? You can prove it was somebody from the royal family, right?" The guy's voice sounded avid.

Ramon's wacko-dar tingled, and he shook his head. "I doubt it. There's a pretty extensive record of information from the time. Everyone thinks their theory is conclusive, but gathering new data's difficult, if not impossible. I confess I don't believe there's a royal family connection. It's more likely that so-called Jack the Ripper was some poor insane person who hated women and killed five in a row before he died or was incarcerated." He shrugged. "But honestly, no one wants to hear that, so I doubt I'll take on the project." He smiled to soften the blow and made to turn again.

The guy frowned darkly. "You're not gonna prove that those rich bastards used those poor women as guinea pigs? Come on, you're the one who should do it. You can get 'em."

Oh dear. "Yes, well, we all have to draw our own conclusions. Thanks for being a fan and saying hello."

He turned his back on the young man and faced the bar. Sadly, writing about the mysteries of history did tend to attract conspiracy theorists and crazies. It went with the territory.

The bartender delivered the glass of bubbly, and Ramon reached for his wallet. Mr. Silver Fox put a hand on his forearm. "Allow me." He dropped a couple of twenties in front of the bartender.

Ramon raised an eyebrow at the proprietary hand, and the man withdrew it. The guy was great-looking, probably in his early fifties, wearing a lot of money on his body. Still… "You're kind, but I have just enough time to drink my champagne. Then, I fear, I must fly." He took a healthy mouthful. *Much better than the beer.*

The man leaned on his hand and gave Ramon a wistful look. "I can't persuade you to fly to my nest?"

That earned both of Ramon's raised eyebrows. "Even if I were that kind of girl, I have an early day tomorrow."

"How very sad. I haven't seen you in here before, and I'd remember, believe me."

Ramon nodded. "No, you're right. I don't come in often." Mostly because it was a four-hour drive to his real life, but no point admitting that.

"Even sadder. Perhaps I can persuade you to make a return visit soon?" Silver Fox smiled softly. "So I can determine if you *are* that kind of girl." He stuck out a hand. "I'm Martin, by the way."

Ramon shook his hand lightly. "Ramon."

"I gather you're famous. At least with one ardent admirer."

Ramon wrinkled his nose. "Only the tiniest bit. I write articles and have a popular blog."

"I'll look for them. What shall I search?"

"Ramon Rondell." He downed the last of the champagne. "Now I must go." He turned on the stool—and froze. Martin said something, but he didn't quite hear it. The crowd facing the dance floor had parted, and Ramon stared at what they'd all been watching so enthusiastically.

A male couple dancing.

No, actually it was a guy dancing, and maybe there was a partner there somewhere. The young dancer was tall, over six feet by at least a couple of inches of superlean body that moved like he was made of rubber. Except for the ass. Holy crap, the most perfect, taut, iron-hard butt, with those irresistible dips in the side that showed even through his jeans. The only thing more perfect than those buns of steel was the face of magic—all brightness and sparkle, with heavily lashed eyes that crinkled as he laughed, dimples that could have sharpened pencils, and a flush of pink across his adorable cheeks. His blond hair flopped forward and he'd flick it back, making even Ramon's practiced head toss look amateurish. Altogether gorgeous, but more than that. The man had an energy, a charisma that captured and held every eye, and a way of grinning and ducking his head that said *Don't take me too seriously*.

"You like that?"

The voice came from over Ramon's shoulder, and he looked back. "What? Excuse me?"

Martin gazed at the dancer in cool appraisal. "Is that your type? The type you'd be 'that kind of girl' for?"

The question gave Ramon a little shiver. "I was interested in the dance style."

"Right." Martin popped a sardonic half smile. "I'm sure he goes from vertical to horizontal very quickly."

Ramon reached in his pocket, grabbed the first bill he felt, and slapped the fifty on the bar. "I like to dougie. Pay the bartender for me, will you?" He turned on his stacked heel and marched catty-corner behind the dance floor and lines of observers toward the lobby. The weirdo who'd asked for the autograph leaned against the wall in the corner. His eyes met Ramon's and glowered almost—odd to think the word— evilly. But he didn't move. Thank God.

With a quick glance behind to be sure no presumptuous stalkers were following, Ramon slipped out the entrance and broke into a jog toward the back lot where he'd parked his car.

He ducked behind an SUV and peeked at the entrance to the lot. *No one.* Even the attendant seemed to be elsewhere. *Good.* Quickly he ran to the gray Volvo, opened the door from a few feet away, and slid into the driver's seat, then closed the door after him and gazed out through the tinted windows. Moonlight illuminated the lot, but nothing moved.

He let out a long slow breath. *Why the hell did I do this? Martin could so easily have been someone from the university. Or even that crazy conspiracy theorist. What if one of them recognized me?* He needed to retire Ramon from public view, but the idea hurt. Ramon didn't make many appearances and he was always careful to look different when he did, but those few outings were fun, dammit.

With an angry snort, he pulled the floppy-haired dark wig off and then the skullcap he wore under it, tossed them in the tote bag on his seat, and ran his hands through his totally ordinary, short brown hair. *Totally ordinary* described a lot of things. He yanked the vanity mirror down, peeled off the false lashes, fished in the tote for the plastic container and stored them away, and then squeezed out the blue contacts he used to transform his mud-brown eyes. A little lotion removed the lip gloss, mascara, and blush. *Wish I had the guts to just throw all this crap away and forget the cosplay. Ramon can write without making personal appearances.* But the idea of retiring nauseated him. Like giving up on joy.

He toed off the shoes that made him two inches taller. He just wore them for cover because he was already really tall. Then he slid off his tight leather pants, pulled his khakis from the tote, and yanked them on easily, since they bagged around his narrow hips. They felt like home. Sighing, he added the brown Oxfords and a cardigan over his shirt—that would do until he was alone—then piled some books from the well of the passenger seat on top of the paraphernalia he'd stuck in the bag. *Ready.*

He glanced in the mirror again. *Who the hell do you think you are, asshole? Easy answer. A tall, awkward, unattractive nerd, too smart to love.*

Finally he cranked the ignition, and the rumble of the old Volvo's engine vibrated through him like it was rearranging his cells. The gray of the car settled on him like a cloud, and he inhaled reality. His pulse scampered and his eyes jerked from side to side.

A minute later, Dr. Llewellyn Lewis of Middlemark University drove his Volvo out of the parking lot, pausing at the street to carefully observe the on-coming traffic.

The dark outline of a person against the next building caught his eye. *Who could that be?*

In a break between cars, he pressed the acceler-ator and pulled onto the street. Shaking his head, he said, "I-I've h-heard one t-too many conspiracies." *Why would you, of all people, have to jump at shad-ows? Especially this far from home.*

Llewellyn drove sedately onto the freeway, point-ed the car south, and settled in for the long ride to San Luis Obispo and a return to real life. Ramon Rondell could stay gone.

"MORNING, DR. L." Llewellyn's assistant, Maria Conchita Gonzalez, looked up from her com-puter and grinned. "Did you have a wild and crazy weekend?"

The heat started instantly, creeping up Llewellyn's neck and burning his cheeks. God, he hated it. "Uh—"

She bounded out of her desk chair in all her ro-bust glory and planted her hands on her denim-clad hips. "Hang on, boss. Didn't we get past the blushes? Aren't we friends?"

"Y-yes." Like a lot of actors, he could only cover his stutter on the stage. When he wasn't wearing his Ramon skin, the stutter made everything harder and more miserable.

"Come on, you've got no reason to be shy around me." She held up a finger. "*A.* I'm your biggest fan."

Amazingly, that was true. When she applied for her position, she'd demonstrated an almost photo-graphic grasp of all his scholarly works.

"*B*. I couldn't care less if your wild weekend was finding a new kind of food for your cats or hanging naked by your heels from the chandelier. Everyone gets to live as they want as long as they don't hurt anyone else."

"Yo-your opinion does represent a mi-minority view." He smiled, however.

She crossed her arms. "Yeah, well, it shouldn't."

"Besides, I d-don't think my chandelier w-would hold me."

She snorted but gave him an appraising glance. "Come on, you're lean as a fashion model." She circled back to her desk chair, then looked up through her lashes like some busty Hispanic elf. "If you decide on that chandelier trick, invite me. I suspect there are hidden treasures under those plain-Jane khakis."

He blushed again, but this time she just laughed. "By the way, the big boss wants to see you." She made quotes in the air. "As soon as you get in."

"W-what does he want?"

"Probably to waste your time on political bullshit, but he didn't consult me."

He started to turn toward the door, and she said, "Dr. L., why don't you put your stuff down first?" She nodded at his old beat-up briefcase and the cardigan sweater he carried even though the fall weather was hot. *It could change.* "Get comfortable. He'll still be there, fussing and fuming. A couple minutes won't matter."

He nodded and walked into his small, dark office. Maria complained that her assistant's desk was in a lighter, brighter spot than his desk, but he didn't really mind. Dark could be comforting. As he'd managed to discard more and more of his teaching duties in favor of his research and publishing, this dark cave had become his sanctuary. Read more. Talk less. He set the briefcase beside the desk and pulled his laptop from it. His baby. Carefully, he placed it on his battered desk and plugged it in, then walked quickly back out the door. "K-keep an eye—"

"No worries, boss. I got this." She grinned, and he returned it. What a great find she was—efficient, brilliant, talented, and so blatantly on his side it was almost embarrassing. Almost. He seldom thought to do anything for himself—well, not counting Ramon—but he'd hired Maria as a rebellious act of self-expression.

"S-s-see—"

She just flashed her dimples, an expression that said *I'll sit here and listen to whatever you have to say no matter how long it takes, and I'm always three steps ahead.*

He smiled and double-timed out the door. If he had to talk slowly, at least he could walk fast.

Skirting through the long dark halls of the old building, he passed several colleagues. This floor housed mostly professors' offices and some of their staff, no classrooms. Professor Dingleton, the only man on earth who could make French history boring and unromantic according to Maria, nodded officiously. "Lewis."

Llewellyn nodded back and kept walking. Around the corner lay "Mahogany Row," the sought-after offices of the department's crème de la crème. Llewellyn could have claimed one of those spaces by right of his research credentials, but all that exposure made him itch.

He stepped two offices down and tapped on the door of Professor Abraham "Don't call me Abe" Van Pelt, head of the history department.

"Come." Professor Van Pelt had definitely learned that response in a movie.

Llewellyn opened the door. "S-sir."

"Come in, Dr. Lewis." He gestured to one of the aggressively masculine leather chairs in front of his desk. Professor Van Pelt's accoutrements—the chairs that matched the leather patches on his jacket elbows, the pipe he never lit, the wainscoting and wooden ducks that hadn't been used in decorating since 1850—spoke more of who the good doctor would like to be than who the short, portly, balding man actually was.

Llewellyn sat. It made him secretly smile that Dr. Van Pelt jacked up his chair until the edge of the desk must have cut into his thighs and sat his guests in very low seats, making their heights closer to equal. Of course, it was hard to offset Llewellyn's gangly six-foot-one frame. He didn't speak. His stutter made Van Pelt nervous.

"Uh, Dr. Lewis, uh, Llewellyn, this coming Thursday, I and some of the other members of the history and English departments will be wining and dining several potential benefactors of our programs. These are wealthy patrons interested in supporting our research. I don't have to tell you how important these patrons are. It's so unusual to find people who want to fund something besides medical research or finding UFOs." He laughed, though it sounded strained. "Uh, I'd like you to join us."

"W-what?" Llewellyn rose half out of his seat, then flopped back when the professor's eyes widened in alarm. Van Pelt knew better. Llewellyn could manage classes when he had to, staff meetings occasionally, but fund-raising dinners? Dear God, the thought made him ill.

Van Pelt held up a placating hand. "I know. I know. But one of the potential donors is a huge fan of your work and will only attend if you'll be there. As you can imagine, we don't want to, uh, trouble you with this, but we must ask. In fact, I strongly request that you make yourself available on Thursday night."

The shaking had already started in his belly. He sucked in his gut to try to control it. "N-no. Not w-wise."

Professor Van Pelt sighed loudly. "Jesus, Llewellyn, don't you think I know that? I've had to hire two extra teaching assistants just to handle your damned classes, but this woman is important, and she absolutely insists she won't attend unless you're there and will speak to no one else. For the good of the department, I have to insist." He stood, which clearly showed how upset he was since it showed off his barely five-foot-four height. "I'm sorry, but that's final."

Llewellyn rose, not meeting the professor's eyes, and walked to the office door.

"I'll email you the necessary information."

Llewellyn just kept walking all the way to the side door to the building. Taking deep inhales, he exited to the small porch and leaned over the railing, trying to catch his breath. It wasn't just the stutter that made him a social mess. He'd entered college in his early teens, too smart and too awkward to make many friends. From there his studies kept him company, and people drifted further away in his awareness. Holding the world at bay meant he didn't have to care so much what anyone thought. *Damn, wish it worked better.*

He heard voices and looked up to see three men walking by on the sidewalk beside the building, all staring at him. One professor of English tittered behind his hand, a second teacher looked appalled, and the third man—the one with the unreadable expression—was the man who'd been dancing his perfect ass off the night before, one hundred and eighty-five miles away.

CHAPTER TWO

"Hey, boss, you look like somebody set your tail on fire. Is everything okay?"

"N-no." Llewellyn leaned against the wall beside the door and tried to breathe. *How can he be here? How? Dear God, will he recognize me? No, no, of course not. He didn't even see me, and that was Ramon. We really don't look alike. People see what they expect.* He kept trying to get air into his lungs.

"What's wrong, sir? Can I help? You're scaring me."

He looked at Maria. Holy God, seeing that guy had freaked him so totally, he'd forgotten all about his actual problem. "Uh, I-I have to g-go to a party." He swallowed hard and pressed a hand to his mouth.

She bounded out of her chair and grasped his arm. "Come on, let's make you some tea." She guided him toward the battered couch by the wall and pressed him down onto it. "Hang." It only took her seconds at the coffee and tea bar she'd set up in the corner to return with a steaming cup of English Breakfast tea laced with milk and a dash of vanilla. Just the smell relaxed him. "Th-thanks."

She sat in the chair opposite the couch with a cup of her favorite coffee that filled the air with the rich scent of caramel. "So shoot. Who's doing this to you?"

"D-don't want to th-think about it."

"Okay, but maybe I can help."

"S-some woman."

She made that great snorting sound again. "Can't you just explain she's barking up the wrong tree?"

"N-not like that." He laughed. "M-money."

"Whoa. I didn't think you were that kind of guy, doctor."

For a second, the previous night flooded back—seeing the gorgeous young dancer, being asked if that's what it took for him to be that kind of girl. He sucked in air. "She's a d-donor. She wants to give m-money for research."

"Hey, that's great from a financial perspective, but can't you just meet her here in this office, like one-on-one? I can serve her tea and shit."

Wow. Could that work? "I d-don't know."

"How about I go ask Dr. Van Pelt?"

He nodded and smiled.

"Be right back." She turned, stopped, walked over and grabbed the teapot, poured him a full cup, then set it back on the warmer. "No worries, boss. We got this," she said as she ran out the door.

Oh man, from her lips to Van Pelt's ears. He sipped his tea. Okay, second problem. Why was that guy from the club in San Jose walking by his building? The men he was with were both in the English department. Could it really be just a coincidence? But damn, there were plenty of gay and gay-friendly clubs and bars in San Luis Obispo. People who drove hours just to go to a club had something to hide—he ought to know. He took a deep breath. *I'll probably never see the guy again.* That made him a little sad, which was stupid, but something about the gorgeous stranger made Llewellyn's nerves tingle—in a good way for once.

Taking his tea, Llewellyn walked back to his desk and settled in for a few hours of total immersion. Research. God, he adored it. While some scholars considered him a dilettante since he jumped from project to project, he loved delving into the archeological and historical mysteries of the ages and revealing new thinking in each. His current fascination was the real fate of Edward V of England and Richard of Shrewsbury, the famed princes in the Tower. Did the much-maligned Richard III really murder them? Funny how he felt kind of sorry for Richard who, recent DNA research suggested, might have come from a male line illegitimate to the throne. Llewellyn knew about illegitimacy and being an outsider. Of course, the princes might deserve more of his sympathy.

He went back to his search engine to look for more obscure comments and references on the case. Even when they were wacko, those kinds of comments could lead to interesting sources. The so-called fan from the previous night flashed in his mind. *Maybe I should pay more attention to his theories. Nah.* Leaning forward, he stared at the screen. The word *Rondell* caught his eyes. He took a breath and clicked immediately.

Well, hell, his least favorite so-called journalist.

Octavia Otto—probably a pen name—was the owner and sometime investigative journalist for the online news source the *Daily Phoenix*. While her news outlet was generally well regarded, the blog had a Digging for Dirt section readers loved. That segment sold more subscriptions to the *Phoenix* than all the other sections combined. One of Octavia's favorite topics? *Who is Ramon Rondell really?*

That day's tidbit was that no two pictures of the elusive Rondell ever seemed to show the same person and asked what Rondell had to hide. *Damn.*

"Uh, boss?"

One glance up at Maria and he cringed even more.

She shook her head. "I'm so sorry. I tried, but Van Pelt says they want this rich woman to attend the dinner, not just meet with you. Something about giving everyone a crack at her." She walked in and sat on his rickety guest chair, which he didn't remove because something more comfortable might encourage guests. "I even asked him if I could come with you, but he said no. Reservations and all that. I'm not senior enough. Damn, boss, I tried. This is so shitty."

Hard to describe the level of shittiness—especially since he'd take a half hour to get the word out. "Thanks. Th-thanks for trying."

She leaned forward. "I don't want to sound like some freaking self-help guru, but you can do this. Hell, you're smarter than any of them, more successful, and I'll even bet you look better in your underwear."

He barked out a laugh.

She grinned. "You know how they tell public speakers to picture their audience members in their underwear?"

"I-I got it." He sighed. "So, wh-who is this w-w-woman?"

"Her name's Anne de Vere."

He shrugged. Still, it was an interesting historical name. He forced his eyes back to his screen, but all the fun had leached from the interviews with scholars investigating the recently uncovered body that was almost certainly Richard III.

Maria rose and left his office, casting one sympathetic look over her shoulder as she departed. He wiped a hand across his face and let his forehead fall to the desk. Nothing was interesting enough to make him want to have dinner with ten people.

Is it better to be late or early? Thursday night, Llewellyn paced a block away from the Faculty Club, as he'd been doing for the previous fifteen minutes, unable to force himself to walk in. *Coward!*

Based on his observation, if he walked in right now, he'd be among the first to arrive, which meant chitchat and horrible social interaction, which he hated. If he waited, he could miss some of that but would have to enter to the stares and judgment of all the people present, while trying to keep from making a fool of himself in front of everyone. There was no good time to walk into that room.

Voices from the next block made him look up. Van Pelt walked beside his wretched teaching assistant, Harley Grove, a weaselly young man better at politics than history and, apparently, a truly boring teacher. Why Van Pelt loved him and yet refused to let Llewellyn promote Maria from research assistant to teaching assistant, he wasn't sure. That was a lie. Van Pelt was inherently suspicious of women and more so if they didn't have blonde ringlets.

On Van Pelt's other side was an attractive, auburn-haired woman Llewellyn had never seen before. The mysterious donor? Van Pelt spoke animatedly, but she barely looked up. Something about her suggested she didn't suffer fools gladly. That was either good or bad for him, but probably now was the time to find out. When she discovered the giant *L* on his forehead, he just might get to leave early.

With as close to resolve as he got in such situations, he walked into the Faculty Club.

A tall, thin maître d' smiled. "Can I help you, sir?"

"V-Van Pelt." Llewellyn pointed toward the disappearing backs of Van Pelt and his companions.

"Oh yes. Very good. I'll have the waiter take you to the table as soon as he returns." He looked back at his reservation list, dismissing Llewellyn, which was damned fine with him. He walked over to the darkest corner and waited.

The door opened and two professors from the English department walked in. The short, gray-haired one—Murphy might have been his name—was one of those he'd seen on the sidewalk with the gorgeous guy. He longed to ask who Beautiful Butt was, but he wouldn't have even if he could have gotten out the words.

The two men spoke to the maître d', who pointed to Llewellyn—who froze.

They turned, and the one who'd seen him gasping for air looked halfway between amused and appalled. The other man, younger, taller, and very pleasant-looking, smiled and stuck out his hand. "Hi. You're Dr. Lewis, aren't you?"

Llewellyn nodded and gave the man's hand a pump.

"I'm George Stanley. I'm the English lit guy."

Llewellyn swallowed. Where was that damned waiter? "P-pleased to m-meet you."

Stanley's smile never wavered. The other man wasn't so cool. He stared at his own shoes, then stuck out a hand like he was undertaking a heinous act. "Murphy. World lit."

Llewellyn nodded and shook. "His-history."

"Oh, of course we know who you are, Dr. Lewis. Honored." Stanley gave him such a warm grin, it killed a butterfly or two.

"Gentlemen, Horace will take you to your table now." The maître d' handed menus to a gray-haired waiter, and Llewellyn and the other two men fell in behind him. All the way to the table in a smallish private dining room, he kept breathing deeply, like he was getting ready to go underwater. *Yeah, drown.*

Van Pelt was seated next to Harley on one side and the red-haired woman on the other. She looked up expectantly. Though two other professors, Shaklee Morse and Ty Anderson, sat on the woman's other side, a chair had been left conspicuously open beside her.

Van Pelt half rose. "Dr. Lewis, please sit here. Anne de Vere, may I present Dr. Llewellyn Lewis, our renowned researcher."

She smiled warmly—she really was quite pretty—and extended her hand. When he took it, she covered his hand with her other one. "I'm so excited to meet you, Dr. Lewis." Her eyes had a very manic sparkle.

"L-Llewellyn."

For a second she looked startled, then nodded with a still-pleasant expression.

He sat, but his whole body felt cold. Like most people who knew him only from reputation, Anne de Vere was likely expecting Indiana Jones, not Elmer Fudd. *Dear God, is there any way to leave? Very tempting.*

Van Pelt cleared his throat. "Uh, Dr. Lewis, I'd also like you to meet Mr. and Mrs. Alonzo Echevarria, who are valued supporters of the university." He pointed to an unlikely looking couple seated across from Llewellyn—a pudgy, florid man of perhaps sixty and an opulently endowed, substantially younger, dark-haired woman.

Llewellyn nodded and shook Mr. Echevarria's hand, a slightly aggressive experience, but didn't try to speak. His wife, who gazed at Llewellyn like she was guessing his weight, didn't offer a hand. Hers was busy with her martini glass.

Anne de Vere leaned toward him. "Dr. Lewis, I'm very anxious to speak to you—"

Some rustling, footsteps, and voices made them all look up. *Heart-stop city, as Maria would say.*

CHAPTER THREE

THE OTHER English professor Llewellyn had seen on the sidewalk outside his building came into the private dining room, followed by the gorgeous dancer from the club in San Jose. Llewellyn sucked a breath—and he wasn't the only one. Next to him, Anne de Vere made a funny little gasping sound, and Mrs. Echevarria practically threw herself across the table; the guy was just that beautiful. Llewellyn might follow suit—or might run out the door. Choices. *Who are you, beautiful boy, and what are you doing here?* He called the guy a boy, but he was probably only a few years younger than Llewellyn's twenty-seven. Prodigies being what they were, Llewellyn had completed his PhD at twenty and had been compiling published research ever since.

The English professor and the beautiful guy were both laughing, and the prof had to pull himself together to address the group, all of whom stared with degrees of avid interest. "So sorry to be late. Had trouble parking." He raised a hand. "Hi, everyone. I'm Justin Rhule, and this is my new graduate assistant, Blaise Arthur."

Llewellyn's head came up. "B-Blaise? Arthur?"

The man's eye connected with Llewellyn's—brilliant blue and more than warm. He grinned. "I should know that wouldn't get past you, Dr. Lewis. My parents have a sense of humor."

Llewellyn's stomach lurched. *He knows who I am?*

George Stanley laughed. "Of course, I'm embarrassed that a mere historical genius had to think of it first."

Llewellyn smiled. Stanley did have a lovely way about him.

Echevarria popped a small crease between his brows. "I'm afraid I don't understand the joke."

"You're not alone." Van Pelt raised a judgmental brow. "Share, please."

Blaise Arthur said, "Forgive us for being obscure. Blaise was a figure in Arthurian legend. Some say he was the teacher of Merlin, and others that he was the chronicler of the Arthurian tales as recounted by Merlin. Nonetheless, my parents couldn't resist naming their Arthur baby Blaise."

Anne de Vere clapped her hands. "Charming." She looked around the table. The only empty chair stood at the end of the long rectangle. "Please, come and sit here, Mr. Arthur." She actually stood and pulled an extra chair from near the wall over to the table and proceeded to scoot her own chair closer to Llewellyn, then slid the extra seat between herself and Van Pelt.

Van Pelt looked startled, Dr. Rhule gaped, and Mrs. Echevarria appeared to be contemplating murder.

Blaise smiled directly at Anne and walked around the table with the same poetic grace he'd shown on the dance floor. Without a single demur, he gave her a small bow. "Thank you so much." His eyes flicked up to Llewellyn's—setting off an electric spark in Llewellyn's belly—and he sat in the offered chair.

Van Pelt cleared his throat. "So you're new to the English department, Mr. Arthur?"

"Yes, sir. I just came south from my home near Palo Alto in response to the offer of the teaching assistantship."

"And where did you do your undergraduate studies?"

"Stanford, sir."

Van Pelt's eyebrow rose. Both the prestige—and the cost—of the university should have garnered some appreciation from him.

Dr. Rhule leaned in from his far distant seat. "Blaise's uncle is a Middlemark alumnus, so we were very anxious to have him—along with his academic accomplishments, of course."

Blaise shrugged charmingly. "I'm afraid my academic status pales at this table."

The waiters arrived, suppressing conversation, although Llewellyn would happily have watched Blaise's lips as he spoke for many hours. Stupid, yes, but at least he now understood that Blaise being in a bar in San Jose made sense without any nefarious or threatening motives. The bar would have been on his way from Palo Alto to San Luis—more or less. Being gay would have been inspiration enough for a small detour. Of course, his being gay was the most interesting part.

Anne angled toward Llewellyn, holding her menu. "What's good here, Llewellyn?"

"I-I don't—" He swallowed. "—know."

Blaise leaned in on her other side and smiled at Llewellyn like they were somehow in this together. "What sort of food do you like, Anne? We three novices can decide together."

She pulled glasses from her purse and perched them on her nose. "I'm fond of seafood and fish, but I'm quite particular about how it's prepared. I prefer simple but still flavorful."

"Ah, don't we all." Blaise gave a half grin and glanced at Llewellyn again. Despite the fact that the statement was likely 100 percent innocent, Llewellyn blushed.

That turned Blaise's half smile full and increased the chance that the remark had been just as lewd as it sounded. "Do you like seafood, Dr. Lewis?"

Llewellyn managed a nod.

"Lobster with lots of butter?"

Llewellyn licked his lips, and Blaise smiled slowly. "You, Anne? Shall we all splurge and try the lobster?"

"Sounds delicious. How about I make it my treat?"

He whispered sotto voce. "How about we let it be the university's treat?"

Llewellyn admired him. When would he ever have the balls to suggest the university should buy him lobster?

Blaise looked up and winked. The waiter arrived beside him, and he proceeded to order for all three of them, saying things like "I know baked potatoes are more traditional, but mashed are so decadent, don't you think?"

Anne almost sighed when she said, "Oh yes."

Even the waiter seemed caught up in Blaise's easy rock-star charm. "What can I get you lovely people to drink?"

"I think champagne goes with lobster, don't you?"

When the waiter walked away, Anne looked between Blaise and Llewellyn. "I know you were just introduced, but you seem to know Dr. Lewis, Blaise."

A blue gaze that could penetrate metal flashed up to Llewellyn before he could shift his eyes. "Everyone knows Llewellyn Lewis, the man who solves the mysteries of history."

Llewellyn frowned. "I-I only try."

Anne put a warm hand on his arm. "No, I totally agree. Your research is amazing. That's why I sought you out."

The waiter placed champagne flutes in front of them and began to fill them with bubbly. If Van Pelt disapproved, he gave no sign. He just drank his iced tea while talking to Harley, who eyed Blaise's champagne with open envy. When the glasses were full, Blaise lifted his. "To new friendships making exciting history."

What the hell did he mean by that? Still, Llewellyn drank.

Anne sipped her champagne and smiled. "I have a mystery I need you to solve, Dr. Lewis."

"L-llewellyn."

"Llewellyn." Her gaze drifted to the glass, and she seemed to watch the bubbles rise. "I have a famous ancestor."

"Ed-Edward." It wasn't a question.

Her face lit up. "Oh yes. I knew you'd understand."

He didn't exactly. *Feared* might be a better word.

Blaise said, "Edward? Edward who?"

"De Vere." She looked at him as if any literate person would know his name, which really wasn't true.

"S-seven-teenth Earl of Ox-oxford."

"Correct." She beamed at Llewellyn.

Stanley spoke from the other side of the table. "You're a descendant of the Earl of Oxford, Anne?"

"Yes, direct. My father was very proud of the association, but sadly he died before anything could be done to establish the earl's true place in history."

"How interesting. I did my dissertation on—"

The waiters began serving food, which halted the conversation, and Llewellyn tried to get excited about lobster, mashed potatoes, and forty gallons of butter. Still, his stomach turned, not only because the room full of people made him break out in hives, but also because he had a very uneasy feeling about Anne de Vere's ancestor.

On the other hand, watching Blaise Arthur eat lobster dripping in dairy products should have been rated triple-X. Tongue, shiny lips, laughter, plus moans and slurps fit for a porn soundtrack all punctuated his thoroughly delightful attack on the sea creature. His pure enthusiasm made others at the table smile, and Llewellyn want to lick the butter from his chin—and anywhere else he could manage to spill some.

I need to get out of here.

Anne ate with fewer sound effects but definite appreciation, probably more because of the company of the sparkling young man than the food, even though it was darned good. Finally she sat back in her chair. "Oh my, that was delicious."

Van Pelt flashed all his teeth. "So glad you enjoyed it." Leave it to the chairman to remind them of who was footing the bill. "Did you like your food, Alonzo? Mrs. Echevarria?"

She stuck out a full lower lip. "I should have ordered the lobster." She gave Anne a sideways look and swallowed another long pull of martini.

"Yes, well, I hope you both will be able to join us tomorrow for a tour of the campus. And you, Anne. We'd love to show off our excellent facilities that help us attract researchers and educators of the caliber you see here. A staff worthy of your illustrious ancestor." He nodded toward the assembled professors.

Llewellyn wanted to crawl under the table. Subtlety was not Van Pelt's strong suit.

Amazingly, Blaise spoke up. "Why doesn't everyone consider the chairman's wonderful invitation over dessert? I notice they have mud pie, and who doesn't love chocolate on chocolate? Perhaps some for the table?" He cocked his head at Van Pelt.

The suggestion, complete with wide blue eyes and a turn of a smile, came across as guileless. Was it? Or did this charmer know his effect on people down to the last goose bump? But it worked. Anne smiled, Mr. Echevarria stopped looking hunted, and everyone took up the discussion of the pros and cons of chocolate, agreeing it didn't have any cons.

"Do you like chocolate, Llewellyn?"

Oh God, chitchat. His horror challenge. He opened his mouth—

Blaise leaned on his hand. "I'll bet Dr. Lewis loves, hmmm—" He gazed upward as Anne giggled, and Llewellyn forced himself not to lean over and kiss him out of sheer gratitude for taking the pressure off him to answer. Well, that was one of the reasons. "I guess coconut. Am I right?"

Actually, he did love coconut. "Y-yes." He nodded.

Anne's eyes got wide. "How did you know that? I mean, you could guess a person loved chocolate, but coconut? Come on."

"I cheated." He connected that direct gaze again. "I read it in some obscure biography of Dr. Lewis."

Was he more flattered or concerned that Blaise seemed to know so much about him?

Anne held up a finger. "Professor Van Pelt, if we're ordering a selection, can we also have a slice of the coconut cake?"

"Well, of course, my dear." Van Pelt waved for the waiter and began ordering desserts and lots of spoons and forks while Llewellyn tried to keep his eyes off Blaise.

Did he do that to keep me from having to answer?

Blaise said, "I'm so interested in hearing more about your relative, Anne."

Leaning forward across the table, Stanley said, "So am I." He smiled with his pleasant dimples.

She looked around the table at the interested faces and shook her head. "Perhaps later. Let's enjoy dessert first."

A couple of minutes later, the waiters arrived with plates piled with mud pie and one giant piece of coconut cake with ice cream next to it. They presented the pies with a flourish toward the middle of the table and distributed utensils liberally, but placed the cake ceremoniously in front of Anne.

She beamed. "Lovely, thank you." She glanced at Llewellyn with a grin.

Blaise picked up a fork and cut a piece of cake, then swiped it through the ice cream. He turned the handle to Anne. "Care to do the honors?"

"No. You."

Slowly he extended the fork to Llewellyn.

"B-but—" Llewellyn's heart beat so hard he almost couldn't hear.

"You're the coconut expert. You have to judge."

The treat hovered a mere inch from his lips, filling his head with the rich scent, while over the top of the frosting, all he could see were blue dancing eyes full of mischief—and lust. *Must be an illusion.*

He started to reach for the fork, but Blaise pulled it back. "Uh, uh, uh. Eat." The laden fork traveled back to his lips, nudged, and with a sigh Llewellyn bit. Flavor exploded and lit up his tongue like a new-movie marquee. Did the presence of Blaise on the other end of that fork make the coconut sweeter? Oh yes. A thousand times yes.

A certain stillness made him pull back. Every person at the table was staring at him with either rapt envy or harsh disapproval. He sucked wind, pulled coconut up his nose, coughed, snorted, and sprayed particles onto the tablecloth—and all over Anne de Vere's lap.

She made a squeaking sound, Van Pelt exploded with "Dear God, Lewis!" and a couple of the professors laughed.

Fire flamed through Llewellyn's head, and the whole room full of judging, critical monsters stood out in harsh relief like someone had turned on a klieg light. Before he could control his body, he pushed back his chair with a loud scrape, leaped to his feet, and ran out of the dining room, across the now packed restaurant where dozens of people stared, and out into the cool, dry California night.

No more. Never again. Van Pelt could take his job and shove it. He didn't need it.

Stumbling slightly, he broke into a trot toward his car.

He almost made it.

"Dr. Lewis. Llewellyn! Please stop. Wait."

Running footsteps came toward him, and Llewellyn powered to his car door. Just as he opened it, a hand gripped his shoulder, bringing him to an abrupt stop. He whirled to find Blaise behind him, wise enough to step back and raise his hands with a smile. "I come in peace."

A more staccato set of footfalls sounded on the sidewalk. *Well, hell, Anne de Vere.* She ran up beside Blaise, breathing hard. "Please don't go yet. It's not everyone I'd run for in these shoes." She stuck out one stiletto-clad foot.

Blaise said, "I'm so sorry, Dr. Lewis. I just don't have good sense sometimes. I never should have put you in such a terrible position. I apologize from my soul."

"N-not your f-f-fault."

"Yes, it is. I completely overstepped my bounds. I feel like I know you, and I acted inappropriately."

Llewellyn took a breath. "Y-you tried to make me f-feel comfortable." He spoke slowly and got most of the words out. He didn't want Blaise to take the blame.

Blaise smiled softly. "Yes, I did."

Anne stepped closer. "Please don't go until I've had a chance to tell you why I came."

He met her gaze, and his whole stomach clenched. *No. No way.* "I—I—"

"Please let me tell you. You must know that Edward de Vere, Earl of Oxford, is one of the people most often named as the true author of the works of Shakespeare."

Blaise looked up at Llewellyn. "He is? I thought it was, like, Marlowe or Bacon."

"No, no." Anne waved a hand dismissively. "The Earl of Oxford has long been regarded as the most likely candidate to have written both the sonnets and the plays."

"Yes, he's one of the top candidates, if you believe such things." The voice came from the sidewalk beside his car, and Llewellyn looked up to see George Stanley, Van Pelt, the Echevarrias, as well as the whole crew of dinner guests, with one or two defections, gathering there.

If I drive away, maybe I could just go to North Dakota and hide for the rest of my life? He swiped a hand over his face. *Right, they love gay freaks there.*

Anne frowned. "Not *one* of them, the most prominent among them, as I'm sure Dr. Lewis will agree." He said nothing, and she didn't seem to care. She was on a roll. "It's been a dream of my family to investigate the earl's position in this mystery for some time."

I could run. Forget the car.

"That's why I've sought out Dr. Lewis. He's renowned throughout the world for uncovering new evidence in some of the great questions of history." Her voice rang out like she was in a Shakespearean play herself. "That's why I want him to prove beyond a doubt that my ancestor, Edward de Vere, the seventeenth Earl of Oxford, is the real author of the works of William Shakespeare."

Llewellyn shook his head back and forth like a befuddled cow. "So many tr-tr-tried. C-can't—"

She raised her voice even more. "And I'm prepared to present the university with a historical research grant of five million dollars in order to prove this claim. One million to go to Dr. Lewis and the rest for dedication of the history building to my ancestor, Edward de Vere."

For a second the whole street—the whole world—went silent.

Someone—maybe Echevarria—murmured, "No."

Then Van Pelt's voice rang out. "Well, that sounds like one of the most exciting and worthwhile historical research undertakings I've ever heard."

Running wasn't enough. Maybe he should vomit.

CHAPTER FOUR

HE'D ACTUALLY run. Stuttering that he had to get home, he'd crawled in his car, told Anne he'd talk to her another time, and raced down the street, challenging the performance statistics of the old Volvo. Bypassing several opportunities to jump off bridges between the club and his home, he pulled into his driveway and dropped his head on the steering wheel. *Kill me now.*

It's what he got for focusing on weird events and mysteries, but dammit, that's what fascinated him. He never promised he could solve them all. He didn't even want to. Just roaming around in all the facts and theories fascinated him and made him happy. Wildass theories and proofs—those were Ramon's job. Hell, Ramon had even written an article on the real Shakespeare and given a gazillion reasons why de Vere was a likely candidate. Ramon didn't have to prove shit.

He could just talk through his fashionable hat. On the other hand, that meant Llewellyn knew intimately just how impossible proving the case would be. So many had already tried.

Lifting his head, he crawled out the door and dragged himself into the three-story house that was the only artifact of his weird parentage—a mother who had been beautiful as a girl but who slowly degenerated into a gray, broken drudge, hating the son her one liaison with a rich, powerful man had produced. Said man, who Llewellyn had never met, gave his mother this house. She'd hated it too.

He loved it.

Before he even got all the way in the door and flipped on the chandelier in the entry, his welcoming committee met him.

"Meeow."

"Mrwaowr."

"Mew."

Silky bodies rubbed against his legs and tried to trip him by weaving in and out of his legs as he attempted to move. With the lights on, he bent down and immediately got Marie Antoinette—the white Persian someone had dropped off at the shelter because she was so damned finicky they couldn't afford to feed her—jumping up on his lap.

Julius—as in Caesar—large, orange, and stocky, tried to make the leap as well and got a swipe of her paw and a hiss that put him in his place, which was flat on his butt on the floor. He might outweigh her by three times, but no one ruled Marie.

Emily Dickinson held back in her dreamy calico way. She never demanded, but wooed with her demure manner and calculating intelligence.

He petted them all liberally, then stood, still carrying Marie, and walked to the big old-fashioned kitchen with shiny new appliances. "S-sorry to b-be so late. I know you're hungry. You w-wouldn't believe what happened today."

He took their dishes he'd left drying on the counter and scooped a healthy portion from the packages of wet food he kept in the refrigerator into each dish. Julius got double and the girls didn't seem to mind. They watched their figures. Marie had to have chicken and nothing——repeat, nothing—else. He gave Marie her dish first—she was alpha, after all—then Emily and Julius together.

Suddenly Marie stiffened, her flat face came up, and her long white fur stood on end. "Urrrrrrr." She stared toward the door in the kitchen that led into the dining room—no open concept when his house was built. Not sure why, Llewellyn inched his hand along the counter toward the knife block, never taking his eyes from the kitchen door.

The front doorbell rang.

He froze. *No!* Could Van Pelt have told Anne de Vere where he lived?

"Hello. Hello, Llewellyn, are you here?"

Well, damn. He slowly released a breath and took another as Blaise Arthur appeared in the kitchen doorway.

Blaise looked from Llewellyn's face to his hand, just inches from grasping the handle of a butcher knife. "Whoa. Hang on, Jim Bowie. Sorry to scare you. Your door was standing open, and I was a little worried that you'd decided to run for Alaska or hang yourself by one of Van Pelt's neckties."

A laugh bubbled up from Llewellyn's belly. That description so perfectly described his options, he just kept chuckling until all three cats looked at him like he was nuts. Marie relaxed her puffed-up fur seemingly one hair at a time, flicked her tail, and returned to her chicken dinner.

Finally he managed to stop laughing. "Uh, how d-did you know w-where I live?"

Blaise cocked his grin to the side. "I followed you, and I must say, I had to move pretty fast to do it."

What the hell? "W-why?"

"I told you. Suicide prevention."

Was he disappointed in that answer? He spread his arms. "A-as you see."

"Feline-feeding duty."

"I'm a cr-crazy cat lady."

Blaise leaned against the door, arms crossed, one nicely muscled leg cocked over the other, and a sexy-as-hell grin on his face. "Neither crazy nor a lady so far as I can see."

"S-so what do you want?"

"There's a challenging question. Just accept my mother-of-compassion routine at face value and offer me a drink."

He still frowned. "B-beer? Wine?"

"Beer would be great."

Llewellyn loved craft beers and took two bottles of Red Headed Stranger from his cooler.

He opened and poured them into pilsner glasses and handed one to Blaise, who stared at the bottle. "Whoa, exotic." He sipped. "Delicious."

"From R-Reno."

"I'll remember it."

Llewellyn gestured to the hall and led Blaise back to the big living room with its high ceilings, elaborate crown moldings, and polished oak floors. He sat in an easy chair and indicated that Blaise should sit on the comfortable couch.

Blaise sipped and gazed around. "This is quite a house. How old is it?"

"N-nineteen twenties or thirties." Why was he chitchatting? *What's he doing here?*

"Is it a family home?"

"S-sort of."

"Are you gay?"

"What?" Llewellyn frowned. "Uh, y-yes. E-everyone knows th-that."

"Yes, I read it, but I wanted to ask." He grinned.

The cats padded in, Marie making a straight shot to Llewellyn's lap, where she turned and stared at Blaise while washing her face and paws.

"She's the formidable one."

"Oh y-yes."

"What's her name?"

"Marie Antoinette."

He laughed. "Perfect. Marie, I'll make it my personal objective to woo you to my side."

That implied some long-term association.

Blaise took another big mouthful. "It looks like you have a nice life." He set the still partly full glass on the coffee table and stood. "I'm glad. Thanks so much for the beer." He walked toward the door. *What the hell?*

Llewellyn popped up, getting a squawk from Marie. "W-why did you ask if I-I'm gay?"

Blaise glanced back over his shoulder. "Because I am."

"I-I know." *Jesus, why did I say that?*

"Am I that obvious?" But he smiled.

Llewellyn shrugged. "No. So?"

Blaise laughed. "See you at work."

He vanished into the entry, the front door closed, and—gone.

With a flop Llewellyn landed on the chair. *What the bloody hell just happened? Why did a guy like that come here?* And much worse, why did Llewellyn so desperately hope he would come back?

FRIDAY MORNING Llewellyn stepped out of the Volvo—and sneezed. Excessive cat fur. The felines had sensed he was upset and slept curled around his head to comfort him. His nose had permanent tickles.

He'd been tempted to call in sick, which disturbed him since he loved nothing better than cloistering himself in his dark hole of an office and chasing down rabbit trails of theory. Today, not so much.

Question one. Where was Anne de Vere? Second, what the hell did Blaise Arthur want with him and how soon could he do it?

Okay, get to it.

He trudged stolidly into the history building, up the stairs, through the door to Maria's office, and stopped, at least one of his questions answered. On the wildly uncomfortable couch under the window sat

Anne de Vere. Beside her perched Dr. Van Pelt, looking like he'd rather be anywhere but there.

Van Pelt glanced up and frowned. "It's about time you got here."

"I-I can leave."

Maria spread her hands in surrender.

Anne stood and shot Van Pelt a vicious glance. "Llewellyn, can we talk, please?"

He sighed loudly. "Y-yes."

Van Pelt jumped up, and Anne extended a hand. "Alone."

"Anne, I can assure you that we'll put the entire history department at your disposal. If it's possible to prove that your ancestor wrote Shakespeare's works, we have the team to do it."

"It c-can't be d-done." Llewellyn shook his head.

Van Pelt scowled. "You don't know that."

"I-I do."

Anne grabbed his arm. Damn, he hadn't even had his tea yet. She gazed at him with big brown eyes. "Please, explain to me why this can't be done. You're the most brilliant historical researcher in the world. I know. I investigated all of them."

Llewellyn nodded toward his office and splayed a hand in that direction. He glanced at Van Pelt. "Excuse us."

Maria rounded her desk and held out a giant mug of tea wafting the smell of vanilla. She handed Anne a cup of coffee and cream. Sainthood was in order.

Anne smiled. "Thank you." Preceding Llewellyn, she crossed into his office and sat on the hard-backed chair in front of his desk. She glanced around his cramped space, then picked up the small ceramic figure he kept on his desk. "J. Worthington Foulfellow."

"How on e-earth d-do you know th-that?" The little figurine constituted the only gift his mother had ever given him with affection, when he was a baby and couldn't yet make her feel dumb just by existing.

"I was an elementary school teacher for a time. One of my students had a figure of J. Worthington she carried in her pocket. Her grandmother had given it to her." She half smiled. "How extraordinary to see him again." She set the figure down. "So tell me why you don't believe my ancestor could be Shakespeare."

He settled on his office chair and took a deep swallow of tea. "Th-there are m-many rea-sons to doubt. D-date of b-birth. But mostly t-talent. The earl did n-not have the genius to do the p-plays."

"You mean because of the sonnets he wrote as a boy?"

Llewellyn nodded.

"But you can't believe that a bumpkin with no evidence of even an elementary education did?"

"N-not my job." He smiled. "Y-your relative might h-have been Shakespeare, but proving beyond d-doubt? Not possible. There are a-always going to be doubts."

"But if you said it was true, or even likely true, people would believe it."

"C-can't lie." He frowned.

"No, no of course not. But I'll pay you to research the issue. If you don't have to do anything else, I'll bet you can find out so many things. You can go to Stratford and Oxford. I'll finance the whole thing."

"It still may n-not be provable."

She took a deep breath. "I understand. But I feel certain I'll be able to help you find evidence that establishes my case. What if I agree to pay you for your time at your regular rate if you fail? At least I'd know and might be content to give up the quest. If the best in the world says it can't be proven, then I may accept it." She grinned. "Of course, I feel certain you will, with my help, be able to prove it absolutely."

All the protests lined up on his lips like planes ready for takeoff—but didn't fly out. The real authorship of Shakespeare's works fascinated him and had for a long time. That's why Ramon had written articles on the subject. To be paid to travel and snoop around into English history did sound a bit like heaven. But still—"I c-can't take your money under false pretenses."

A crease popped between her brows, and she looked a lot less pleasant. "I'll bet Dr. Van Pelt wouldn't have any trouble doing it."

"Pr-probably n-not."

"I'll give you the weekend to reconsider." Still frowning, she stood.

He rose across from her. "I'm unlikely to ch-change my mind, Ms. de Vere. You should spend y-your money more wisely."

"Quite the contrary, Dr. Lewis. If you won't take the case, you will leave me no choice. I'll take my offer to Ramon Rondell! He already believes I'm right." She turned and stalked out of the small space. She paused at the door. "Monday. No later."

What the hell did he do now?

He heard voices in the outer office—raised voices—and it only took seconds for Van Pelt to come sailing into his space on the wings of outraged vultures. "What the hell do you mean by telling Anne that she should spend her money elsewhere? Have you lost your mind? Five million dollars? Do you know what the department could do with that money? I want you to call her this moment and tell her you changed your mind and will do her research and attempt to prove her damned ancestor is the Bard. Hell, I don't care if you promise to prove he's Jack the Ripper, I want you to do this research!" He sucked in air like a Dyson. His voice got low and cold. "Do I make myself clear?"

"I c-can't prove it. Dozens have tr-tried."

"They weren't you. There's not a chance that it's acceptable to turn down this project without even an attempt."

Llewellyn shook his head.

"Lewis, this isn't a choice. If you want to keep your position, I suggest you call Anne before her deadline and tell her you'll take the assignment."

Llewellyn frowned back, but his heart wasn't in it. He loved his job.

"You know I can find a way." He pointed a finger at Llewellyn. "Do it. Make this happen and you'll make your career. You'll be able to write your own ticket for the rest of your life." His scowl deepened. "Besides, you can't possibly want her to give this project to that phony, Rondell. Call her. No later than Monday morning." He turned and walked out, redefining high dudgeon.

Before he could even take a breath, Maria was setting a new cup of tea in front of him. "Jesus, boss, I think you better just try to prove it, don't you?"

"Already tr-tried some. No evidence." He swallowed the tea like it was direct from Zeus, burned his tongue, and spit the balance onto the papers on his desk.

Maria flopped into the chair across from him. "Aw hell, boss, I should have warned you. I'm sorry. Maybe you could go home and start this day over."

"N-never should have s-started it at all."

"Don't say that. Things will get better. Dayum, there has to be something good about all that money." She giggled. "You might even need to take your research assistant with you on trips to England."

He tried to smile back. "Th-there is that."

"Why don't you go for a walk, get some fresh air, and I'll get the tea off the papers?"

"Th-thank you." A new perspective sounded good.

Outside he squinted against the sunshine and strode off toward his favorite secret garden behind the English building, where people were unlikely to bother him. If he looked in a hurry, no one would interrupt.

A couple of students gave him a smile and a nod. Oddly, despite the fact he taught very few classes and avoided most students like Ebola, they treated him kindly—although they did call him Lew-Lew behind his back. He kind of liked that.

As he cut across the lawn toward his destination, he caught a movement in the corner of his eye and glanced up. A man stood beside the corner of the building across the street, staring at Llewellyn. When Llewellyn looked toward him, the figure instantly disappeared around the edge of the computer science center. Odd. Probably a student, but for a second he'd

reminded Llewellyn of that strange guy at the club.
The Jack the Ripper man. That made him think of Van
Pelt, which made him shiver.

Focus on the problem at hand. Like most humans, he hated being told what to do, but hell, was
it worth fighting so hard? If Anne de Vere insisted on
paying for research that would only prove what was
already known—and he got some pleasant travel in
the bargain—how bad could it be?

Of course, he didn't much like to travel, and
spending time on a useless endeavor rubbed his fur
the wrong way. Plus, staying near here in the immediate future might be interesting. He smiled. The kind of
interesting he could use more of.

He cut between the buildings toward the garden,
rounded the corner, and stopped. His heart made a visit to his toes.

CHAPTER FIVE

LLEWELLYN STARED past the low bushes only to see Blaise Arthur relaxing against the trunk of a tree, while George Stanley leaned in and laughed as he reached up and brushed something from Blaise's hair.

Yes, the scene could be totally innocent. They both worked in the building, they were colleagues, it was a pretty day nearing lunch hour. And they were both young men, one of whom—and from the looks of the scenario, both of whom—were gay. It made sense. Blaise and George were damnably attractive, charming, conversant, and bright. Why wouldn't they seek each other out?

Llewellyn turned and walked away from the garden. Surely he hadn't been counting on anything from that quarter? He'd learned to have low expectations a long time ago.

Interesting, though, how the drive to stay home felt less demanding.

It took longer to get back to the office than it had to leave. A couple of people waved and he nodded, but some of the sun had gone out of the day. *Stupid. Stupid.* When he walked back in the office, Maria looked up, startled.

"You barely got enough sun to produce any vitamin D."

"I'm, uh, th-thinking I might t-take the job." He walked past her into his office and sat behind the desk. He wanted to close the door, but that was so much of a statement, he couldn't bring himself to do it.

He searched *Edward de Vere* on his computer and began sorting through the string of references, from scholarly to absurd.

"Uh, boss?"

He looked over the top of the screen.

Maria stood in the doorway. "I was kind of hoping that you'd get comfortable with the idea of taking on the project, not that you'd make yourself miserable. If you really don't want to do it, hey, we can run off to Canada and join the Mounties."

"I c-can't ride." But he grinned.

"Small, itsy-bitsy detail."

"And I don't look good in r-red."

"Yeah, well, that queers it. Seriously, don't do this if you really hate it."

"It's n-not that—exactly." Damned if that wasn't true.

She made herself as comfortable in his guest chair as the unforgiving wooden frame would allow. "So what is it?"

He shrugged. Much too stupid to discuss.

She leaned forward, her intelligent, pretty face as earnest as he'd ever seen it. "Llewellyn, you're one of the smartest, most capable people I've ever met. Everyone knows that except you. You can do what you want and make shit happen. Seriously, just do it. Nobody at Middlemark or anywhere else is more deserving of a happy, full life than you. Please remember that. *Illegitimi non carborundum.* Don't let the bastards get you down."

He snorted. "It doesn't mean t-that."

She hopped up and winked. "It does if you think it does."

Llewellyn finally gave up and laughed, then leaned back in his chair as she walked back to her desk with a little flick of her long hair.

God, he loved her so much.

So back to the question. Yes, he liked Blaise Arthur, but there was no reason Blaise would prefer Llewellyn Lewis to George Stanley or much of anyone else. He could have rolled out Ramon Rondell if Blaise hadn't gotten such a close look at Llewellyn. As it was, Blaise said he liked Llewellyn, or at least that's what he implied. But obviously, he liked George Stanley more.

Llewellyn's heart gave a hammer, and he exhaled reality. Obviously Blaise wasn't thinking about him, so Llewellyn could return the favor. *Forget Blaise.* He inhaled, looked at the screen, and started reading, then paused.

If he planned to forget Blaise, finding someone he liked to have sex with sounded like a wise plan. Maybe Ramon just had the shortest retirement in history. Maybe he needed to return for one last encore.

BLAISE SCRUNCHED down in the driver's seat and peered at the old house over the edge of the car door. Better not be too suspicious-looking. It was still afternoon, and since it was Friday, a lot of cars were coming and going on the street.

Llewellyn's Volvo pulled into the driveway. Professors often left the office early on Friday, so he'd taken the chance and preceded him there. Llewellyn left his old car in the driveway and keyed open his entry. Just like the other night, he knelt down to greet his cats before he even closed the door behind him. That was an unwise practice that could get him mugged or worse.

Blaise took a breath. *Relax. That's big-city thinking. Yes, and guilty-conscience thinking.*

Chances were good nothing interesting would happen. Llewellyn, not known for his wild nightlife, would settle down in his house with his cute cats, and Blaise would twiddle his thumbs for zip. He clicked Play on his phone and turned on the Chainsmokers for a little dance inspiration. Just as he leaned his head back for a rest, Llewellyn's front door opened, and he walked out carrying a tote bag. Blaise scrunched and watched.

Tossing the tote in the passenger seat, Llewellyn walked to the driver's side and was backing out as fast as Blaise could duck down. As the Volvo pulled past, Blaise started his Prius and drove a half block in the opposite direction, then U-turned like the Flash and followed the gray car from a safe distance. Probably going for dry cleaning, but still, there was hope.

After twenty minutes of driving, the dry-cleaning theory was out and a lot of options came to mind. The

Volvo had proceeded up Highway 1 from San Luis and was now approaching Morro Bay. Blaise smiled. *You little devil.*

Five minutes later, Blaise wasn't so sure about his assumptions when Llewellyn pulled into the parking lot of a pretty ordinary restaurant attached to a hotel and, carrying his tote, walked inside. Was he having a dinner meeting? The man had so few social interactions, it seemed unlikely.

Staring out the window from the other end of the parking lot, Blaise waited. *Nothing. Hell.* He jumped out of the car and hurried to the front of the restaurant. *What do I do if he sees me? Think fast, but right now I just don't want to lose him.* Trying to look casual, Blaise sauntered into the entry, from which he could see a lot of the big open room. No Llewellyn.

The hostess said, "Can I help you, sir?"

"Oh, I was passing and I thought I saw my friend, Professor Lewis, come in. Tall, slender, brown hair, kind of smart-looking."

"Carrying a bag?"

"Why, yes, I believe he was."

"A gentleman came in, but I think he walked directly through into the hotel."

"Oh. Darn. Thanks for your help." He walked out the exit and hightailed it to the hotel lobby entrance—and stopped. Okay, this would be harder to explain. *I just happened to be stopping into a Morro Bay hotel. Yeah. No.* He leaned against one of the pillars in front and waited.

Ten minutes later, he'd about given up, but he took a couple of steps back and tried to look casual behind the pillar when he heard the click of heels on the granite floor.

A quick peek revealed the back of what appeared to be a truly stunning man—very tall, reed thin, shiny dark hair that fell over his shoulders and around his ears. He moved like a dancer on his way to a tour de force performance. Oddly, he wore a sweat suit. But he moved with confidence toward the building next door. Oh, that made sense. He was headed to the spa— the notoriously gay-friendly spa.

Blaise smiled. Some lucky guy over there was in for a fun evening.

Blaise turned back toward the entry and peered into the lobby. No one. Glancing around, he quietly entered the hotel, but there was no sign of Llewellyn. *Hey, Llewellyn was carrying a bag. Maybe he checked in. Or maybe he went to the spa too. Wouldn't it be wild if he was hooking up with the looker in the sweat suit?* Blaise snorted. *Not likely.* From what Blaise had seen, Llewellyn Lewis would never think he deserved a guy with as much charisma as that dark-haired man. So brilliant. So shy. Jesus, his mother had to be nuts.

He gazed across the parking lot. How bad could a night at the gay spa be?

He left the hotel and trotted across the crowded lot. In the lobby of the spa, a cute guy looked up with a smile—that escalated as soon as his eyes met Blaise's. "Hi there. Can I help you?"

"Yes, I'm a first timer. Uh, at this spa, I mean. What services do you offer?"

"We have a complete menu of massages, facials, and wraps. We also have two nice whirlpools. One is inside and coed. The other is outside and"—he grinned—"gentlemen only. That designation also applies to the large steam room. It's *very* steamy."

"I think I'll just use the whirlpool and steam room to start. If I decide on a massage…?" Blaise made a waving gesture with his hand.

"Just let the head attendant know in the locker room. He'll check with me." The attendant took Blaise's credit card and supplied him with a robe, flip-flops, and a towel. "I'll leave your account open in case you decide on more services. Enjoy yourself—" He gave Blaise a slow, significant once-over. "—immensely."

Blaise flashed him a wink and took a step toward the entrance to the locker room, then turned back. "Uh, did a tall, slim guy with brown hair and a kind of a studious look come in during the last few minutes? He, uh, stutters sometimes."

"No, sadly. I'd remember. I love those shy, silent types."

Me too. "Thanks." *Well, damn.*

"I hope that won't be too disappointing for you." The guy grinned. "I get off in a couple hours." He raised his brows significantly.

"Kind, but I may not last that long."

"Oooh, I hope that's not true."

Blaise just laughed and stepped into the locker room—carefully. If Llewellyn was in there, he'd need a good story for how he happened to be at the same off-the-beaten-track spa. Of course, there weren't that many gay hangouts on the central coast, so….

No professor types in the lockers at all. The dark-haired guy wasn't in there either.

Blaise undressed and pulled on the cushy robe and flip-flops, then ventured into the wet areas of the massive men's lounge. Guys wandered through, some giving Blaise the eye and signaling they'd be happy to follow with additional body parts, but no one was pushy. A big sign above one of the doors said IR Sauna. Still draped in his robe, Blaise stuck his head into the wood-lined interior. Nobody there. He pulled back out and closed the door. Obviously, sauna wasn't the happening event in this spa.

A number of men walked in and out of a glass door, creating billowing gusts of fog. *Target.* Discarding his robe in favor of a towel around his waist and another over his shoulders, he followed two guys inside and immediately saw the attraction—steam so thick you couldn't see your own body parts, much less what others were doing with theirs. The hissing of the jets covered a lot of noises, but a certain number of moans and grunts emerged from the mist. Still, it was likely the flow of steam wouldn't stay this high.

He felt in front of him with both a foot and a hand. *Whoops.* Contact with bare skin made him snatch back his arm. "Sorry."

"Anytime." That comment was accompanied by a low chuckle.

He kept feeling the air. The chances of sitting on someone's lap unintentionally were high. That might be part of the plan. If you tumbled into a stranger's embrace, they got to keep you. Blaise had certainly played such silly games in his life, but right then he had another priority. Find Llewellyn, if he was there.

His foot contacted a smooth surface, and a couple of steps revealed it to be a low, tiled bench. He slid

closer and sat, occupying enough space to keep bare
bodies away from him. As he'd guessed, after a couple
of minutes, the flow of steam lessened and the density
cleared enough so he could make out a very large room
with two tiers of seating occupied by a number of men,
some draped in towels and some bare-assed. None of
the guys he saw appeared to be in couples, so all the action must have been coming from the back of the room
farthest from the door, where the fog stayed thick.

Blaise wiped a hand over his face and peered between his fingers at the steamers. *Damn, no Llewellyn.*
Blaise wasn't a hundred percent sure what he would
have said—or done, for that matter—if Llewellyn had
been there, but he might wish it involved a trip to the
back of the room. Funny that Llewellyn had no confidence in his attractiveness, but he turned Blaise on
like a light switch—all that shy brilliance, to say nothing of the beautiful ass he tried to hide.

Whoa. That woke up his dick.

He inhaled some of the eucalyptus-scented steam
to get it under control. Towels didn't cover much. His
attraction to Llewellyn was a weirdly disturbing side
effect of his assignment. Not one he'd considered
when he drove south. Still, he couldn't seem to resist
that sexy brain—and the possibility of mendacious
mystery.

The flow of steam started hissing again, and
Blaise dropped his head into his hands, stretching his
neck side to side. On his turn to the left, he opened
his eyes and connected with a glimpse of piercing
blue, soft, gently turned pink lips, and a shock of dark
hair. Blaise heard his own indrawn breath, and then
the steam closed in. Maybe what he needed was to

take his mind off his Llewellyn obsession and turn it to more low-hanging fruit. He chuckled at his own analogy.

LLEWELLYN'S HEART slammed against his ribs as he backed away from Blaise into the thick blanket of vapor collected at the back of the steam room. *What the bloody hell is he doing here? Damn the man.* With a slap he bumped into a bare body, veered to the side, stumbled over someone's feet, and slammed his hip into the hard tile of the bench. "Ow."

A hand emerged from the cloud and touched his arm. "You okay?"

"F-fine. I mean, yes, thank you."

The hand vanished, and he took a deep, wet breath. *He didn't recognize me. He couldn't. Calm down. I was just another potential screw in the steam room to him.*

A moan close to him on the upper bench made him jump. *Some hot lover you are. Come here to get laid and run from every contact.* He sighed. Obviously Blaise had no such compunctions. That felt weirdly disappointing—which felt weirdly weird. *He's gay. This is a gay meetup. Just because I'm a hopeless social dud doesn't mean he is. Hell, he's not cheating on me. Maybe he's cheating on Stanley.* That made him smile a little.

His demanding brain screamed at him. *What are the chances Blaise Arthur would show up here on the exact night and the exact time I do? Well, not me exactly, but still.*

And there it was. He wasn't him, so Blaise hadn't shown up on the same night as Llewellyn Lewis. He'd shown up on a Friday, after school, otherwise known as date night.

Need to get out of here. But there was a lot of scary real estate between him and the door. Jesus, he could picture himself shriveling into a prune while waiting for the imaginary coast to clear. *You're not you. Just do it.*

The steam stopped hissing. *Okay, wait for it to start again.*

One of the men near him on the bench got up and moved away in the slightly improved line of sight. Then two more walked past him only inches away, holding hands, one of the guys' dick stretching out the front of his towel.

Llewellyn swallowed. Just what he needed, to be hornier.

The steam started again. *Give it a second.*

Someone passed him and seemed to sit somewhere near him on the bench. Llewellyn scooted a couple of inches over to his right, but a body suddenly sat there. *Okay, leave.*

Something touched his leg, and he jumped and slid away. Before he could figure out the way to the door, a leg pressed against his.

"What? Sorry." He scooted in the opposite direction and slammed into another expanse of nude flesh. "I'm so sorry."

"It's okay."

Sweet Jesus, he'd know that voice anywhere.

A voice so near his ear the person could have kissed him said, "Are you looking for company?"

He froze. Company with Blaise Arthur? His brain burst in a flying fit of imagination—lips, tongue, body, hands. He wanted all of them. At that moment, desperately.

He'd hesitated so long, Blaise must have taken it as assent. From the mist, a hand caressed Llewellyn's bare back and slowly slid to far more vulnerable parts.

Llewellyn felt his own chest rise in a deep sigh. All he wanted was more.

Blaise caressed his face and slid his fingers up to tangle in Llewellyn's long hair.

Wait. Not Llewellyn's. Shit!

Fortunately Blaise wasn't ready for resistance. Llewellyn pushed hard against Blaise's chest, throwing him off balance so he fell backward against the tiled bench. Llewellyn leaped up and ran toward the door, running into several people but elbowing his way through. "Sorry. Excuse me."

He threw open the steam room, ran to the locker room, shoved in the key, and opened the locker. It took seconds to pull on his sweatpants, grab his bag, and tear out to the lobby of the spa. Fortunately, he'd paid coming in. He waved at the receptionist. "Sorry. Emergency." He ran out the door, across the parking lot, and was in his hotel room before he stopped to take a deep breath.

Leaning against the inside of his door, he slowly banged his head back against it. *Oh my God. Blaise Arthur.* He pressed a hand on his abdomen and felt it rise and fall with his panting breaths. *Blaise Arthur came on to me. Keep breathing or I'll die of amazement.*

Seconds ticked by as his heartbeat returned to normal. *Uh, wait.* Breath. *He didn't come on to me.* Breath. *He caressed Ramon Rondell.* Breath. *Not even that. He came on to an anonymous stranger in a steam-filled room full of lust and debauchery.*

Llewellyn walked across the room to the bed and sat on its edge. He'd asked for a faceless, nameless night of sexual adventure, and that's what he'd gotten.

BLAISE STOOD outside the spa, staring into the dark parking lot and over to the hotel. *Damnation.* He'd left that fucking account open, and it took forever to pay and get out of there. *Gone.* He'd lost them both—Llewellyn and the dark-haired man. *No, asshole, you lost Llewellyn because of the dark-haired man. When you saw Llewellyn wasn't in the steam room, you should have left. Mother will kill me.*

He started trudging over to the parking lot of the hotel, his too-tight jeans reminding him of his explosive response to the guy in the steam room. In fact, it wasn't really his style. He was no sex-starved adolescent, unable to control his libido. But the dark-haired man had suddenly been in front of him, and Blaise just reacted. He let out a single laugh. *Memorable.*

He crawled in his Prius, pulled out his cell phone, and settled down to get his ass chewed.

CHAPTER SIX

"MERWAOWR."

"I'm awake."

"Mew."

"Mewwwr."

Llewellyn opened his eyes and stared into large green ones. "Good morning, Marie." Interesting how he stammered less when he talked to the cats. As agreed in his feline contract, he scooted up against the headboard and let the furries snuggle and rub against him. Julius did most of the rubbing, Marie took his lap, and Emily purred against his side. He'd only get a few minutes of snuggle time because Julius wanted his breakfast, thank you very much.

He closed his eyes and petted all the fur he could reach. Pretty tired. He hadn't planned to come home last night since he'd paid for the handy hotel room, but somehow staying there made him antsy. What if he saw Blaise? Would Blaise put coincidence together and figure out who he'd groped? That was one step from realizing Llewellyn had been wearing a wig and makeup—although most of it had washed off by that time. Damn, that'd be hard to explain. Plus it still weirded him out that Blaise had turned up in the same unlikely place as him. Even making big allowances for gay men on weekends, it still stretched the bounds of probability.

A little smile crept over his mouth. But just because Blaise Arthur represented a potential threat didn't mean he wasn't epic. Hell, he'd happily lie there and let Blaise grope him all day. His dick gave a little hop.

"Merwaooowr."

He opened his eyes; Julius was practically stomping his feet. A not-so-subtle reminder from the universe to get off his ass and stop mooning over a guy he not only couldn't have—but shouldn't. "Okay, g-guy. Breakfast time. Then I'm settling in to a weekend of w-work."

He sat up and the cats all got the cue, leaping to the floor and meowing. Although he usually kept his drapes drawn, last night he'd been so tired and upset, he'd forgotten. In the interests of his neighbors' modesty, he threw on some jeans and padded out to the kitchen, bare-chested and barefoot.

Eyeing the tea maker with longing, he veered to the cat food cabinet for his first stop to keep the beasts from attacking. *Whoops.* No cans of Julius's favorite and not even any of Marie's food. "Hang on." He checked the refrigerator. *Very bad news.* It wasn't like him to be so disorganized, but the last few days had been pretty intense.

If he only gave the cats dry food, they'd pout for a week. Okay, so a trip out for cat food and a giant tea latte; then he'd lock the doors, close the curtains, and forget the outside world with its expectations and demands until Monday. Right, Monday, when he had to make a life-altering commitment that could threaten his professional standing—or get him fired from his cushy position that let him do whatever research he wanted with few intrusions. "Sorry, guys." He grabbed the bag of dry food. "This will hold you until I get back, okay?"

As he crossed the big living room toward the stairs, he caught a glimpse of movement outside the window. *Dark hair. Female. Probably Maria.* She didn't usually bother him at home unless it was important.

Walking into the entry, he pulled open the door— and stopped. "Uh, M-Mrs. Echev-varria."

"Please, call me Carmen." She smiled, giving her mane of black hair a toss.

"H-how c-can I h-help you? I w-was just going out."

She looked at his bare chest meaningfully.

"After I-I ch-change." He forced a smile.

"Don't do that on my account." She smiled. "May I come in? I'll only take a moment of your time."

"Uh, v-very well." He stepped back and she swept in, getting an immediate audience from three cats. She cringed back. "Oh dear. I'm quite allergic, I'm afraid."

"W-we can s-sit outside." He pointed to the two chairs on his big Craftsman-style front porch.

She eyed the felines. "Well, I was hoping for more privacy, but it would be best, I suppose."

"I-I'll dress."

She walked out again, and he let the door close behind her, then ran down the hall, threw on a shirt and some Birkenstocks, and stopped in the bathroom to pee. Breathing out, he gathered his brain. Why the hell was this woman at his home, and how had she learned where he lived? Van Pelt's face floated across his mind. Right, anything for the money.

Sighing, he walked back to the kitchen to put on a pot of tea, then exited his front door with three fuzzies yowling they wanted better food. *Cats in hell want cold milk too.*

He took the other seat on the porch, separated from Carmen Echevarria by a table. "I-I p-put on some t-tea."

She leaned forward, displaying an acre of cleavage. "Oh, I won't be staying long. Let me tell you why I'm here. You recall that my husband and I are considering a donation to the university in a considerable amount."

"I-I don't know any de-details."

"Yes, well, we were—are. Unfortunately, our intentions rather conflict with those of Anne de Vere, and we hoped that you might, uh, see our side of the issue."

"Wh-why con-conflict?"

"We wish to have our own name on the history building. It's my husband's field of study, and he wants our children to have this legacy. We think it's more appropriate if Ms. de Vere names the English building after that historical imposter. Why subject the history building to such an indignity?"

"I—I'm s-sorry. I c-can't make that decision."

She reached over and patted his arm. "Of course, but if you refused to do the research, there'd be no reason for the de Vere person to even be considered. I know you don't want to do it anyway. All you have to say is no." She smiled so big her back teeth showed.

"B-but—" He stared at her shark grin. She'd just offered him a way out of his mess. A perfect way. "I-I'd have to discuss it with D-Dr. Van P-Pelt. Are y-you making the s-same donation?"

"Uh, no. We were planning a gift of a half million. We might be persuaded to increase to three-quarters."

"I see. I'll t-talk to Van P-Pelt." As if he'd give up four million dollars.

She frowned. "It would be a lot neater if you just refused and let Van Pelt realize that we're the solution to his dilemma."

"N-no."

She looked up startled.

"S-sorry. I c-can't decide it my-myself."

"Even if we put in some money for you? You wouldn't actually have to do any research to earn it."

He swallowed hard. *Oh dear God.* "Even th-then."

She gave him a sideways glance. "You certainly aren't a pushover, are you? No wonder you're such a successful researcher."

He just gazed at her as she stood.

"Discuss it with Van Pelt, then. Remember, according to Alonzo, even suggesting de Vere is Shakespeare will make you a laughingstock in many circles. Not the best for a famous researcher. Bad for the reputation."

He stood beside her. "Th-thank y-you for c-coming by."

She shook her head, then walked off the porch.

Well, hell, he didn't really need that temptation further clouding his vision. Just when he'd pretty much decided to take this stupid case. *Damn. Okay, cat food.*

He reached inside the door—ignoring the cater-wauls—grabbed his wallet, foldable shopping bag, and house keys from the hall table, and set out walking toward Higuera Street. *Cat food or tea first?*

Buy the food first, and then he could relax over a cup of tea for a few minutes at his favorite tea shop before he returned home.

On the side street that led to his house, he stopped at the small shop that specialized in pet food.

The bright-eyed salesgirl gave him a smile. "Hey, Dr. L."

"H-hi, C-Carly."

"Are those four-footed food fanatics at it again?"

"Y-yep." He smiled back. He could manage one-on-one interactions so much better than groups.

She knew right where to go. Whistling through her teeth, she walked to the back and returned with six cans of Julius's favorite that also satisfied Emily, and several packages of the homemade food Marie Antoinette chose and was all she would deign to eat. "Need anything else? Litter? Cat toys?"

"I-I'm their c-cat toy."

She laughed. "I know how that is." She rang up his purchases while he unfolded the nylon bag from its self-contained pouch, then put the food in. "Thanks so much, Dr. Lewis. Give those critters a pat for me. See you at school."

He nodded and waved as he left. The brilliant fall sunshine greeted him and warmed his face as he ambled toward the tea shop. He loved the place, with its little sidewalk café and choices of all the best teas in the world. Of course, he always got the same thing. As he walked up, a couple vacated the perfect table—a medium-sized round café table in the corner of the patio, near the flower baskets and the fountain. He grabbed it and settled in with a sigh.

"Hey, handsome, how's it hanging?"

He grinned at Lizzie Meredith, who along with her wife, Jay, owned Jazzie Tea. "H-hanging l-loose."

She plopped down in the chair opposite him. "Lew-Lew, how come you stutter?"

His eyes must have widened in surprise, but he shouldn't have been shocked. Lizzie said whatever came into her mind. "I-I d-don't know."

"Were your parents really smart like you?"

"N-no." Maybe his father was, but how would he know?

"Well, there you are. I'll bet nobody wanted you to show off your brains and make them look stupid, so they told you to shut up a lot."

His mouth opened, closed, opened again. "Y-yes."

She chuckled. "I knew that degree in psychology would come in handy someday." She stood and wiped her palms on her baggy gray denims. "I'll get your tea, sweetie."

He stared after her sturdy butt. *Son of a bitch.* Talk about nailing him in one amateur therapy session. Yeah, and Ramon never got yelled at, so he didn't stammer. A bit convenient, but what an interesting idea.

"Llewellyn?"

His head snapped up. "W-well, shit."

"Excuse me?" George Stanley half laughed.

"S-sorry. S-so many coincidences."

"Excuse me?" He full-on laughed then and slid into the chair Lizzie had occupied earlier.

Where's the tea? Although truthfully, the morning sun shining off George's fair hair and fair skin was diverting. Still—"H-how do y-you happen to b-be here?"

"I was staking out your home and followed you here—by way of cat food."

"Y-you what?" His shock had to show all over his face.

George laughed nervously. "Yep. Desperate times and all that. I figured I likely wouldn't see you if I didn't take the issue into my own hands."

"W-what issue?"

"Persuading you to go out with me." He looked around. "How do we get some coffee around here?"

Llewellyn was still way back there—on the "going out with me" part.

Lizzie came bustling out at that moment, carrying a large steaming cup of English breakfast tea latte with vanilla. She stopped. "Oh. Aren't you cute?" She set the tea in front of Llewellyn. "This your boyfriend, Llewellyn?"

"N-no."

George leaned back in his chair. "Trying to be. May I have a caffe latte—if you carry caffe, that is?"

"Yes, we carry the beans, though we prefer the leaves. Whole milk or two percent?"

"Two percent's fine. And tell him to go out with me or you'll withhold his drug of choice."

She gave him a long once-over. "Why are you worthy, boyo?"

"Well, let's see. I'm moderately smart—nothing compared to him, I fear. Moderately attractive—again, a pale comparison. I have a great regard for the English language and a stupendous respect for history, but nothing like his talent." He sighed dramatically. "You're right. Completely unworthy."

Llewellyn chuckled. *Cute, if contrived.*

Lizzie planted a fist on her square hip. "Not short on fake humility, I see." She snorted. "Besides, you drink coffee. I'll get it." She walked away.

"Wh-what's this about?" Llewellyn gave him as level a stare as he could muster.

George's expression got more serious. "Just what I said. I'd like you to accept an invitation to dinner."

Llewellyn stared at the handsome face. Man, he wanted to say "When did you trade in Blaise?" but he couldn't say it as coolly as he imagined it. Plus Blaise and George could have been just what it appeared—a friendly meeting between two colleagues. Bringing it up would be really gauche. "Wh-when?"

"Would I be super insulting if I asked about tonight? I mean, I'd never assume you don't have a date."

Lizzie strode back with a paper cup of steamy, milky coffee and plopped it in front of George. "You should try tea. It's better." She slid a check on the table, gave George another evaluating look, and walked away.

George watched her go with a wry smile. "Man, she's a tough room."

"Y-yes, okay."

"What?"

"I'll g-go."

"Oh, you mean dinner? Wow, that's great. Do you have a favorite restaurant, or shall I pick?"

"You."

"Okay. I'll pick you up at seven, if that works for you."

Llewellyn cast a sideways glance. "R-right. Y-you know where I l-live." He sipped his tea. "H-how did y-you get my address?"

"Gosh, I'm not sure. Somebody in the department, I think." He grinned. "I've been asking around about you for a while."

Llewellyn smiled and drank more tea.

"Well, I have to get back. I've, uh, got some meetings today. But I'll look forward to seeing you at seven." He grabbed the check in front of Llewellyn, glanced at it, then looked at his own. He pulled money from his pocket and laid it on the checks. Grabbing his coffee, he shuffled from foot to foot. "Glad I ran into you."

"I th-thought you f-followed me."

"Yeah, well, even better. See you tonight." He hurried off. Even his back looked relieved to get away.

Interesting. George seemed uncomfortable with Llewellyn, but whatever he had on his agenda must be worth a few hours of discomfort and a dinner bill. George had been at the university for at least a year and Llewellyn for far longer. No "asking around" had ever come to his attention. The fact was, he appeared to have become the gay-boy flavor-of-the-month only since Anne de Vere started throwing around her millions. Hell, men were following him. That was a creepy thought.

With a deep breath, he swallowed the last of his drink and left an additional tip for Lizzie. Grabbing the coveted cat food, he started home. The night would be interesting, but right then he just resented not having been able to enjoy his tea.

CHAPTER SEVEN

BLAISE STOOD behind the bush and watched Llewellyn open his door and do the now-familiar kitty dip. This had been a high-exercise morning. He'd happened to drive by Llewellyn's and seen George Stanley creeping around, then that Echevarria chick arrived and hung out on the porch for fifteen minutes, coming away looking not altogether happy. Then Llewellyn had left the house on foot with George on his tail, so Blaise had parked and taken off in pursuit. When he saw Llewellyn's trajectory, Blaise had hurried into the tea shop and stood inside by the window when Llewellyn took his seat on the patio—and when George accosted him.

So that little shit Stanley was taking Llewellyn out to dinner. Why? When Stanley had coaxed Blaise out for coffee the previous day, he'd come on pretty strong to him. But he'd also asked a few well-placed questions about Llewellyn, usually with an almost mocking tone. He'd called him Lew-Lew and made fun of the fact that his TAs had to do all his teaching because he was too shy. *Then he sits there and praises Llewellyn to the skies in that tea shop. What the fuck is his game?*

And that woman.

Hell, am I any better?

Clearly, there are way too many games afoot.

As Llewellyn's door closed behind the man and his cats, Blaise slipped between the houses to his car on the next street over. Chances were he wouldn't learn much more—until seven o'clock.

"H-HEY, GUYS, you're g-getting fur on my j-jacket." Llewellyn grabbed his sports coat from the bed, displacing Marie Antoinette, who gave him a withering glance. "S-sorry." He smoothed the dark jeans he didn't usually wear and stared in the closet door mirror. "D-do I look okay?"

"Mewwwr." Marie gave him her fuzzy back.

"Y-yeah. S-silk purse. Sow's ear. I know." He turned his back on his reflection. Funny that he was so willing to look like a mud fence when clearly Ramon had sprung from his soul in protest. Some part of him screamed to be admired and desired, but he couldn't seem to get the two parts together. Llewellyn wasn't ready to let Ramon in on a permanent basis. Hiding was much easier, and he had a helluva lot of practice.

His cell rang on the dresser. Probably George canceling. He grabbed it, looked at the screen, and considered not answering. "Hello, sir."

"Lewis, what the hell are you doing?"

"Uh, getting r-ready f-for dinner."

"I mean about Anne de Vere, of course!"

"I-I need to sp-speak to y-you, s-sir. B-but I-I'm late for an engagement."

"What about? I can't imagine that there's anything to talk about."

"H-have you sp-spoken to C-Carmen Echevarria?"

"No."

Damn. "C-can we t-talk tomorrow or M-Monday?"

"Anne's going to run out of patience and go to Ramon Rondell."

"N-no, she's n-not."

"How do you know that?" His voice reeked suspicion.

Because I won't take her call. "B-because she said she'd g-give me the w-weekend. Plus she wants v-validation. C-can't get that from Rondell. Are you prepared to rename the b-building?"

"For four million, I'll paint the damned thing orange. And how can you scoff at that much money in your bank account? Of course, since you'll be conducting the research under the auspices of the university we'll have to explore your claim to the money now, won't we?"

Of course you will.

The knock on his door sent all three cats in curious pursuit. "I-I'll talk to you l-later."

"Don't blow this, Lewis. It won't be well received." He hung up.

For a second Llewellyn thought about sitting down and typing out his resignation. After all, Ramon did pretty well, and he didn't have a lot of expenses. Llewellyn, not Ramon. But he thought of how much

he liked Maria, and the nice comfy tenure that protected his position—and the nice comfy cave of an office
that protected him. True, he didn't much like Van Pelt,
but the man wasn't usually awful. Right now his biggest motivation had a hold of him—greed—and that
did bad things to everyone.

The knock came again, louder and more insistently. Llewellyn tossed off the impulse to do something
rash and trotted to the door, where Julius was sniffing like a bloodhound and the girls were waiting with
trembling impatience for a visitor. "I-I s-swear, you're
all d-dogs."

He opened the door. George stood there, looking—well, actually kind of delicious. Not three-
course meal, nutritional delicious, but a well-prepared
appetizer. "H-hello."

George's eyes widened and traveled briefly down
Llewellyn's torso, stopping somewhere around the hips.
Okay, these jeans did hug areas he usually disguised.
George looked up quickly. "You look really nice."

"Th-thanks. Y-you too."

"Who have we here?" George bent down and extended a hand to the felines. Julius gave him an immediate sniff, Emily hung back as was her way, and
Marie flipped her tail and walked away in disgust.

"S-sorry. She's a pr-princess."

"I'll say." He stood and wiped his hands on his
tan jeans.

"Oh, I f-forgot my jacket. B-be right back." Leaving George in the entry, he hurried into the bedroom,
pulled on his khaki jacket, and stared at himself one
last time. *Regular old Llewellyn.* He turned and lifted
his jacket hem. *But okay ass.*

When he got back to the entry, George wasn't there. He glanced to his right into the living room and found George staring at the books on one of his many shelves. He looked up. "I thought I had a lot of books."

"M-my friends."

"You have quite a few volumes on Shakespeare, I notice."

"Y-yes."

He smiled, but it seemed—what? Tight. "Have you started researching for Anne?"

"N-no. Those are from before."

"Oh. You did previous research on this topic?" His brows rose with a lot of interest.

"N-no. Just Shakespearean h-history." That wasn't a lie, exactly. Ramon had done the research. "Sh-shall we g-go?"

"Oh, sure." George walked with purpose toward the door, and when Llewellyn followed, the cats fell in behind. In the entry Llewellyn shrugged apologetically, then knelt and gave each of the cats a pet, reserving the last and most lavish for Marie Antoinette. "S-see you later."

George kind of chuckled as Llewellyn stood. "It must be nice having pets—I guess."

"It's w-work."

"Yeah, I can see that."

In George's Camry, they listened to music and didn't talk much. He'd chosen an Italian restaurant downtown. They could have walked, but Llewellyn was just as glad to drive. Sometimes walking with someone was awkward, since his legs were so long and he didn't like to dawdle. There was also the question of touching—holding hands or arms. George said, "You sure have a nice house. I was lucky to get a two-bedroom apartment."

"F-family house."

"Oh wow, that's great. It looks real historical. When was it built?"

"L-late twenties, early th-thirties."

"Craftsman."

"Y-yes."

"Next time you'll have to give me a tour."

Llewellyn nodded. Interesting that a next time appeared to be on tap. That made two.

The restaurant turned out to be one Llewellyn considered moderately good. George had made a reservation, which earned him points with Llewellyn, and they got a nice booth in the back.

They ordered Chianti and chatted about school, weather, and San Luis, but some shoe wanted to drop, and Llewellyn kept waiting for it. The only time George had seemed really engaged was when he looked at the Shakespeare books. Not a good sign for their social future.

A waitress bubbled over and took their orders— George for lasagna and Llewellyn for chicken piccata—and then left them with wine and breadsticks. George grabbed one and held it up in a mock swordfight. "En garde."

Llewellyn played the game and broke George's breadstick.

"Ah, you got me." George held up his tumbler full of red wine. "To us."

Llewellyn clinked glasses but didn't smile. They both drank.

"So, are you going to do the research for Anne de Vere?"

It could be an innocent question. He'd been there when she made her grand announcement. "I d-don't know. V-Van Pelt sure w-wants me to."

"Want my advice?"

Ah, they'd arrived at the point. "S-sure."

"I did my dissertation on Shakespeare, and I really think you'll be a laughingstock if you try to push the old Oxfordian turkey of an argument."

He nodded. "P-perhaps."

George frowned. Probably not as dramatic a response as he'd wanted. "Seriously, all major scholars have given up the argument. There's just too much evidence that Shakespeare was Shakespeare. I mean, all his friends acknowledged him as a writer. Even his wife."

Llewellyn glanced up through his lashes. Finally, a subject that squeezed some juice out of the man. "You d-don't think it could have been an inside j-joke?"

"You mean everyone getting in on the conspiracy? Hell, no. Why would they?"

"Fun. M-money."

"You think the earl bribed all those people to pretend that old Will was really the Bard? Even Ben Johnson? You don't believe that." His eyes widened and his cheeks got pink.

Llewellyn shrugged.

"Honestly, even his printers and publishers acknowledged his authorship. No one in his own time thought differently. It's just a stupid conspiracy theory cooked up long after his death."

"M-maybe."

The waitress brought their food, and George sat back in the chair as she placed the gooey, rich-smelling dish in front of him. As soon as she'd given Llewellyn his chicken and left, George said, "You're going to take it on, aren't you?"

Llewellyn frowned a little. "M-maybe. Wh-why do you c-care?"

George stared at him like maybe a cobra had crawled onto the table. "I guess that much money can dilute anyone's integrity."

That got a much bigger frown from Llewellyn, and George saw the reaction.

"Sorry. Didn't really mean that the way it sounded."

"Oh?" He raised an eyebrow, neither of them eating.

"I'm just worried about you. You have such an untarnished reputation, and since this is a field I'm so familiar with, I feel it's my duty to warn you. I'm sure when you look into it further, you'll agree with me."

"Maybe." He still gazed at George.

With a loud bark, George laughed. "Sorry. Guess I was coming on a little strong. It's just that I lived with old Will for a few years, and I must have some investment in him being the unschooled genius rather than the urbane nobleman."

"A-amazing no m-matter what."

"Yeah, but doesn't it thrill you that one of the greatest writers in the world ever was a dirt-poor guy with an elementary education? I know it included classics and such, but still."

"M-many playwrights were l-lower c-class. M-most."

"My point exactly. And Shakespeare, for God's sake." He shook his head. "It boggles my mind."

"Y-yes. Perhaps that's m-my point exactly. It boggles the mind t-too much."

For a moment, George's face sobered intensely; then he smiled big. "Let's not let all this great food get cold."

Llewellyn cut his chicken and chewed, but George's intensity had taken some of the *casual* out of casual dining.

After pretending to chat and laugh for another hour, they left the restaurant. On the sidewalk, George said, "Would you like to go to a show or dancing?"

"N-no, thanks. Got t-to admit, this week's taken it out of m-me. Probably best to have an early n-night."

"I guess Van Pelt can be pretty intense."

"Y-yes."

"So he really wants you to do this thing?"

"Th-there m-might be other options."

"Really?" If he'd been a dog, his ears would have stood up. "What?"

"I c-can't say now."

He actually glanced from side to side. "Hush-hush?"

"Y-yeah."

"I'll be watching with interest." He led the way to the car with more enthusiasm than he'd shown for the last hour.

In front of his house, Llewellyn said the obligatory words. "W-would you like to come in?"

George showed teeth. "Aw, thank you, but I know you're tired. We'll get to know each other better next time." He winked, and Llewellyn almost laughed at the lack of subtlety. But seconds later George pulled away from the curb as Llewellyn let himself into his house—and they hadn't said another word about a second date. *Thank God.*

Instead of stooping to pet the kitties, he hit the overhead lights, walked into the kitchen, and poured himself a beer, then threw off his jacket and collapsed on the couch, patting his lap for Marie and whoever felt up to challenging her for the position. He instantly had a lap full of fur as he downed the cool, bittersweet liquid.

What the hell had that whole dinner been about? George just fell into line as one more person who seemed to have some stake in his research. Jesus, he'd gone from being an obscure academic toiler to the primary shaper of everybody's dreams.

Like some harbinger of doom, somebody knocked on his door.

He cringed. *Who the hell is that?* He could go weeks and never have a visitor, and suddenly he was LAX.

The cats went wacko, leaping up and meowing loudly as Llewellyn stood and crossed warily to the front door. "Who is it?"

No answer. *Well, hell.* He needed a peephole—and a doorbell that worked. Right, and a better dry cleaner and more vacations days. *Shit.*

He opened the door.

Uhhhh—

Grinning, Blaise Arthur leaned against the doorframe. "Since your date didn't, can I come in?"

"Wh-what the h-h-hell are you d-doing here, and how do you know I had a d-date?" All those words rushed out before a wave of remembrance washed over him—heat and desire so deep he could have drowned in it. With a soft gasp, Llewellyn turned on his heel and walked back into the living room, sat on the couch, and took a long swallow of beer.

When he looked up, Blaise stood in the arch of his living room. He hadn't stopped grinning. "That was the shortest date on record."

"And y-you know this because—"

"I came to see you and watched you arrive home." He glanced at his watch. "I happened to notice it was 9:00 p.m." He grinned even broader, which looked so adorable on his beautiful face it almost made Llewellyn sigh.

"H-how do you know w-we didn't start at noon?"

Blaise laughed, and it manifested as music for Llewellyn's balls. *Control your dumb self.* He drank the rest of his beer.

"Want another?" He nodded toward Llewellyn's glass. "I thought I'd get one for myself."

Llewellyn's mouth opened, and all that came out was laughter.

Blaise turned and walked away. Llewellyn heard a distant rattle and pop, and a couple of seconds later, Blaise walked back into the room with two beer bottles. He handed one to Llewellyn and sat beside him on the couch. "I like your beer."

Llewellyn shook his head but said, "Th-thanks."

All three cats stared at Blaise, and Julius broke the ice by rubbing against him. Emily gave him a tentative sniffle, then settled beside him. With a flick of her tail, Marie Antoinette approached and gave Blaise a long look-see. Then, with the sound of heavenly harps playing in the background, she delicately stepped onto his lap.

Llewellyn heard his own gasp.

Blaise looked up with wide, shiny eyes and reverently applied a gentle hand to Marie's long, pristine white, silken fur.

In a world of awards, recognition, and prestige, Blaise had just been given the ultimate recommendation.

CHAPTER EIGHT

"Wh-why are you here?"

"To pet Marie Antoinette, obviously." He grinned, and it was pretty easy to see why the cat succumbed to his charms. *Jesus, that face.*

"S-seriously."

He looked up from the focused petting ritual. "I guess I could say I was worried about you and the pressure you must be under."

"Y-you could say that, or it's t-true?"

"Caught that subtle difference, did you?" He chuckled and looked down at Marie, who was now sprawled across his lap in wanton feline abandon. "I'd guess it's true."

"Yes."

"Van Pelt?"

"E-everyone."

Blaise looked up sharply. "What do you mean?"

Llewellyn held up one hand with fingers spread and counted them. "Anne de V-vere, V-van Pelt, Echevarria, George. I don't even know who's p-putting pressure on V-Van P-Pelt from the administration."

"Why does George have a dog in the hunt?" He got a little too close to Marie's butt, and she gave him a warning look. He moved his hand fast.

"He d-doesn't. J-just thinks he knows Sh-Shakespeare was Shakespeare and w-wanted to keep me from making a m-mistake."

"What do you think?"

"I've traced v-very good arguments on b-both sides."

"You have?" He looked startled.

Careful. "Y-yes. C-can't research historical mysteries without running across it."

"I suppose." But his eyes lingered on Llewellyn's face an extra second. "Maybe you'll discover something brand-new on one side or the other of the argument. That'd be exciting."

"C-could happen. It's extensively researched already."

"But that's what you do, right? Uncover new evidence."

Llewellyn shrugged.

"Or tell them all to go to hell and live however you want to live."

Llewellyn snorted. "There's n-no s-such thing."

"Sure there is. If you don't want much, it's a lot easier to achieve. If you're not attached to what you do have, you don't care if it's gone."

"Is t-that how y-you live?"

"Hell, no, but it sure sounded Zen, didn't it?" He laughed.

"S-so now tell the t-truth."

"About why I came here?"

Llewellyn nodded.

Blaise stared down at Marie. "What do you think, beauty? Shall I tell him?"

She rolled on her back and presented belly, purring.

"I'm taking that as an affirmative vote." He gave her a few strokes to her silky underfur, then lifted her and set her beside him on the couch.

"Mew!" She jumped off the couch with a flick of the tail and stalked to the other side, where Llewellyn sat.

So did Blaise. He stood in front of Llewellyn, gazing down, some kind of battle going on behind his eyes. "I don't really give a shit about Shakespeare. But don't tell the English department that, okay?"

Llewellyn's throat was so dry he barely got out the word. "Okay. W-what do you c-care about?"

Blaise rested a knee on the couch right beside Llewellyn's hip. "This." In one swooping move, he leaned in and captured Llewellyn's lips with his mouth as his palms cupped Llewellyn's cheeks. That left them both off balance in more ways than one, and Blaise half pressed, half fell on top of Llewellyn as he rode him down onto the cushions of the couch.

Usually Llewellyn had to consciously relax his mind to be able to enjoy a kiss or any other kind of sexual attention. Not this time. One touch of those perfect lips blew every neurocircuit, and Llewellyn's body went up in flames—as if he were in a steam room.

Llewellyn parted his lips as the scent of clove and orange seeped into his nose and traveled along his nerves like a drug. He couldn't control his tongue or his hands. They wanted to be everywhere at the same time, his tongue pressing and exploring the soft, pliable recesses of Blaise's mouth. Like being drunk, which he'd only experienced once or twice in his life. He slid his fingers under the hem of Blaise's sweater, and the touch of soft skin—as silky as Marie's fur—seared through him.

One little trickle of thought tiptoed into his brain. When they'd caressed in the steam room, it had been anonymous. Nothing more than a hookup, even though Llewellyn knew with whom he was hooking. Now Blaise knew him. Llewellyn. He'd chosen him. The truth of that choice thrilled him, but—

He must have tensed because Blaise responded, slowing the kiss and pulling back. "Problem?" He smiled down into Llewellyn's eyes.

"W-why?"

Blaise shook his head but didn't lose the grin—or the erection that pressed through his jeans into Llewellyn's groin. Man, did that feel good. Blaise made a cute grimace. "You're full of questions."

"It's my j-job."

"I think you're sexy."

"I think you're cr-crazy."

"Would you be open to having a relationship with me?"

"I-I don't know. Define 're-relationship.'"

Blaise pushed up on his arms and then rose to sitting. *Wise but disappointing.* "It'd be like most relationships, I guess."

"I w-wouldn't know." Llewellyn sat up too, hiding his sigh.

"Oh. Well, we'd have some drinks, go to dinner and a movie, and see what happens. If we like each other, maybe we keep going."

"Going w-where?"

"Jesus, Llewellyn, haven't you ever been in a relationship with a guy?"

"N-no." He stared at his hands. That was mostly true. Ramon did one-night stands from time to time.

"How come?"

Llewellyn shrugged. "I-I'm sh-shy. I stammer. I'm p-plain. Too much work for n-not enough reward." He smiled but gazed at his hands. Still, he could feel Blaise staring at him.

"Now I'm the one who thinks you're crazy. Just to be superficial, you're tall and lithe and have a killer ass and beautiful eyes."

Llewellyn gaped at him.

"You're wicked smart and interesting as hell and you have cool cats. Your stammering doesn't bother me, and I figure if you get comfortable with me, you'll stammer less. But it doesn't really matter. I like what you have to say."

"I-I saw you w-with G-George St-Stanley."

"Saw me what?"

Llewellyn raised a shoulder. "F-flirting."

He frowned. "When?"

"D-did it happen m-more than once?"

"Just tell me." He looked serious.

"In the g-garden. Outside the d-department."

"If you were paying attention, you may have noticed that George was doing all the flirting. With both of us—you and me—I might add."

"T-true."

"So?"

"Y-You're a T-TA. I'm a professor."

"Yes, but I'm not your TA. Or your student. And don't give me the whole age-difference crap. We're only a few years apart, you being brilliant and advanced. Besides, I'm not proposing. Just proposing a date or two."

"And a r-roll on the couch." He glanced at Blaise sideways with a grin.

"There is that." He sighed grandly. "But if you find that objectionable, we can always switch to the bed."

Llewellyn finally laughed. *Why exactly am I fighting so hard? He's adorable, he's sexy, he's funny—he's suspect. Whoa.* That last thought took him by surprise. He gazed at Blaise's handsome face. *But if he is questionable, the best way to answer the questions is to be around him, right? Yeah, that's a helluva good excuse.*

He must have smiled, because Blaise scooted slowly toward him with wicked intent gleaming in his eyes.

Llewellyn heard himself giggle, which made him blush. And then he heard a knock on the front door.

You are effing kidding me.

Blaise whispered, "Were you expecting someone?"

"N-no. B-but I s-seem to be everyone's b-best friend lately."

The knock came again, more insistently.

Llewellyn exhaled loudly and turned toward the door. Blaise laid a hand on his arm. "We could pretend we're not here." He grinned, but his voice had the ring of truth.

Llewellyn turned his head toward the front door—where three cats were loudly meowing.

Blaise laughed and shook his head as Llewellyn walked to the door, sighed, and opened it.

Okay, worst possible scenario. There stood Anne de Vere, clutching what looked like a scrapbook or photo album to her chest. "I'm so sorry, Llewellyn, but I just can't let this go without a fight. You have to see my point of view. I—" Her eyes seemed to travel past Llewellyn. "Oh. Hello, Blaise."

Blaise came up beside Llewellyn. "Hi, Anne."

"I'm sorry. I just didn't think." She looked back and forth between the two of them. "I thought you didn't know each other."

Blaise said, "We didn't—then."

"I see." Her brows gave a little dip.

He smiled but said, "No, you probably don't. I was concerned that Llewellyn was getting an awful lot of pressure over this offer you made, and I came to see how he's doing."

"Oh. Pressure." She looked uncomfortable.

"Yes. Most people don't ignore the amount of money you're tossing around, you know. It's difficult for Llewellyn to make his own decisions." Despite the implied criticism, he said it kindly.

"I didn't mean to place undue stress—"

Blaise made a cute snorting sound. "Yes, you did. You want this to be as tough to turn down as possible. I get that. I—"

Llewellyn waved a hand toward the living room. "W-why don't you c-come in?"

"Are you sure?"

He nodded, and she crossed in front of him, walked to the living room, and took a careful seat on the couch. Funny that Blaise's polite chastisement had made Llewellyn feel sorry for her. He glanced at Blaise, who stepped closer.

"Shall I go?"

Llewellyn said, "Anne?"

"What?" She looked at Blaise. "No. Of course not." Even though she was wearing black slacks, she pressed her knees together like she was in a skirt and hugged the album she was carrying against her chest.

Llewellyn took the chair closest to the couch without actually sitting beside her. "D-do you have s-something t-to show me?"

"Yes." She thrust the album forward.

He accepted it and opened it on his lap. If she noticed he seemed to be humoring her, she didn't let on.

She pulled her glasses out of her small purse and balanced them on her nose like they helped her think. "Dr. Lewis, these are copies of a series of documents that have been in my family for many years. Apparently the originals have been lost, but obviously someone in my family had them because these are photocopies, not a technology available in the sixteenth century. I'd like you to look at them. If you have a magnifying glass, it helps."

"Uh, y-yes." He walked to his closest desk and pulled a magnifying glass from the top right-hand drawer. He used them all the time. Returning to his chair, he picked up the album and opened it with something between the anticipation of discovery—and dread. The first two pages were posted with a handwritten document, clearly from sometime in the previous few decades, talking about how the family deeply believed that Edward de Vere created the works credited to William Shakespeare and that the following evidence proved it.

With a deep breath, Llewellyn turned the page.
Okay, interesting. The photocopies were not very
good—light in spots, crooked on one of the pages, and
faded—but appeared to be of an old, handwritten document using language and calligraphy that would have
been characteristic of the sixteenth or seventeenth
centuries. Obviously it would be difficult if not impossible to verify the authenticity of a bad photocopy, but
Llewellyn picked up the magnifying glass and tried to
read. The document was the beginning of what looked
like a play. He cocked his head and leaned back to
catch more of the light. The play seemed to be about
a fantasy setting, maybe somewhat similar to *A Mid-
summer Night's Dream.* Though parts were hard to
make out, the language was, no doubt, sophisticated,
funny, and lyrical at once. Very much like what one
would think of as Shakespearean.

Llewellyn looked up. "How long have you had
this?"

"I was given it about six months ago. It's what
prompted me to do the research that led me to you."
She beamed. "Isn't it amazing? We know that Edward
de Vere wrote that, and it's virtually Shakespeare.
Don't you agree?"

"It's quite imp-pressive. But Anne, y-you know
no one c-can prove de V-Vere wrote this. C-can't
prove it's n-not a forgery."

Blaise said, "Not meaning to butt in, but do you
think someone in your family had the originals, or that
they received the copies from an outside source?"

She sighed. "I haven't been able to find out."
Her face brightened. "But I'm hoping Llewellyn can

discover that. I think people are more likely to talk to him since he's a famous researcher."

Llewellyn stared at the pages. They went on and on with beautifully crafted, flowing dialogue. Some of the lines were even scratched out. The quality of the ink on the paper suggested it had been written with something far less consistent than an ink pen. In spite of himself, he felt a sizzle of excitement. "This m-might give me a place to start."

She pressed her hands against her chest. "Oh my God, I knew you'd love it. Now you understand why I'm so certain about Edward." A laugh escaped like a fountain. "Isn't it wonderful?"

Blaise chuckled. "I feel like I'm caught in a *Twilight* remake." He raised his left hand. "Team Edward." Then his right. "Team William."

She frowned at him.

He flashed the smile that sank a thousand female hearts. "Sorry. Just being a wiseass."

"W-why didn't you show m-me this right away?" Llewellyn asked.

She sighed. "I wanted to know what your attitude on the case would be without benefit of new evidence."

"Why?"

"I suppose I didn't want you to take the case just because of the money." She smiled. "And you didn't disappoint. Even for the money, you wouldn't promise to prove the unprovable." She pointed at the album. "But now you understand my certainty."

Llewellyn handed the album back toward Anne, but she held up her hands. "No, please keep it. Spend more time reviewing it. I think you'll find that it becomes more and more persuasive the more you read."

"I-I'd rather n-not."

"Please. If for no other reason that you're a researcher and this is a fascinating source of research."

Blaise leaned forward, elbows on his knees. "I know you were considering giving this project to Ramon Rondell."

Llewellyn felt himself flinch, and Blaise's eyes widened just a little at the reaction.

Blaise looked back at Anne. "Obviously you've changed your mind."

For an instant her expression said she'd been bluffing, but she composed her face more neutrally. "Of course, I'd rather have Dr. Lewis do the job if possible. Rondell does some amazing work, but he's so sensational, his results aren't always appreciated by the academic community."

Blaise grinned. If he'd said "Ya think?" his attitude couldn't have been more obvious. "But as you say, he does do some amazing work, based more on solid research that you'd expect from such a headline grabber."

"I agree. That's why I'd consider him." She smiled.

"What do you know about him?" Blaise glanced at Llewellyn, then back at Anne.

She shook her head. "Rondell? Very little, actually. Amazing how anonymous he stays. I suppose someone like that would get hounded by nutcases if he was well-known." She looked at Blaise directly. "Do you know anything?"

Blaise shrugged. "No. Of course, he's never been an object of study for me. I don't even know what he looks like."

She shook her head. "Me either. I've seen several pictures, but they're all different. Some show a really handsome guy, some an almost ugly man. A few pictures are blond, most brunet. Some even show him fat. Obviously he's used different photos at different times—" Her phone buzzed and she pulled it from her purse. A crease popped between her reddish brows. "Excuse me." She clicked. "Yes." The crease became a furrow. She glanced at Llewellyn and then at Blaise. "I've told you how I feel. Nothing has changed. I'm sorry, I'm quite busy. We'll have to talk later." She hung up without saying goodbye. "Sorry. My sister." She smoothed her pant legs unnecessarily. "Now, where were we?"

"Rondell," Blaise offered.

She pressed her hands together in front of her chest. She seemed upset by the call. "Of course. I trust I won't have to rely on Mr. Rondell, whatever he may look like. I'm so delighted." She stood. "I'll let you relax. I'm sorry to have intruded. Could you possibly call me a cab?" She looked at Blaise. "Unless you happen to be leaving, Blaise. I could hitch a ride with you."

For a moment a look of dismay crossed his face, but the charming smile overtook it. Hell, maybe the unhappiness was just Llewellyn's imagination. "Of course, glad to be of help." He stood and walked to where Llewellyn had risen beside Anne. He held out his hands and took both of Llewellyn's. "It's good for you to get some rest and not worry about any of this until tomorrow at the earliest. I'm sure if Anne sees Van Pelt, she'll tell him that you have a reprieve on decision-making while you examine this new information."

"Absolutely I will." She wrapped an arm through Blaise's and smiled at Llewellyn. "I'm so excited to have this in your hands." She gave Blaise's arm an obvious squeeze. "I'm so appreciative of this ride, Blaise." Without letting go, she said, "I'll see you soon, Llewellyn." She firmly led Blaise out the front door. Blaise managed one helpless glance over his shoulder.

Llewellyn closed the door and leaned against it. *Helpless. Hmm.* He could have said no.

His phone buzzed and bounced on his coffee table, and he hurried over and grabbed it. *Blaise? No. Too soon.* He didn't recognize the number. "H-hello."

"Dr. Lewis?"

"Y-yes."

"You need to know that Anne doesn't speak for the de Vere family. She has no right to promise you that money, and we'll see to it that you and the university never receive it. It's a fool's errand. Give it up."

"Who—who is this?"

"My name is Miranda de Vere. Trust me. I know what I'm saying. My family will take action to stop this insane compulsion of Anne's. That's all I have to say." The line went dead.

He stared at the phone.

How in hell could one nerd of an obscure historian suddenly be at the heart of refighting the Wars of the Roses?

CHAPTER NINE

BLAISE OPENED the car door for Anne. She smiled as she slid in, then looked up at him. "Thank you."

He nodded and closed the door, then walked around the car slowly, convincing his body it wasn't going to get some more Llewellyn sweetness and heat. But Anne clearly had an agenda—among many agendas flying all over Middlemark University. He couldn't quite pass up the chance to find out what it was. *Dammit.* He'd rather be pushing Llewellyn down onto a bed right now. That thought stopped him, and he glanced up at the house before he opened the driver's side. *Is Llewellyn a top? Bottom? Switch?* The throb in his groin said he didn't much care. Blaise liked it all ways, and he'd bet on Shakespeare's identity, whatever the hell that was, that Llewellyn had a preference in bed. Blaise sighed softly. The lights still burned. Probably Llewellyn diving into that album

Anne had given him. *Sure would like to get a look at it.* That could well be possible—one way or another.

He opened the door and slipped behind the wheel.

She gave him a look. "I thought maybe you'd changed your mind about driving me and were thinking of going back to Llewellyn's." But she smiled.

Pushing the Start button, he shook his head. "No, I just wanted to make sure everything seemed okay in the house." He pulled away from the curb.

"Why wouldn't it be?"

He shrugged. "Dr. Lewis impresses me as a supersensitive type."

"I suppose. But he has undertaken some very complex projects that required great persistence and championed them through the hypercritical hierarchy of historical researchers. That takes thick skin."

"Oh yes." He turned on a classical station, and they soaked up a little Beethoven until he turned left toward her hotel near the university. "I can imagine Llewellyn having thick skin as long as he doesn't have to meet his critics face-to-face. Obviously human contact isn't his strong suit."

"I thought you liked him."

"I do. Very much."

"You're quite critical."

He looked at her as he pulled into the hotel parking lot. "Did I sound that way? Not intentional. I'm one of his biggest fans."

He rolled into the portico of the hotel and stopped.

She said, "They have a nice bar. Would you like to come in for a drink?"

His brain did an instant calculation. How much information could he get out of her? Was there any chance of going back to Llewellyn's? "Sure. I'd love a drink."

She smiled big as he pulled away from the entrance and found a spot to park, then walked her back to the bar off the hotel lobby. Saturday night and the place was jumping. Some of that jumping involved people from the university, since it was nearby. He glanced around, recognizing some professors with their significant others and some in groups.

A bar waitress walked by with a tray of drinks, saw Blaise, smiled, and nodded toward the back corner. "A party's leaving back there."

"Thanks."

They skirted through the crowd and found the table just as a busboy was wiping it. They sat, and the same waitress showed up promptly. "Hi. What can I get you?" Her eyes never left Blaise's face.

He looked at Anne. "What would you like?"

"Do you have champagne by the glass?"

"We have splits." The waitress managed to drag her gaze from Blaise.

"That will be fine." Anne looked a little annoyed with the begrudged attention.

The waitress turned immediately back to Blaise. "And you?"

"Beer will be fine." He thought of Llewellyn's wonderful craft beer. "Whatever you have on tap."

"Can I get you some snacks?"

He glanced at Anne, who shook her head.

"No, thanks."

The waitress looked sad not to have any more excuse to hang around. "Okay, I'll be right back with drinks." She actually waggled her fingers in a little wave.

As the girl walked away, Anne said, "You must get that a lot."

He cocked a grin. "Attentive service, you mean?"

"Females hanging on your every syllable."

"Maybe I should wear more pink and spandex so they don't get the wrong idea." He grinned.

No reply.

He cocked his head at her.

"What are you saying?"

"That I'm gay. Sorry. I assumed you knew that."

A crease popped between her brows. "How would I?"

"Good question. Thanks for not assuming."

Then a little dawn seemed to break on her face. "So that means you and Llewellyn—"

He shrugged. "Could happen."

"I'm so sorry I pulled you away from an assignation." She didn't look extremely sorry.

He chuckled. "I'm impressed. You actually used 'assignation' in a sentence."

That coaxed a laugh from her.

Blaise shrugged. "I'm sure he's more interested in your materials than he'd be in me anyway."

"That seems unlikely."

"Thank you."

She sighed noisily. "What a waste."

"Forgive me if I don't agree, but thank you again."

"Maybe I meant Llewellyn." She half smiled.

"Still true."

"How does your family feel about you being gay?"

He gazed into space. "Well, let's see. They don't like that I decided not to go into business. They hate my taste in movies. But, hmm, nope, I never heard them say anything about me being gay except to ask what guy did I plan to take to the prom."

"Sorry. I guess that was kind of a silly, old-fashioned question."

"No, sadly. I wish it was. But a huge percentage of homeless kids are gay and trans, so it's still a pretty relevant issue."

The waitress came back with their drinks, Blaise paid her although Anne tried, and she went away reluctantly.

Anne sipped her champagne. "You got me hooked, I'm afraid."

"Good." He smiled. "We all deserve champagne."

"But you're not drinking it."

"I actually love beer. I save the bubbly for celebrations." He clinked her glass. "So tell me how the family, uh, interest in your ancestor's literary credential came about."

"Is 'interest' a polite word for obsession?" She smiled and sipped her champagne.

At least she had humor about it. "Your word, remember. Not mine."

She leaned back in the chair. "It started with my grandfather. I'm not sure where his interest came from, but we have records of his having spent thousands of dollars trying to get people to say that Edward was Shakespeare."

"Is 'get' a polite word for bribe?"

"Exactly." She shook her head. "Seriously, he actually was obsessed. He honestly didn't care if it was true or not. He just wanted the cachet of being a relative of Shakespeare." Her phone rang in her purse, and this time she really frowned. She opened the bag and glanced at her screen. "Sorry, I need to take this." She clicked the phone and put it to her ear, angling her body a little from Blaise, but she didn't leave the table. "I'm busy. What do you need?" Her frown got deeper.

Blaise pulled out his own phone and swiped through his emails so he wouldn't appear to be listening.

"I've already told you, I have no intention of stopping, and I'm perfectly within my rights to spend it. He would have wanted it this way, and I, at least, want to honor both his wishes and his memory." She listened, and her hand tightened on her phone. "I'm sorry. I really am." She clicked off and put the phone back in her bag with more force than was technically required. "Sorry." She looked up and smiled. "Family. Can't live with them."

"Can't kill them." He grinned, and she laughed.

"Exactly." She took a breath. "Anyway, at my grandfather's knee, my father got interested too, but he bothered to actually do the research and discovered both the strengths and weaknesses of the so-called Oxfordian conspiracy." She sipped. "He found what he believed to be more weight on the positive than the negative sides of the argument. Then, somehow, he saw the documents I gave to Llewellyn, and that tipped him over the edge."

Blaise frowned. "Not the actual documents you gave him, right? Those are a copy."

"Oh, of course. What I have are photocopies, but whether my father actually saw the originals or even owned those documents, I don't know. I was very young during most of this. I'm the youngest. He tried to interest my siblings in proving the story before he ever got to me. By that time he was old and infirm." She smiled. "But he was so thrilled that I was interested in carrying on his quest. It was the last thing he talked about before he died."

Blaise swallowed a mouthful of beer. "Five million is a lot of money. If your sibs weren't interested in the case, how do they feel about that much money going toward something they don't care about?"

"They feel as you might expect. That was one of my sisters on the phone." She slowly turned the champagne glass and gazed at it with a small frown. "But my father left money specifically for this case, so they can suck eggs." She grasped the stem of the glass, and it wobbled to the point of spilling some of the liquid.

"It must be hard having your own family against you."

"It is, but my brother and sisters are just greedy. This was my father's dying wish. I don't understand how they can do anything besides move heaven and earth to fulfill his wishes." She wiped her fingertips across one of her cheeks, then smiled and took a big swallow of her champagne.

Blaise drank down the last of his beer, and the waitress appeared like she'd been suspended from the ceiling watching. "Can I get you another?"

"Uh, no, thanks. Anne? More champagne?"

"Oh no. I'm getting kind of tired."

He handed the waitress two twenties. "Thanks for all your help."

When she walked away smiling, Anne asked, "Did you give her that to allay her disappointment?"

He just laughed and stood, then held her chair as she pushed back. They walked toward the door, skirting between tables.

"Anne?"

Blaise looked to the side and came face-to-face with Van Pelt, who sat at a table with three other similarly middle-aged academics. He jumped up and gave Blaise a long, rather annoyed look. "Uh, hello. I didn't know you'd be here."

Pretty dumb statement, since how would he know, but Blaise said, "We made a last-minute detour to come in for a quick drink."

Van Pelt's eyebrows crawled down toward his eyes. "Detour from what?"

None of your business, asshole.

Anne raised an eyebrow a little but said, "Blaise and I ran into each other earlier, and he offered to give me a ride home."

Van Pelt opened his mouth to speak, and she held up her hand. "I want to tell you that I'm giving Dr. Lewis an extension on my deadline. I gave him some additional data I want him to investigate before making his final decision about whether to take my case."

Van Pelt adopted a smile probably meant to be ingratiating, but somehow it came out condescending. "Ah, my dear, it's not really a case now, is it? You're not on trial."

She gave him a narrow-eyed glance. "Yes, well, I have to go. Good running into you." She slid her arm through Blaise's and gave him a tug.

Blaise nodded. "Good to see you, sir." He walked away with Anne practically pulling him. They exited into the lobby, and Blaise escorted her to the elevator, then stopped.

She sighed. "Thank you. That man annoys the hell out of me. In fact, I find academics rather hard to take across the board."

"And yet you want a building on a university campus to be renamed for Edward de Vere." He grinned to soften his incredulity.

"Yes, that was my father's wish. He really wanted the legitimacy academic recognition would give." She released a long stream of breath between her lips. "But you and Llewellyn are academics, so I shouldn't tar the whole profession with the same brush."

Blaise leaned against the granite wall and cocked his arms. "In truth, while Llewellyn's a researcher, I'm just a grad student, right? I'm still making up my mind what I want to do, and teaching may not be it."

"Oh? What else would you do?"

He shrugged, though he didn't feel quite as casual. "Maybe write ad copy or be a journalist. Who knows?"

"Well, that would be academia's loss." She put a warm hand on his arm. "Sorry I wrecked your date."

"No worries. You didn't." *Not exactly.*

She pushed the elevator button.

He said, "By the way. You mentioned that what you have is a copy of the de Vere original documents your father might have seen."

"Yes."

"But what you gave Llewellyn is a copy of your copy, right?"

The elevator door slid open, and two people walked off. Anne took a step into the elevator and turned. "Oh no. I gave him my copy. To reproduce it again would make it almost unreadable. Besides, who could be more responsible than Llewellyn?"

The door slid closed on Blaise's openmouthed expression.

LLEWELLYN WALKED down Higuera Street, sipping on his tea latte carefully since it was still hot. He'd sat up for hours after Anne left the previous night and he'd received that bizarre phone call. He'd wanted to call Anne and confront her, but what would she say? Of course, that she was right and her sister was an idiot.

Instead of calling her, he'd pored over the document Anne gave him, attempting to make sense of it—the whole time trying not to hope Blaise would come back. *Stupid.* Of course Blaise didn't return, suggesting that his intentions toward Llewellyn might be something other than lust. *Maybe.*

Oh crap, why can't I just go back to my quiet research and stop all this nonsense?

"Lew-Lew. Llewellyn."

He turned toward the voice behind him and found Lizzie striding toward him, carrying a large thermos. "H-hey."

She thrust the thermos toward him. "I couldn't get over how tired and upset you were when you got your tea. I thought you needed some more to tide you over."

"Th-thank you." He stared at the giant thermos, and heat pressed behind his eyes at her kindness. "S-so nice of y-you."

"No worries, Doc." She gave him a pat on the shoulder. "You know, it's funny. I've had a few people ask about you in the last day or so."

He frowned. "R-really? Who?"

"One was that guy I saw you with yesterday. The kind of cute one? He came by this morning and asked if you'd been at the shop. Then he left. Didn't even buy anything. What can you expect from a coffee drinker?" She snorted. "Then there was some other guy who at least bought tea, and there was some red-haired woman. It's weird. In the years I've known you, I don't remember anybody asking about you and then, bam."

"N-not sure which f-fact's m-more disturbing." He gave her a snarky grin. Hopefully he didn't show how damned much that news upset him. Probably the woman was Anne. The guy? Was it Blaise? Why would they ask about him at a tea shop? "Th-thank you again."

"My pleasure, sweetie. Bring back the thermos whenever." She gave him a wink, turned, and walked away with her sturdy stride.

He linked the thermos on the second finger of his left hand and headed for home, sipping his tea a bit more luxuriously since he knew there was more where that came from.

Why would Anne go to Jazzie Tea? How does she even know it exists or, more pertinently, that I go there? I need to be a private detective, not a researcher.

He turned on his street and tried to enjoy the warmth of the sun on his face before he went back into his cave and stared at a computer screen all day, trying to find some source for the document Anne had given him. It couldn't just appear in her hands with no one in the past having seen it. There had to be records somewhere—if it was real, of course.

He walked up to the porch, half expecting to see Carmen Echevarria. Oddly, after her big play, he hadn't heard from the Echevarrias. Not as if he needed any more lobbyists.

He slipped the key into the lock, opened the door, and got met by the usual carpet of meowing fur. "H-hi, my furries." He held up his thermos. "I'm s-sorry. I got something for me, but n-nothing for you this t-time." He knelt, set the thermos on the floor, and started his official petting duties. Julius rubbed and Marie Antoinette took a dive for his lap—just as the slam of metal against his head shot pain through his body and everything went black.

CHAPTER TEN

"LLEWELLYN. MY God. Llewellyn, what happened?"

Oh man, head hurts. Llewellyn tried to open his eyes. *Stop. Bad idea.* Light flashed like a strobe in his brain. Felt more like an ice pick. He squeezed his eyes shut again.

"Mew."

"Emily, get over here. Julius, inside the house. Shit! Marie." The voice came from somewhere above Llewellyn.

"B-Blaise?"

"Llewellyn, don't move. I'm calling 911." The sound of scrambling and scuffling. "Marie, goddammit. Get back here."

"Wait. D-don't need an ambulance."

"Yes, you do. Marie. Get over here."

Llewellyn tried to laugh. "Sh-she'll never come if you ch-chase her."

Blaise's voice got closer. "Just like a goddamn female."

"P-person."

"What?"

"N-not just f-female."

"True." Soft hands touched Llewellyn's face and his head. "What happened? Did you faint? Slip? When I got here, you were lying there, and I thought you were dead." His soft lips pressed against Llewellyn's forehead. "I need to call an ambulance because there could be something really wrong. Maybe you passed out. Maybe—"

Llewellyn slid a hand over Blaise's where it rested on his cheek. "H-hit."

"What?"

"Somebody hit m-me." He struggled up onto his forearm. "From behind."

Blaise slid his knee under Llewellyn's head. "Wait. Stop moving so fast." His cool palm caressed Llewellyn's forehead. "Just lie here for a minute while we assess the damage, okay?"

Llewellyn closed his eyes and sighed. Maybe just for a minute. No one ever took care of him. His brain whispered, *Whose fault is that?*

Blaise's fingers began to explore his head, sifting through his hair. "So you think you were hit? By whom?"

"N-no idea. I-I was petting the c-cats."

"Any chance you could have fallen and banged your head on the edge of the door?"

Well, damn. "N-no." He rolled his head to the side and managed to pull himself to sitting. "I'm n-not an idiot."

"Of course not." His hands on Llewellyn's back didn't feel quite as nurturing in light of his dismissal. "It's just that when you black out, it's sometimes hard to keep track of events."

"Th-thanks for the d-diagnosis." He got his feet under him and slowly rose.

"Why would someone hit you?"

"N-no idea." Although after the phone call, maybe he had a clue. He looked at the two cats inside the entry, then glanced at Marie, who sat halfway across the lawn, staring at him challengingly. "S-stay there. I don't give a d-damn." He glanced at Blaise, who still knelt on the porch, and let the command include him. With as much cool as he could muster, he turned and walked inside, pushing the door closed behind him.

He moved slowly across the entry, into the living room, and made it to the couch, where he flopped down. *Should call the police.* Of course, they'd be even more skeptical than Blaise. Stuttering nerd of a professor saying he got struck from behind for no reason whatsoever. *Right.*

"Merwaow." Julius swaggered across the floor and jumped up beside Llewellyn, butting against his hand for a pet.

"Y-you're pretty c-cocky without Marie, aren't y-you?" He stroked his orange fur.

"Merwawwr."

"Y-yes, I know. I have to let her b-back in even though she's acting like a p-pill." The door looked a mile away. "Y-you open it."

"Mewow."

After one more chuck under Julius's chin, he stood, staggered to the door, and opened it. *Okay, seriously cute.* Blaise sat on the top step of the porch, his back to Llewellyn, with a white fluffy tail hanging off the side of his lap. The movement of his arm suggested serious petting going on.

"W-want to c-come in?"

Blaise didn't even turn around. He just stood, fluffy tail rising with him, turned with Marie in his arms, and walked in the door. When he got to the couch, he sat, still stroking Marie. She stared at Llewellyn like, *So there.*

Llewellyn just wanted to sit back down before he fell down. He made it to the chair and sat, which gave him a different perspective on the room. What he needed was a new perspective on life. *Wish I had some tea.* He glanced around for the thermos Lizzie had given him. Maybe still in the entry. *Hell, is it cold? How long has it been since I opened the door and—*

He froze, his eyes glued to the coffee table. *No.*

Like his head was on a swivel, he stared around the room.

"What's wrong?" Blaise sounded kind of annoyed. Him and Marie.

Llewellyn pressed a hand to his chest. "The b-binder from Anne. It's g-gone."

"What do you mean?"

Llewellyn rose. "G-gone. It was there." He pointed at the table where he'd been studying it the previous night. The night Blaise hadn't come back. The night weird strangers had threatened him.

Llewellyn rushed around the room, his head throbbing and his gut in a ball of sick. Nowhere. It wasn't there. He faced Blaise. "S-someone took it. Whoever h-hit me. Robbed."

"Good God, why? Who'd want it, besides you and Anne?"

Llewellyn shook his head. "Who—who even knew it existed?"

"Shall I call the police?"

Should he? Sweet Jesus, he was knocked out and robbed. "D-do you think they'll p-pay attention? I have a big lump, but I c-can't p-prove I was hit. They could think I fell." He frowned. "Like y-you did." He wiped a hand over his neck. "And there's no v-value to a copy of a c-copy of an obscure d-document. W-will the p-police care? Will they even b-believe me?" He looked up at Blaise, who stared at Llewellyn with a weird expression. "Wh-what?"

"I hate to tell you this, but—" He exhaled noisily. "That wasn't a copy of a copy. I think it was Anne's only copy."

His stomach leaped into his throat. "N-no. She n-never told me."

"When I was taking her home, she said something that made me worry, so I asked her. She said, 'Where could it be safer than with Llewellyn?' But if she wanted to be sure it was safe, she should have told you. I assumed she had, or I would have called you."

"Wh-when would she h-have told me? You w-were here." Llewellyn's hands actually shook, and his voice rose. *Anne's priceless family artifact. Gone.*

"I don't know." Blaise locked his hands behind his neck. "I didn't think. I just—"

"I guess we sh-should call the police." He sighed. "B-but f-first I should c-call Anne."

Blaise stood and waved a hand at the couch. "You lie down and let me take care of it, okay? Come on. You might have a concussion."

"N-no."

Blaise frowned.

"I-I mean, n-no concussion. I will lie d-down."

As soon as he was horizontal, Marie jumped on his chest and the other two bracketed him, all purring loudly. Drifting through the vibration and the warmth, he vaguely heard Blaise saying, "Anne, I know this is hard to believe, but someone hit Llewellyn on the head and stole the manuscript."

Yes, they certainly did. He drifted off.

THE DETECTIVE leaned forward in Llewellyn's comfortable living room chair. "Ms. de Vere, why is this document so valuable?"

"It's my only copy." It came out as a wail.

"That's not what I'm asking. Who would want to hit Dr. Lewis on the head in order to steal this photocopy you describe? Who would want it?"

"Many, many people." She was practically crying.

Blaise said, "The document provides evidence that an English nobleman might have been the real Shakespeare. It's a claim that people have been trying to prove for years. As I understand it, this document isn't definitive since it's a photocopy and its authenticity is hard to prove, but it does take a step toward establishing the connection between the Earl of Oxford and Shakespeare."

The detective, whose name was Holiday, wrinkled his nose. "Excuse me, but who cares?"

Anne's head snapped up. "Who cares? Dear God, it's one of the greatest mysteries of all time. The person who proves Shakespeare's real identity will be renowned and respected."

"But Dr. Lewis is the one trying to prove it, and he didn't hit himself on the head." He gave Llewellyn a look that definitely questioned the whole head-hitting thing. The police had brought an EMT, who had verified Llewellyn had a lump, but it was impossible to establish how he acquired it.

Blaise cleared his throat. "Uh, Detective, Ms. de Vere has offered five million dollars to Middlemark University if Dr. Lewis, or anyone, I suppose, is able to prove that de Vere is Shakespeare."

"Holy shit. Uh, excuse me."

"Exactly." Blaise nodded. "That's enough for somebody to do some head hitting."

"But who benefits from it not being proven?"

Blaise shrugged.

Llewellyn took a breath. "Y-yes, that is the b-big question. I haven't h-had a chance to t-tell Anne, but her sister called me l-last night and said the rest of the f-family doesn't want the research to g-go forward. Sh-she was very upset."

Anne huffed. "Damn. My sister's an idiot. All my siblings are. And they have no say, since my father left money specifically for this purpose and put me in charge of it." She looked at Llewellyn. "So whatever she told you is hogwash."

Holiday wiped a hand over his forehead like he'd never heard a stupider case. "Still, by stealing the document you had, somebody's assuring this research doesn't continue, so I guess they're successful."

Llewellyn shook his head. "F-fortunately, I-I did read it all." He pointed at his temple. "Very g-good memory."

The detective shrugged. "But your memory isn't proof."

"The document isn't p-proof. Must f-find the original."

The detective stood. "I've got to be honest. This is kind of an obscure case for our little police department. The object of the theft could be easily destroyed by one good match. Aside from Ms. de Vere's offer, which certainly can't be collected by most people, it's hard to see who gains. If it was stolen by your relatives, it's really a family matter or a question for an estate lawyer, not the police. I'm afraid we could invest a lot of time and get no results and, well, we have bad guys to catch. I'll file a report on the possible assault, and aside from that if you learn anything more, feel free to call me."

Moments later he was gone.

Llewellyn, Anne, and Blaise sat in silence. Finally Llewellyn said, "I-I'm so sorry."

Anne glared at him. "How could you leave it just out in the open where anyone could find it?"

"I-I—"

Blaise lifted his head. "Be fair, Anne. You never told Llewellyn this was your only copy, and who would ever dream that anyone gave a shit, anyway? You didn't even come clean about your family. Plus, he left it in his own living room. Not exactly a thoroughfare." He got up and stalked across the room to where Marie Antoinette sat on the window seat, looking out onto the porch. He stroked her fur like it calmed him down. It probably did. "I know there's a lot of money at stake, but who'd actually attack someone to get an obscure historical document?"

She stood. "I have to go. I'm just too upset to deal with this right now."

Blaise glanced at Llewellyn, then at Anne. "Do you need a ride?"

"Okay." She marched to the door, not looking back.

Blaise stood also, but Llewellyn stayed in his chair. Blaise murmured, "Can I come back?"

Llewellyn shrugged. "If y-you want."

For a second Blaise gazed at Llewellyn's face, then turned and followed Anne out the door.

In the quiet, Llewellyn leaned his head back on the cushions of the chair and took a breath. He had three cats on and around him in seconds. Marie crawled as high on his chest as she could get, ending up with her head over his heart. He petted her idly.

So Blaise is coming back. How do I feel about that? A warmth in his nether regions certainly communicated how his body felt about it. But no matter how much he might crave some more of those kisses, it was hard to forget a couple of facts. Except maybe for Anne's sister, Blaise Arthur was the only other person he was aware of who knew he had the Oxford document, and Blaise was the one who was there when Llewellyn woke up.

BLAISE PARKED two blocks from Llewellyn's house and clicked off the ignition so his call transferred from the car system to his phone. "Yeah, there's a lot going on. More than I thought. Even if I could get the first story wrapped up soon, which seems unlikely, I have to see what else happens."

"Don't take forever." His mother's voice growled, but he knew she loved him.

"I won't. But trust me, this is great stuff."

"You sure you're not the one getting the great stuff?" She gave a snorting laugh, but it didn't sound happy.

"I wish. Talk soon." He hung up. *More like I hope.* With a sigh he left the car, trotted up the walk, and climbed the porch stairs, then took a deep breath and knocked softly on the door.

Nothing.

He tried again. *Damn, Llewellyn changed his mind. I guess I kind of deserve it.*

He grabbed the door handle to give it a sharp yank just for satisfaction—and it opened. His heart slammed against his ribs. Shit, if he'd gotten hit over the head last time, what—

He tore open the door, rushed in, and—stopped as he stared across the living room at the sleeping beauty. Blaise knew Llewellyn was asleep because he was snuffling a soft snore, and the cats were purring almost as loudly, creating a symphony of buzzing.

Whew. Beauty was right. Funny how hard Llewellyn worked to look plain, but that bone structure was sheer perfection, and those big brown eyes could suck you into eternity. Blaise cocked his head.

"Mewr."

Llewellyn's eyes fluttered open. For a dreamy moment, his lips turned up. "Hi." Then his eyes widened the rest of the way, he gasped and leaped up. The cats squalled and jumped in three directions, and Llewellyn teetered and fell backward to the couch again. "How the hell did you get in here?"

Blaise crossed his arms. "You left the door un-locked after Anne and I went out."

"I f-fell asleep." He wiped a hand over his face.

Blaise walked across the room and sat next to Llewellyn. He didn't move away. *Maybe a hopeful sign?* "You need to be more careful. After that bash on the head, you don't know who to trust."

"Th-that's the truth." He gave Blaise a sideways glance.

Blaise put a hand on his arm. Llewellyn looked at it but again didn't pull away. Blaise tightened his grip a little. "You're suspicious of me, right? I knew you had the document when hardly anyone else did."

Llewellyn nodded. Man, it was challenging deal-ing with a serious mind.

"I know. All I can say is, I didn't do it. Honest-ly, why would I? What would I gain?" He looked up. "And I'd lose you. I mean, not that I have you or anything."

Llewellyn just stared.

"Please tell me if you suspect me."

Llewellyn blew out a breath. "N-no. Not really. You had n-no reason."

"Right." His shoulders relaxed. "Would you like a beer?"

He nodded.

Blaise walked into the cool, old-fashioned closed kitchen with the shiny new appliances and peered into the refrigerator. *I'm a shit.* With a deep breath, he grabbed two bottles, opened them, and carried them back to the living room. Llewellyn was walking back from the hall, his khakis still rumpled from sleeping in them.

"I-I ch-changed my shirt. Got dirt fr-from the porch."

Blaise handed him the bottle, followed him back to the couch, and sat. He swigged the good beer. "I'm so sorry this happened to you. I don't just mean getting mugged. I mean all of it."

"Y-yes."

He slid a hand across Llewellyn's shoulders—so surprisingly broad and strong for a guy who portrayed himself as wimpy.

CHAPTER ELEVEN

GOOSE BUMPS on top of goose bumps.

Tingles traveled out along his nerves from the soothing touch of Blaise's hand until the hairs on his arm weren't the only things standing up. Why did Blaise just turn his whole existence upside down? When Blaise was around, Llewellyn wanted things it was stupid for him to want. Things that only happened to the special, lucky guys. Forever things.

In spite of himself, he sighed and slowly lowered his head to Blaise's shoulder.

Blaise dropped his cheek against Llewellyn's hair. For minutes they just sat like that, their beer bottles dripping on the coffee table. Weirdly, it was the most peaceful moment Llewellyn had experienced in… at least days. Since that fateful night when he'd first seen Blaise dancing.

Gently, Blaise slipped a hand under Llewellyn's chin and turned his head toward him. Almost like he was stealing his breath, he moved his lips ever so slowly toward Llewellyn's, pausing a half inch away. Llewellyn's lips quivered, the scent of the beer they'd both drunk filling his head. Dear God, could he climax just from the anticipation of kissing Blaise?

Finally, finally their lips touched. Softer than Marie's fur.

And *bam!* Blaise grabbed Llewellyn's head and devoured his mouth like a five-course banquet menu.

The silly analogy used in novels, that people went up in flames—not silly anymore. Llewellyn's nervous system overloaded before Blaise's tongue had even explored the deeper recesses in his mouth. He heard himself moaning and whimpering. Embarrassing, but he couldn't stop.

His brain knew there was something off about Blaise. Some truth that needed exploring. He didn't care. He wanted to delude himself all the way to the bedroom. He'd trade his greed to know the answers for a night in Blaise's arms.

Blaise pressed him backward onto the couch, and Llewellyn didn't resist. In fact, both his khaki-clad legs surrounded Blaise's hips and held on like a giant, skinny monkey. Totally getting with the program, Blaise grasped Llewellyn under the butt and started thrusting—a move that would have been a lot more fruitful without clothes. Still, it felt so very good Llewellyn never wanted it to stop.

Blaise did.

He froze and reared back, breaking all that hot, delicious contact, grabbed Llewellyn's arm, and pulled him up. With a breath he wrapped one arm behind Llewellyn's back and leaned to grab him under the legs.

"Whoa!" Llewellyn pressed a hand against Blaise's chest. "I ap-preciate your optimism, but I'm almost as t-tall as you. You'll never g-get me off the ground."

Blaise grinned. "Wanna bet?"

"N-no. I'll walk." The smile spread over his lips by itself. "En-thusiastically."

"Race you." Blaise took off like a rabbit toward the hall. Of course, he didn't know where the bedroom was, so that might slow him down. Still, Llewellyn walked slowly after him.

When he got to the master, Llewellyn leaned against the doorjamb and watched the show. His back to the door, Blaise tossed clothes in several directions, and oh my, the landscape being revealed. His T-shirt was already draped over the easy chair Llewellyn used for late-night reading. Creamy, beige skin stretched over broad shoulders, well-developed lats, and a narrow waist commanded the view until the jeans dropped off, leaving—oh my, that same creamy, beige skin stretched over the most delectable pair of buns, hard and high. It was difficult to drag his eyes from them until Blaise leaned forward to slide the denim down his legs and uncovered the enticing gap between those buns, to say nothing of some hangy-downy bits that attracted Llewellyn's gaze.

With difficulty, Llewellyn held himself still and didn't hurl himself on Blaise's back, because who got a view like this—ever?

Finally Blaise stood nude and seemed to realize he was under scrutiny. He looked over his shoulder. "Doing research?"

"My p-passion."

"See anything you'd like to get passionate about?" He fluttered his lashes, which looked incongruous and cute on his alphaish, all-American-boy face.

"The whole p-package."

Blaise jumped and turned, landing with his groin framed by his fingers. "This package?"

"Among other th-things."

"To take advantage of what's offered, Dr. Lewis, you need a helluva lot fewer clothes."

Confronting. He stared at his shoes, then turned and started walking toward the en suite bathroom he'd had added to the old house after he inherited it.

"Uh, where are you going?"

He didn't turn. "To und-dress."

"No way, Jose. Get back here and let me watch. Fair's fair."

"N-not the s-same."

"So true."

Llewellyn glanced back and nodded.

Blaise flashed his dimples. "Better. Now get over here and let me help with the unveiling."

"N-no. Not wise."

Blaise walked across the room, nude and apparently unselfconscious. Hell, he had no reason to be. *Perfection.*

Blaise reached out and grabbed the front of Llewellyn's polo shirt. "You fond of this shirt?"

"N-not really." Llewellyn stared down at Blaise's hand.

"Good." His fist tightened and he yanked the shirt upward over Llewellyn's head, fabric ripping somewhere along the way. Llewellyn's arms dropped automatically and surrounded his own bare torso, but Blaise pushed his hands away and leaned forward to kiss his chest.

Embarrassing, but so very nice.

Blaise's kiss stole across Llewellyn's skin until he nibbled his way to Llewellyn's nipple and closed his mouth over the tingling bud. Never had Llewellyn seen the attraction of that kind of foreplay—oh, what a mistake. Who knew the nerves in his chest were directly connected to his even more intimate regions?

He shivered. Blaise chuckled and murmured, "So beautiful and so sensitive."

Llewellyn shook his head, but the shaking head turned to thrashing as Blaise licked and pecked his way down Llewellyn's abdomen. He simultaneously undid the button of his khakis and began sliding the loose fabric down Llewellyn's hips.

Some piece of Llewellyn's brain deeply regretted his choice of baggy white boxers that morning, but even that couldn't swamp the throbbing desire to get that questing mouth where it appeared to be going. *Throbbing. Appropriate word.*

For a minute the kissing stopped—*damn!*—as Blaise leaned down and untied Llewellyn's walking shoes. "Step out." Llewellyn did as requested, and the pants slid to his ankles. Blaise slipped his fingers in the ugly shorts and snapped them down in one bold move. They bagged around Llewellyn's ankles. "One more step." Without even thinking—most reasonable thought having signed off for the night—Llewellyn moved forward and, just like that, stood nude.

His hands moved to cover his very prominent erection, but Blaise got there first. He dropped to his knees and stared right at what Llewellyn would have liked to hide. He cocked his head. "Well, isn't this a big deal."

Llewellyn made a snorting sound. It was all he could manage. Yes, he was better endowed than most people might guess, but it didn't need to be discussed in polite conversation. He twisted a little, but Blaise held his hips.

"Appreciation's in order."

Llewellyn sucked his breath. *Appreciation? What kind?* "Ohhhhh."

Blaise took Llewellyn in his mouth and ap- plied gentle pressure—but it was enough to suck his brains right out of his head. Flashes of electricity shot through him and lit him up until all he could feel was between his belly and his thighs. No chance for his legs to hold him. His knees weakened; he stumbled and Blaise caught him, and together they flailed to the bed where Llewellyn fell, Blaise pounced, and that was all, game over, thank you sports fans.

Llewellyn cried out and his brain exploded as Blaise just kept sucking him into a new dimension. Gasping, Llewellyn lifted his whole torso off the bed as pleasure so intense he could barely stand it seared through him. He collapsed back to a gasping blob.

Gradually, his heart returned to normal—no, wait. It was kind of unlikely his heart would ever return to normal. But he stopped gasping enough to notice the warm heat of Blaise's cheek resting against his thigh. "I'm s-sorry."

Blaise snapped his head up like a jack-in-the-box. "What? Why?"

"I w-wanted to w-wait and—y-you know."

Blaise scooted up beside Llewellyn and turned on his side, chuckling against Llewellyn's ear. "Oh. don't worry. We'll get to 'you know' eventually."

"I could—" He glanced down toward his intruding penis.

"Unh-unh." Blaise folded his arms around Llewellyn and snuggled against him. "Just sleep. We'll think about the rest later."

I should—

His eyelids fluttered… and closed.

WHEN HIS eyes opened, Llewellyn stared into the dark in front of his face and felt the warmth of another body cuddled next to him. *Amazing.* Never before in his life. He'd never spent the night with a lover. Even Ramon had slept alone. As a child, he hadn't spent a night sleeping beside his mother as most children had. His life was a cuddle-free zone. He never thought he'd missed it.

Blaise made a little muttering, snuffly noise. It sounded vulnerable. With a moan he rolled onto his back, exposing a significant target area.

Llewellyn smiled and began to scoot toward Blaise's still half-masted erection as Blaise flopped an arm above his head, stretching his muscled body like a cat in the sun. Make that moon.

Oh my.

Llewellyn licked his lips. This was a sexual practice Ramon had perfected, so Llewellyn felt comfortable gently kissing Blaise and then sliding him into his mouth all the way to his throat. Funny. He'd done this a number of times, but it had only been mechanical. A way to maintain his reputation for prowess and mastery. This time he noticed everything—the sweet, musky smell, the feeling of soft, soft skin stretched taut over the hard cylinder. Most of all, he noticed how perfectly Blaise fit into his mouth—even though he was more than a mouthful.

"Oh baby, baby. What's going on down there?"

"If y-you d-don't know, I must—"

"Be doing it wrong? No way."

Spurred on, Llewellyn returned to his task, and Blaise popped his hips, moaning and mewling until he froze and backed himself slowly from Llewellyn's mouth. "Wait. If we actually want to do this together this time, you better quit that. You're too wonderful."

Wonderful. Hell, he knew who was wonderful.

Blaise scooched back and sat up, then smiled. "Oh good." He nodded toward Llewellyn's very prominent condition. Falling forward onto hands and knees, he crawled closer, then nuzzled Llewellyn's ear. "Can I offer you top or bottom?"

The word slid out on a sigh. "Bottom, p-please."

"So polite. Please direct me to the condoms and lube."

"L-lube's in the b-bedside t-table. I—I don't have c-condoms."

Blaise cupped his cheek. "Why?"

"N-never need them." He stared at his hands, lying on either side of his erection.

"Not from lack of attention?" He looked incredulous, which was damned flattering.

"Y-yes."

Blaise whispered, "We better buy a large economy-sized box, because we're going to need them all the time from now on."

"W-we are?" He grinned.

"Yeah. Meanwhile, I have one in my wallet." Scrambling, he opened the drawer, grabbed the lube, and tossed it to Llewellyn. "Do you mind using it yourself? It would be more romantic if I did it, but I find I'm several furlongs beyond anxious."

Anxious barely describes it. Llewellyn opened the cap and squeezed sticky fluid into his hand. He began shoving it in the appropriate channel as Blaise jumped off the bed with parts bouncing and grabbed his jeans from the floor. Rummaging in the pockets, he found his wallet and produced the coveted item from it. He held out the package. "I hope it's not so old it disintegrates."

With another energetic leap, he landed back on the bed, gloved himself, and fell forward, taking Llewellyn down with him and kissing when they landed. Suddenly Llewellyn's mouth felt complete— even more than when Blaise's dick had been in there. Llewellyn caressed every corner of Blaise's lips he could reach. Sweeter and sweeter.

Blaise pulled away an inch. "Come on, beautiful." He reared back, grasped Llewellyn's hips, and pulled him to the edge of the bed, then draped Llewellyn's legs on his shoulders.

Llewellyn's eyes widened. "F-face-to-face?"

"I want to see your eyes. To know how you feel."

"O-okay."

Blaise positioned himself, and Llewellyn's heart hammered. As the pressure started, Blaise gazed into his eyes, and Llewellyn felt the heat in his own cheeks. Blaise smiled. "You're so cute."

"N-not—ohh."

Blaise slid in deep, and nerves that hadn't been touched in so long sprang to life. That applied to all kinds of organs in his body—including his heart. "Oh G-God, Blaise."

"Yes, oh yes." Blaise pressed his chest close to Llewellyn's, heart to heart, every move claiming another small piece of emotional real estate.

Fight it. Don't be stupid.

Fuck it. Stupid sounds wonderful. Mostly what smart got him was lonely.

He wrapped himself like a monkey around Blaise's beautiful body, rising to meet every new thrust, letting the mewling sounds fly out of his throat and not caring where they landed.

Blaise increased the pace. *So good.* Almost too much pleasure. Llewellyn could fly apart from the pressure to scream his joy. The deep drives followed by little jerks of Blaise's hips slid over Llewellyn's gland, sending shock waves into his brain and belly on every pass. The heat built and built until the need to explode centered in his groin—like planets and stars must be circulating around his cock, getting ready for another big bang.

Blaise's jamming hips got erratic, and his noises emerged louder and more frantic. "Llew—gonna—oh God. Soon. So close. Soon. Can you—"

With a gasp Blaise grabbed Llewellyn's most sensitive organ in his hand and gave it a long, slow pull.

"Yes!" No amount of foreplay prepared him. The orgasm ripped through him like a tidal wave of feeling in shudder after shudder of pure fire, spasming his belly and shooting up his spine until his head exploded. "Oooooh, gooood."

Blaise held himself on straining forearms and, at Llewellyn's cry, let go, slamming them both to the mattress. The weight on Llewellyn from shoulder to calf felt so damned amazing.

It was hard to gasp for air with a hundred-and-seventyish-pound body on top of him, but he sure didn't want Blaise to move. Finally, though, Blaise rolled to his side, off Llewellyn, but he reached out, wrapped his arm around Llewellyn's neck, and pulled him closer. *Nice.*

Maybe he'd rest for a few minutes. Llewellyn's eyes closed, and he dissolved into the smell of musky sex and spicy man. *Yes, damned amazing.*

CHAPTER TWELVE

WHERE AM I? The thought barely registered in Blaise's brain before good feelings swamped him. His body tingled in all the right places, and his usual restless energy had magically been replaced by a deep, satisfying lassitude. He didn't want to think, much less move. Of course, thinking was the real problem.

Llewellyn's head lay heavily on Blaise's shoulder, his breath hushed deep and soft from his slightly parted lips. Beautiful full lips. So not nerdy. A lot of things about Llewellyn didn't go together. Didn't add up. *That's good for me, I guess.* He sighed softly. His left arm had gone to sleep, but he didn't want to wake Llewellyn. If he were honest, he'd like to tighten his hold and never let go. *If Mother knew, she'd kill me.*

Just then Llewellyn muttered in his sleep and rolled onto his side, taking the pressure—and the warmth—away from Blaise. *Damn, he probably heard my thoughts.*

Moving very slowly, he slid away from Llewellyn to the edge of the bed, swung his feet to the floor, and got up, glancing back at the sleeping beauty. *It's good he's getting some rest. I'll bet he doesn't sleep enough. Yeah, look who's talking.*

Naked as a mole rat, Blaise felt his way toward where he vaguely remembered the bathroom door was. It took some feeling around on the wall, but he connected with the door handle, stepped in, closed the door to block the light, and flipped the wall switch. Despite the age of the house and the old-fashioned style of most of the rooms, the bathroom was obviously remodeled. Shiny marble countertops and subway tile set off a claw-foot tub and a separate walk-in shower. He peeked in. *Multiple showerheads. Fun.*

He used the facilities, then opened the medicine cabinet, looking for a toothbrush. The mirrored shelves contained a basic collection of just-your-usual—aspirin, aftershave, extra razor blades, mouthwash, and toothpaste. Just one toothbrush. Clearly not expecting company. Blaise dumped a capful of minty mouthwash into his mouth and swished, then spat. He washed his hands, then opened the drawers for fun. Not much to see. The only real puzzle was a small tube of eyelash glue. Funny. Maybe Llewellyn used to date women?

Blaise closed the drawer, then stepped to a door on the other side of the bathroom and opened it a crack. *Oh, a closet. A big one.* Llewellyn really had remodeled this area of the house thoroughly. The room looked like it might be an addition. Interesting, though. How big a closet did a man need for five pairs of khakis?

With a glance toward the bedroom, Blaise stepped into the closet and turned on the light. *Wow. What a great design.* Built-in shelves crawled up the back wall, with a peninsula sticking out, also containing shelves of various sizes. On the wall, two rows of hanging bars actually held a fair number of clothes. Yes, the khakis were front and center, along with various white shirts and even a few sweater vests. *Seriously, Llewellyn.* But when Blaise walked to the back areas of the shelves, there were suits and a couple of leather jackets. A slanted show rack held a few pair of handmade loafers that Blaise had never seen anywhere near Llewellyn's feet. Who'd have thought he was a secret clotheshorse? But where did he wear this stuff?

Maybe he only wears them in here? A full-length floor-standing mirror was positioned in one corner, and Blaise tried to imagine Llewellyn prancing around in his closet, modeling his fancy wardrobe. Did not compute. *Should I tell him I saw the clothes and ask if he'd like to go on a date with me where he can wear some of them?*

Better not.

He reached to turn off the light when a tote bag caught his eyes. A copy of one of Llewellyn's historical research pieces sat on top, and Blaise picked it up to look through it. A book on the process of research. He flipped the pages. Even on a totally academic subject, Llewellyn had an engaging writing style that clarified the most complex topics and made the reader feel cared about. Yeah, that was one of the reasons Blaise was there.

As he leaned to replace the book, something silky, black, and shiny shone beneath where the book had been. Nosiness ran in his family. First he cocked his head. He still couldn't tell what it was, so he reached in and ran a finger over the enticing object. *What the hell?* He grabbed it and pulled out a longish dark wig. *Is Llewellyn a secret cross-dresser?* The image made him smile—the quiet, conservative geek strutting out in women's clothing. Blaise glanced around the closet. Nothing in there suggested a female wardrobe. Quite the contrary. Most of it was pretty fashionable men's couture.

Maybe a Halloween costume? *Not likely.* It was very beautiful quality hair, and it had been apparently hidden in the tote bag. Blaise held it out and stared at the wig. *Wait. The steam room. The kiss.* When he'd grabbed the guy in the spa, at first he'd thought it was Llewellyn, but then he'd gotten closer and seen the dark hair. Dark hair that looked a lot like the wig in his hand. *Well, damn. Tricky devil.* Maybe Llewellyn used a disguise to go hang out in gay men's clubs and bathhouses—to protect his rep as a serious academic—or maybe to escape from it. Or maybe—? *Shit.* Blaise's stomach flipped. He wanted to hide the wig at the bottom of a well and forget he ever saw it.

Sighing, Blaise carefully replaced the wig and set the book on top of it. He turned off the light and crept back into the bathroom. When he'd flipped the light switch off, he very quietly opened the door and peeked out. Llewellyn still snored very softly.

"Merwaowr." Julius got up from his spot on the chair where he lay on top of Blaise's shirt and bounced to the floor to rub against Blaise's legs.

"Shh." Blaise glanced at Llewellyn, but he didn't seem to register the cat. Probably used to the meowing, since cats were essentially nocturnal. Marie Antoinette had taken up a position on the pillow Blaise had been lying on. She gave him a level stare, daring him to try to take it back.

Sadly, he wasn't going to battle her for supremacy. He had places to go and phone calls to make—which kind of ripped his heart out. Tiptoeing, he grabbed his jeans from their heap on the floor and slid his T-shirt off the chair, still warm from Julius's big body. He peered around in the nearly dark room but couldn't find his boxer briefs. Oh well, it wouldn't be the first time he'd left his underwear behind.

Llewellyn gave a little moan and turned on his back. Marie Antoinette adjusted her position so she was curled around his head. Blaise wanted to pull out his phone and take a picture, it was so cute.

He sucked a deep breath and let it out slowly. *Wish I didn't have to go. Wish I didn't have to do a lot of things. Damn, wish I hadn't snooped.* Frowning, he turned abruptly and walked out of the bedroom, pushing the door closed so Julius couldn't follow him.

In the living room, he opened a desk drawer and found a notepad and a pencil. He wrote—

So sorry to leave. I really didn't want to, but I have an early meeting tomorrow. You were sleeping so soundly, I didn't want to wake you. Marie Antoinette took my place keeping you warm.

His hand paused over the *L* word. With a scribble he signed, *See you tomorrow. Blaise.*

Trying not to think, he powered out the front door, pushed the button, and closed it behind him so it would lock automatically and he wouldn't be tempted to go back in.

He'd parked the extra distance away so as not to get Llewellyn's neighbors talking, but hell, how many people would talk about Llewellyn Lewis if Blaise completed his mission? *Maybe I don't have to say anything? Hell, the clothes, the wig could mean a lot of things.*

Yeah, but anything out of character was significant. He knew that as well as he knew his name—uh, names.

He dialed. It rang three times.

"Damn, it's the middle of the night. Is there a reason?"

"Maybe not."

"I'm awake now. Talk."

"I looked in Lewis's closet. He's got a lot of upscale clothes that I've never seen him wear. Nothing even close to the usual baggy khakis. It seems odd that he'd have this alternate wardrobe if he never wears it."

"I agree. Anything else?"

Maybe I don't have to say anything.

"Blaise?"

He sighed. "Yeah, there's something else." He took a breath and told her about the wig.

A half hour later, Blaise walked to the back entrance of the history building. Time to test the theory that the security credentials that let him in one building also worked on all the others. He pulled out his magnetic card and took a deep breath—

A NOTE. He left a note. Llewellyn stared at the top of his dresser at Blaise's obviously quick scrawl. He so wanted to feel good about that scrap of paper, but no go. Everything felt off. He'd had sex with Blaise Arthur, and it had been better than… anything.

Now here he stood staring at his tote bag in the closet and tingling. Had it been moved? *Something's different.* He glanced around. Who could have been in here? The person who stole the document? *Was I unconscious long enough for the assailant to come in the closet, move something, and then put it back?* Seriously, would somebody violent enough to hit him in order to steal the papers then be so subtle as to try to cover his tracks? Why?

And if it wasn't his attacker, who? Blaise could have sneaked in, but double why? If he saw the wig, surely he would have asked about it or teased him. *Why don't I trust him? Easy. Because why would that guy be interested in me? And why does he show up everywhere I am?*

Hell. He sank down on the chair he used for putting on his shoes and stared around. *Having this shit makes me paranoid, which is seriously dumb. Ramon needs to stop making personal appearances.* The thought made his chest hurt. He'd created Ramon Rondell when he was twelve. A dashing, charming, eloquent superhero of a guy who embodied everything Llewellyn wasn't—and knew he'd never be. He knew because his mother told him all the time. As he got older, Ramon grew up and got a job, but he still had a life of his own. *Time to give it up.*

With a bigger sigh than he wanted to admit, Llewellyn got a garbage bag from the kitchen. Marie followed him with interest as he gathered all Ramon's clothes and accessories and shoved them in the bag. He tucked the wig in the middle of the jackets and pants, then took the whole thing out to the Volvo and stuck it in the trunk. He'd donate it all first chance he got.

Back in the closet, he stared at the small, neat row of khakis, then at the note from Blaise he'd set on his dresser. Right. Back to Llewellyn's ordinary life, giving up the grandiose dreams. He reached for a pair of khakis.

A HALF hour later, Llewellyn leaned around the corner of Maria's office. "H-hey."

She looked up, and her eyes widened. "Hey, boss, what the hell?"

"There's n-nobody else around?"

"No. Get in here." She raced from her desk, grabbed his arm, and pulled him inside, then slammed the door and locked it.

He sat on the couch, and she brought him a mug. He sipped and sighed. "I should bring you tea. You're the one who's been fending off the attacks of the a-avaricious academics."

She sat opposite him, holding her own cup. "I love it. The case of the avaricious academics."

"So what's going on?"

"Van Pelt was here Friday night and first thing this morning. I mean, seriously, boss, that man's never kept such an ambitious schedule in his life."

"The a-ambitious, avaricious aca-cademics."

"Exactly." She nodded at his closed door. "He was determined to wait in your office until you arrived, but I locked it and told him I didn't have the key." She grinned.

"Th-thank y-you."

She stared at her coffee. "Have you decided what to do?"

He sighed. "I s-suppose I'll take her m-m-money. Maybe I c-can get you made a t-teaching assistant."

"I'd rather help in your research."

"Y-you c-can do both. You'll be a g-good teacher and make m-more money."

"That's fine, Llewellyn, but this isn't about me. Do you feel okay about this research? I know you said it's impossible to prove, but that's been said about a lot of things. Do you think it's true in this case?"

"P-probably. B-but I s-saw Anne over the weekend, and she g-gave me a document that w-was very interesting. If it was real, it could be s-significant."

"Cool. May I see it?"

"It was st-stolen."

"What? When? I thought you said you had it."

He nodded. "I d-did. Someone, uh, stole it f-from me."

"What the hell?" She threw herself backward in the chair. "Please tell me what happened."

He glanced at his hands. "I d-don't want to freak you out."

"You're already freaking me out."

The words rushed out as much as they ever could with him. "I g-got hit over the head and the manuscript was stolen."

"Holy shit, boss! Are you okay?"

"Y-yes. B-Blaise found me and c-called the cops."

"Are they investigating?"

"Not really. They're n-not very interested in a photocopy of some old p-papers about Shakespeare."

"Wow. So if you don't have this document any-more, why are you taking the case?"

"I-I remember it, and w-we can t-try to find the original." He smiled. "Y-you and me."

She let out a hissing breath. "Well then, good, I guess. No one deserves that money more than you."

"N-not me. The school."

"No. She told me she was giving a million to you and the rest to the university. Even after you pay my as-sistant fees"—she grinned—"you'll have quite a bit left."

He sat back and sipped. Truthfully, he wouldn't mind having that much money at his disposal. Imag-ine all the research he could do. "Okay."

"Cool. She's gonna be thrilled. Shall I call her?"

What a frightening commitment to prove some-thing he suspected was virtually not provable. "Y-yes."

She picked up the office landline and dialed.

Llewellyn heard a phone ringing and grabbed for it, but it wasn't his. Probably in the hall.

Frowning, Maria hung up a few seconds later. "No answer. I'm surprised, honestly. She's been like a ghost around this office. I thought she'd spring for her phone if it rang."

"She was at m-my house y-yesterday and w-was pretty upset about the theft of her p-property."

Maria looked up. "Why? Doesn't she want other people to see it? It was a copy, right?"

"Y-yes. Her only c-copy."

"Bullshit." She stared at him with huge eyes. "Why would she do a dumb thing like that?"

Good question. He shrugged. "Not s-sure. Any-way, t-try her again in a few minutes. Th-that will give me t-time to change my mind." He smiled and stood.

A hammering on the outer office door made Maria snort. "Gee, I wonder who that could be?" She stood, crossed to the door, and opened it. As Van Pelt rushed in, Maria said, "Sorry, sir. Didn't realize it was locked."

"Lewis, what in the hell's going on? I've tried to reach you all weekend."

"A lot h-happened."

Maria handed Van Pelt a cup of coffee, asked him to sit down, and proceeded to tell him about the theft, which gave Llewellyn a chance to sip some tea.

Van Pelt's expression threatened rain. "How could you be so careless?"

"C-careless?" *Maybe throwing the tea in his face would wake the man up.*

Maria glanced at Llewellyn and stepped forward anxiously. "Sir, Dr. Lewis had no idea that was Ms. de Vere's only copy. It was, after all, a copy." She tried to cover her snarky expression, which made Llewellyn want to laugh. "And I'm sure no one could have guessed that some asshole would be willing to hit Dr. Lewis on the head to get it."

Still frowning, Van Pelt said begrudgingly, "Are you hurt?"

"J-just a bump."

"So I suppose this theft lands us dead in the water, correct?" He crossed his arms tightly over his chest. "I'm sure you will now refuse the commission despite the value to the institution—"

"I'll do it."

"You shouldn't have to think for one second—what?"

"I'll d-do the research—w-with no guarantees."

"You will?"

"The d-document was v-very persuasive. I'll do it."

"But the document—"

Maria said, "Dr. Lewis has a near-photographic memory. Now he needs to find the original to prove what Anne de Vere had was real."

"Well, my God, that's wonderful." His smile should have cracked his face. Van Pelt was a self-interested SOB, but at least his personal identity included the university.

"I just tried to call Ms. de Vere to tell her, but she didn't answer." Maria waggled the phone.

Van Pelt's mouth hung open. "Well, for God's sake, call her again. Now!"

Maria dialed the phone but shook her head again. "She's not answering. Maybe she gave up and went back to wherever she's from."

Van Pelt scowled. "Did you tell her no absolutely?"

"N-no. She was upset about the d-document. She left."

"The last I spoke to her, I told her I'd persuade you." The crease between his eyebrows returned. "What if she didn't believe me? What if she's so upset she sought out that bastard Rondell?"

"I-I doubt it." He stared in his teacup. Interesting that she hadn't even tried calling Rondell. Perhaps she had no contact for him, or it had been an idle threat.

Maria said, "Sir, she did a lot of research before coming to Dr. Lewis. She has to know that Rondell's reputation is too sensational to have his findings taken seriously."

"You never know what desperate women will do."

Maria raised an eyebrow, and before she could snarl something as snarky as Van Pelt deserved, Llewellyn said, "We'll k-keep tr-trying."

"You bet your life you will." He crossed to the couch and sat. "May I have some more coffee, Ms. Gonzalez?"

She gave Llewellyn a look, but she poured more coffee and added the artificial sweetener they kept for Dr. Van Pelt. "Here you go, sir." She took Llewellyn's cup and refilled it. He cast a longing glance at his office door, but inviting Van Pelt to wait in there seemed too intrusive on his personal space.

Maria brought him the tea, then dialed her phone again, shaking her head as she listened.

Van Pelt felt his coat pocket and pulled out his cell. He cocked an eyebrow. "Thought I heard my phone."

"N-no, I thought—" Llewellyn's heart gave a flip. "C-could it b-be Anne's ph-phone? I hear it whenever M-Maria calls."

Maria looked up from her computer. "Could she have lost it when she was here? That would explain why she's not answering. She lost her phone."

He shook his head, remembering the ringing from her purse the night before. "N-no. She had it yesterday. C-call again. K-keep it ringing."

Maria grabbed the phone and dialed.

Van Pelt yelled, "I hear it. Where is it?" He stepped into the hall. "No, it gets fainter out here."

Maria hissed, "I think it's in your office, boss."

Oh damn. He guessed he had to open up his inner sanctum. Pulling out his key so Maria didn't look like a liar, he unlocked his office door, then slid the key back in his pocket.

Van Pelt crowded behind him. "I hear it. It's definitely inside."

Llewellyn pushed open the door and stepped aside to let Van Pelt hurry in.

Van Pelt's scream came seconds after the sharp smell hit Llewellyn's nose. "Holy shit! She's dead!"

CHAPTER THIRTEEN

"AM I correct that you and Ms. Gonzalez have the only keys to this office, Dr. Lewis?" The detective—Holiday—was back, and he wasn't a holiday of any kind. He poised his pen over the classic notebook, and Llewellyn sighed.

"I-I d-don't know. I think—m-maybe?"

The detective shifted in his chair. Clearly Llewellyn's stammering made him uncomfortable, but what the fuck could he do about that? The straight-backed chair pressed into Llewellyn's spine. Since his office was declared a crime scene, the police had moved him and Maria into an empty classroom at the end of the hall—far from Maria's comforting teapot.

Maria spoke from the other corner of the room. "That's not true."

Holiday looked toward her and discovered her comment was directed at him. "Excuse me?"

She sprang up from where she sat with a police-woman, crossed the big room, and planted her hands on her hips. "Dr. Lewis doesn't know about the keys, since I'm the one who got them from administration. A ton of people have the key to his office, including housekeeping, and presumably every professor who's ever occupied the space. When I got the key, I asked if I could have the locks changed and was told, quite emphatically, that I could not." She gave him a weak smile. "Sorry, Dr. Lewis. I never told you because I—" She looked at Holiday. "—well, because Dr. L. is very protective of his research, and I didn't want him uncomfortable about who might be snooping around in here. On top of that, anyone with a university access card can get into the building."

"Do you think someone was snooping, as you call it?" Holiday was a rough-hewn tree stump of a man, younger than his craggy looks suggested on first glance. Also more attractive, whenever he let up his affected scowl enough to appear pleasant.

She shrugged. "I don't have any reason to. Or I didn't until today. Obviously someone used a key to break in."

"Using a key is not generally considered breaking in." Holiday raised a dark eyebrow.

She took a deep breath, her prominent chest bobbing, which made Holiday swallow hard. She gave him her snarkiest look. "Since the only people authorized to be in there, no matter who has a key, are Dr. Lewis and on rare occasions me, I'd call it breaking in."

"Unless one of you killed her."

"Oh, come on, you don't believe that." She waved a hand. "That woman was asphyxiated, right? That's really hard to do."

"How do you know that?"

She flattened her lips in a grimace. "I do research for a living, duh. In high school I used to work for a writer. You wouldn't believe the stuff those people have to look up."

"Like how to kill someone?"

She pulled out a chair from the table where Holiday and Llewellyn sat. The policewoman who'd been questioning her rose from the table she was sitting at in frustration. Maria leaned on her hand. "Yes, frequent topic of research. Do you know how to get out of a car underwater? Or what kinds of poisons can kill you with no trace?" She grinned at him. "You don't really think I did it." It wasn't a question.

"If you did do it, what would be your motive?" He seemed to be trying not to smile.

"None whatsoever. See, told you."

"A jealous rivalry for the professor's affections?"

She snorted. "Hey, it'll take you about thirty seconds to find out Dr. Lewis is gay, so you can let go of that theory."

He turned back to Llewellyn. He might have already known Llewellyn's orientation—or not. Poker face. "And you were out Saturday night and Sunday morning, Dr. Lewis?"

"Y-yes. I-I went to an early d-dinner on Saturday. Home by n-nine. Sunday I went for tea b-before I got hit and y-you arrived. But you saw Anne a-after that." That had been the first thing Holiday asked him.

"So let's explore last night, shall we?" Holiday turned his head purposefully to Maria. "You should go back to your questioning now."

She glanced at Llewellyn with compassion in her eyes. "Okay." With occasional looks back, she returned to the other side of the room and the stern-looking policewoman.

Holiday shifted all attention to Llewellyn. "So after I left yesterday, you say that Ms. de Vere stayed for a few moments and then was driven home by Mr. Arthur."

"Correct. He can v-verify that."

"I'm sure he can." He gave a tight-lipped smile. "And then Mr. Arthur returned."

"Y-yes."

Holiday's eyes flicked up at the stutter, which unfortunately, in this context, made Llewellyn sound guilty as hell. "Can you tell me why he came back?"

"H-he called it s-suicide pre-vention. Making s-sure I wasn't too upset about what h-happened. Or hurt too badly."

"Were you in danger of suicide?"

"N-no."

"So Mr. Arthur's a *friend*?"

The way he said "friend" sounded like "niece" in *Pretty Woman*. "W-we only met recently. But we're f-friendly."

"What time did he leave?"

Damn, what to say? They had to be questioning Blaise at that moment. What story would he tell about their night together? *Stay as close to the truth as possible.* "I-I was v-very tired, and I fell asleep. I'm not s-sure what t-time Blaise left. Mr. Arthur."

"You fell asleep?"

"Y-yes."

"How can you prove that you didn't leave the house after Mr. Arthur left?"

"I-I d-don't know. I d-don't even know w-when that was."

"May I search your home?"

"What?" His head snapped up, and he frowned.

Holiday made notes on his ridiculously clichéd notepad. "Purely standard practice. May we search your home?"

Llewellyn shook his head. "Wh-why? No prob-ab-ble c-cause."

Holiday shrugged. "Just asking."

"C-cats."

"Excuse me?"

Maria called from her side of the room. "He has cats who don't like strangers."

In the case of Julius and Emily, that was overstating the case, but far be it from him to argue.

Holiday smirked. "Attack cats?"

"Oh yeah." She laughed. "You'll choke to death on fur."

Holiday gave Maria a glare, although there seemed to be a flare of interest deep in his dark eyes. "Have you finished intruding on our questioning, Ms. Gonzalez? Perhaps you'd like to continue to answer your own questions now?"

"I already answered all mine." She walked back to their table, grinning, and plopped into the chair she'd occupied before. "I wasn't here after about 4:00 p.m. on Friday and came in at eight this morning. I knew, uh, people might want to wait for Dr. Lewis in his office, and he doesn't like that, so I walked to the door and locked it. I never even looked in."

"And the proof of that is—" He raised his brows.

She sighed loudly. "I don't know. I locked the door and then I think I rattled the handle, so my fingerprints will be on it. I go in that office all the time, so—" She glanced up at him. "You tell me how I can prove I wasn't in there this morning."

"You can't." Holiday wrote something in his omnipresent booklet.

A plainclothes guy waved at Holiday from the door. Holiday stood. "You're both free to go."

What? Llewellyn's mouth must have fallen open.

"If you have to leave town, notify me first, please." Holiday walked over to the guy at the door, and they disappeared into the hall.

Llewellyn glanced at Maria, and they both laughed.

She pressed a hand against her mouth. "Sorry, I'm just giddy."

"M-me too."

She put a hand on his arm. "You should go home and rest. It sounds like you didn't get a lot of sleep."

Oh my, she had no idea.

They both got up—him slowly since he'd been sitting too long in a very uncomfortable chair. When they walked out the door of the classroom, a wall of humans greeted them, spearheaded by Van Pelt. He was white as the proverbial sheet. "Dear God, how could this happen? This is insane."

Since he had no answer, Llewellyn stayed quiet, but his eyes searched the group for Blaise.

Van Pelt grabbed his elbow and started pulling back toward the room he'd come out of.

Llewellyn drew back. "W-what?"

"I need to speak to you."

He stared at Van Pelt's hand until the professor dropped it from his arm. Then Llewellyn walked into the room with Van Pelt right on his heels. He heard the door close, and he turned. He knew what was coming.

"This is terrible."

He nodded.

Van Pelt cleared his throat. "Now that Ms. de Vere is dead, what do you think will happen?"

"Th-they'll try to f-find her k-killer."

"I know that." He let out a noisy breath. "And sully the university's reputation in the process. Dear God, who wants to send their precious darling to an institution where they murder people?"

"Sh-she wasn't a st-student."

He stalked to the windows and back, raking his hand through his thinning hair. "But what's going to happen to the money, Llewellyn? What will they do with our money?"

"The s-siblings don't w-want to sp-spend it. They're against the idea."

"Damn, damn, damn. The department could do so much with that money." He glanced up. "Who do you think killed her?"

"I d-don't know."

"Do you think the police will take this seriously?"

"Y-yes. It's m-murder."

He started pacing again. "If it will only turn out to be someone from outside the university. Someone from her family, maybe?" He leaned on the table and stared at Llewellyn. "Do you think you could help find out who did it? Get this over with as soon as possible?"

"H-how?"

"You're a researcher, for God's sake!"

"I d-doubt the p-police will w-want help."

He dropped into the chair. "But they have dozens of cases. Getting this solved, out of the headlines, and dissociated from our school and department is our priority, not theirs."

"I-I'm sure it is."

"Today it is." He stood and walked toward the door. "Just search and scrape and do whatever it is you do. I'm making it part of your job." He looked back. "Do you think you could have proved that Edward de Vere was Shakespeare?"

He shrugged. "Maybe I still c-can."

BLAISE LOOKED up and didn't even try to hide his sigh when Detective Holiday walked into the small living room of his apartment. The guy who'd been questioning him for the last hour stood, and Holiday walked over.

"Thanks, Ed. I'll take over."

"Yes, sir." The young cop glanced back at Blaise, then hurried from the room. He'd actually been pretty friendly during their endless questioning.

Blaise looked up at Holiday and tried to smile. *Wish I could talk to Mother.* But the cops had banged on his door before he'd decided what the fuck to do. No chance to call.

Holiday sat down opposite Blaise and nodded, still staring at his notes. Another guy stood near the front door of the small, cramped space. In Blaise's defense, the apartment wasn't supposed to be permanent, but he'd never tell Holiday that.

"Mr. Arthur, am I correct that you took Ms. de Vere somewhere after you left Dr. Lewis's house?"

"Yes. I took her back to her hotel."

"Is there anyone to corroborate that?"

Blaise shrugged. "I dropped her off. Maybe a bellman might recall her arrival, or perhaps she stopped at the front desk."

"We're already checking." He looked up with intense focus. "And then you went back to Dr. Lewis's." It wasn't a question. *Good.* So Llewellyn told them something like the truth. But how much like it?

"Yes. I was concerned for him. Anne was really upset about the theft, and I knew he felt badly—although I don't know what he could have done differently, since she never said it was her only copy. Plus I wanted to be sure he was okay. You know, the bump on the head."

"Who do you think robbed him?"

Blaise shrugged. "No idea. I wonder who Anne told he had her document. Her family, maybe? We'll never know."

"You knew."

Sigh. "Yes, I was there when she came to see him with the document."

"Which was Saturday."

"Yes."

Holiday cocked a significant brow. "For new friends, you do spend a lot of time together."

Well, shit. "That's how new friendships are, don't you think? Lots of getting-acquainted time."

Holiday didn't even raise his eyes to that. "What's your interest in the, uh, Shakespeare identity question?"

"None whatsoever, beyond the fact that I'm a teaching assistant in the English department. I didn't even know who de Vere was until Anne and Llewellyn told me."

"Is it a big enough issue for someone to kill over?" He made a note and frowned.

Blaise shrugged. "Honestly, two days ago I would have said no. Who really cares but a bunch of academics? Sure, people would be interested, but I suspect it was the money more than the historical mystery that prompted the murder."

"You mean the money the university will *not* get?"

"Right. I guess the question is, who didn't want Anne to give five mil to Middlemark?"

Holiday raised that brow again. "That is the question, isn't it? Her siblings were pretty upset, I gather."

"Yes."

"I understand Dr. Lewis wasn't very excited about taking on this case."

Be careful. "No, I heard him say several times that many had tried to prove de Vere was really Shakespeare and had come up empty. I think he didn't want to take her money under false pretenses."

"But he was very adamant about it, I'm told."

"She asked under very public conditions. He's quite shy. I think he freaked and ran."

"Does he freak often?"

Well, shit. Blaise let out a long sigh and didn't care if Holiday heard. "Dr. Lewis had nothing to gain by killing Anne de Vere, and maybe a million bucks in his pocket if she lived. Plus if he had a reason to kill her, he sure as hell wouldn't have done it in his own office."

"Perhaps that's the perfect cover? The least suspicious spot."

"Oh, come on."

"What time did you leave Dr. Lewis's home last night?"

Pounce. Did I really think I'd escape that question? "I'll be honest. It was very late. I fell asleep, uh, watching TV and woke up in the middle of the night. Everything was dark. I tried to find my, uh, shoes and sneak out without waking Llewellyn. I think it was around 2:00 a.m. I didn't even look at the time until I was almost home, and that was close to 2:45 a.m."

"And who could prove that, I wonder?"

"No one that I'm aware of, unless Llewellyn woke up and heard me leaving. But come on, Detective, what possible reason could I have for killing a woman I didn't know until a few days ago?"

"I'm sure I don't know." He smiled, which somehow looked scarier than the frown. "Who's Ramon Rondell?"

It took every ounce of training he'd ever gotten from his mother to keep his face neutral. "He's a sensationalist writer and blogger who focuses on wildass possibilities for famous historical mysteries. You know, like who's really Jack the Ripper and shit like that."

"I thought you weren't interested in history?"

Blaise crossed his arms and scowled darkly enough for Holiday not to miss it. "Rondell's pretty famous, as I'm sure you know. He's pop culture. Plus Anne de Vere said if Dr. Lewis didn't take the research assignment, she'd go to Rondell. It was an empty threat, since she really wanted the credibility of Dr. Lewis's credentials, and Rondell doesn't have those."

"Yes." He flipped his notebook closed and stood like he'd just dropped by to say hi. "Thank you so much for your help. We'll be in touch."

"Uh, okay." He really wanted to ask if he needed a lawyer, but that made him sound guilty as hell. *Better ask Mother. Why, oh why did they ask me about Rondell?*

All the cops walked out of Blaise's apartment at once, leaving it quiet—and ominous. Blaise didn't even bother to get up. Jesus, this seemingly simple project had gotten damned complicated.

Blowing the hair off his forehead, he pulled the phone from his pocket. *Okay, Mother, put on your big-girl panties.* He hit speed dial and listened to it ring twice.

"Hi, dear. What's up?" His mother sounded busy. Nothing new about that.

"Murder."

"What?"

"Remember I told you that this woman had offered Lewis and the university five mil to investigate the whole Shakespeare thing?"

"Yes."

"Somebody killed her."

"What the hell? Why?"

"There could be a lot of reasons. Five million of them, I'd guess, but that's not why I called. The police are questioning me."

"Why?" She sounded… neutral.

"Somebody stole some documents that Anne de Vere gave to Llewellyn. I found him knocked out on his porch, and then I was there when Anne barged in and, uh, I took Anne, the murder victim, back to her hotel, and then was with Llewellyn pretty late."

"We spoke last night. Why didn't you tell me about the theft then?"

"I didn't think it was vital information at that moment. I was a little busy, as you remember." And he'd gotten to the point where telling his mother one thing he didn't have to made him sick.

"And what were you doing with Llewellyn Lewis so late?"

"That's not material to my question. I want to know if I should hire a lawyer."

"Good heavens, Blaise. You don't need a lawyer because you were fucking a guy who might be under investigation."

"Uh, I was with Llewellyn when Anne was getting murdered."

"Okay, and you know that because of time of death?"

"No." He swallowed really hard. "I know that because I went to Llewellyn's office after I left his house to see if I could find any evidence we could use—and saw her body."

"Blaise, what the everlasting living fuck have you done?"

CHAPTER FOURTEEN

LLEWELLYN ADJUSTED his feet on the arm of the couch and took a deep breath, pressing up against the weight of three furries. Normally Marie Antoinette had exclusive claim to lying on Llewellyn's chest or lap. If she declined those positions, the other two could jockey for rights. Tonight appeared to be the exception. Apparently he needed so much fuzzy therapy that all three of them had taken up purring spots on his body parts. He didn't dare move. Not that he was in any hurry to go anywhere.

Oh God, he had to be living in a nightmare. He just wanted to wake up and discover that no innocent person had been killed in his office.

A scratching sound he would have blamed on the cats if they hadn't all been clustered on top of him came from the dining room area. Had the wind come up? It sounded again and seemed too regular to be a bush scraping the window. He raised his head.

"Mew." Emily, of all of the cats, was objecting.

He sighed. Since he'd been awarded this feline fandom, he hated to look it in the butt, but—*I better go check.* Lest he forget, someone had bashed him over the head, though a far lesser evil than Anne's murder. "Sorry, m-my friends." He sat up.

Julius gave him a squall, while Emily looked hurt, and Marie turned her back on the peon who didn't appreciate her gifts.

Llewellyn rose and walked tentatively toward the dining room. He peeked around the corner at the windows as the scratching came again. Llewellyn crept closer and jumped a foot when the scratching turned into knocking, soft but consistent.

What the hell? Bending down, Llewellyn pressed his face toward the far window in the dining room and came face-to-face with Blaise. Llewellyn gasped. Blaise pressed his palm against the window, then pointed toward the back door.

Glancing over his shoulder like some hidden enemy might have crept up on him, Llewellyn hurried to the back door and unlocked it, then pulled it open an inch. Blaise was right there. Llewellyn pressed his mouth against the gap in the door. "Sh-should you b-be here?"

"No. Let me in."

Llewellyn half wanted to slam the door closed and half wanted to pull Blaise in and kiss him. His dumber instincts won. He opened the door, flipped off the lights in the kitchen to make less of a target, and pulled Blaise in by his arm, then closed the door and locked it. Before he could even stop himself, he pushed Blaise against the wall and covered his mouth with a hungry kiss.

Blaise wrapped two very satisfying arms around Llewellyn's back and returned the kiss with something between passion and desperation.

For minutes they drank comfort and strength from each other's mouths; then Llewellyn pulled back. "I th-think the police must be w-watching me. It's not g-good for you to be here."

"They're just as suspicious of me." He smiled, though it wasn't quite as sparkling as usual. "Besides, if they were really watching closely, I doubt I could have gotten in here."

"I'm s-so sorry."

"For what?"

"That you got p-pulled into this."

"I jumped in."

"Because of m-me."

Blaise cupped his cheek with his long fingers. "Catnip can't apologize for being addictive. There's nothing I could have done to stay away."

Llewellyn snorted loudly and waved a hand at Blaise. "Stop."

"Are the curtains closed in the living room?"

"Y-yes."

"Good. Can I get you a beer?"

"Just g-got some more delivered."

"Good, since I've been drinking it all up."

Blaise pulled two bottles from the refrigerator, uncapped them, slid an arm around Llewellyn's shoulders, and walked him into the living room. They sat side by side, and the cats jumped up, with Marie insinuating herself between them.

Blaise clinked the bottom of his bottle against Llewellyn's. "To finding answers."

"Yes."

Blaise looked at Llewellyn. "Have you heard from Anne's siblings?"

"Since the murder? No."

"I just wonder what they're thinking. Anne said the money was left specifically for the project by her father, and the sibs can't say shit."

"E-even if she's d-dead?" His breath rushed out as he said it, and he dropped his forehead against the cold wetness of the bottle.

"That's a question, isn't it? If the money reverts to the sibs, it's clear motive for murder."

"C-could be."

"One thing's for sure."

Llewellyn turned his head so the bottle rested against his cheek. He slid it so the top slipped between his lips and drank a mouthful. It made him realize how thirsty he was. Another long pull from the bottle tasted so good he wanted to finish it all, but that wasn't wise. Keeping his wits sounded like a damned good idea right now. "W-what's for sure?"

Blaise held out his bottle. "Want more?"

Llewellyn shook his head.

Blaise sat back. "What's for sure is that somebody really didn't want Anne to prove de Vere is Shakespeare."

"Or d-didn't want her to sp-spend the m-money to prove it."

"Right, but the outcome's the same. Nobody proves Shakespeare isn't Shakespeare."

"R-right."

"What do you think that might indicate?"

Llewellyn curved a half smile and cast his eyes sideways at Blaise. "Th-that maybe Sh-Shakespeare isn't Shakespeare."

"And Edward de Vere is." Blaise's throat worked as he swallowed some beer. Even that was sexy.

"V-Van Pelt wants me to investigate the m-murder."

His blue eyes widened. "You're shitting me?"

Llewellyn shook his head.

"Holiday won't like that."

"I t-told him everything I know."

"So it's not like you're withholding evidence."

"R-right."

"And just because the police department doesn't have a brilliant researcher like Dr. Llewellyn Lewis on staff isn't your fault."

"S-so true." Llewellyn actually smiled. "I d-didn't really l-like Anne that much. B-but I hate to think s-someone k-killed her because of me."

Blaise set down his bottle on the coffee table and turned, taking both of Llewellyn's biceps in his hands. He squeezed a little. "Funny, I'm always surprised at how fit you are. You manage to come off as such a nerd."

Llewellyn tried to control his frown. Ramon kept fit. Not great for people to notice. "G-good genes."

Blaise tightened his hands. "She wasn't killed because of you. She was determined to find someone who would do this research for her. She came to you first, but she would have moved on to Rondell if you'd flatly refused."

Yes, and I'd still be responsible for her death. He sighed.

"Okay. So you've been given carte blanche to investigate and do backup for the cops."

"N-not that Van Pelt's s-say-so counts for much with the cops."

"So how do we start?"

"W-we?"

"Of course. Like you said, I'm involved in this too, and I need to find out who really did it so I can get back to work."

"Work?"

"Teaching assistant, remember?"

Llewellyn gazed at Blaise's beautiful face. Why couldn't he get rid of the itch that said there was something off about Blaise? Not enough to quell his ravenous attraction for the guy—but enough to keep him from getting totally comfortable. "R-right." He stood and walked to the desk to get his laptop, then carried it back to the couch. "L-let's search the s-siblings, shall we?" He set the computer with its EMI-reducing laptop pad on his lap, then input "de Vere family" into his search engine.

Blaise peered over Llewellyn's shoulder. "Four siblings. That agrees with what Anne told me. Two sisters and a brother."

Llewellyn clicked a couple more times. "B-but did you know that one was a tw-twin?"

"No. She never said that." Blaise frowned.

Llewellyn turned his head. "Not just a tw-twin. Anne's twin."

"Holy shit. Why wouldn't she have mentioned that?"

"M-maybe the sister is against her, and she h-hated that?"

"Possible. Where do they live?"

"S-San Francisco."

"All of them?"

"All."

"Hmm. So maybe we should be making a trip to the big city."

"Y-yes. Maybe."

"We're not supposed to leave town without letting Holiday know."

"H-he can't stop us unless he ch-charges us."

"Yeah, but we don't want to tempt him."

"T-true." Llewellyn couldn't help it. He yawned.

"You're exhausted."

"T-tired."

"Hell, with what you've been through, I'm surprised you can keep your eyes open. How about I tuck you in?"

Llewellyn needed to glue his lips together and not say—*damn*. "Will y-you stay?"

"You couldn't get me to leave."

Something in his chest—tight and hard—unraveled into a sweet warmth, and the fatigue spread through him like melted butter. He took a step toward the bedroom and stumbled.

"Whoa." Blaise caught him. "Come on, smart guy. Time to sleep."

It was really nice to just be led—especially to the bedroom. By Blaise.

In the room, Llewellyn sat hard on the edge of the mattress, toed off his tan shoes, and started

unbuttoning his shirt. Blaise pushed his hands away.
"Let me." He knelt in front of Llewellyn and efficient-
ly removed his clothes. Llewellyn knew because air
started hitting bare skin in various locations.

At the moment he most wanted to be totally
aware, he couldn't keep his eyelids in a full upright
position. Moments went missing before he noticed a
blanket being pulled up under his neck. "W-wait. I—"

The next time he had a conscious thought, there
was a warm weight pressed against his back and soft
breathing on his neck.

Don't want to get used to this.

*Oh hell. For one short night, Lewis, just enjoy
yourself.* With a deep sigh, he let his eyes close and
his brain believe this was something he deserved.

PURRING IN his ear. Blaise opened his eyes. It
was still dark, but whiskers tickled his nose. How did
one cat get whiskers in his nose and still manage to
vibrate his earlobe? *Ah, two cats.*

Have to pee.

Llewellyn had turned on his side, so Blaise could
slide to the edge of the bed. Claws dug into his shoulder.
"Ow. Damn, Julius." He whispered it, but those claws
still hurt. He reached up and grabbed the cat, who had
to weigh a good fifteen pounds. He set the giant beast
on the floor and padded to the bathroom nude. Inside,
he flipped on the light and used the bathroom.

The closet door stood cracked open. Some piece
of his heart wanted to say *fuck it* and *fuck them all*. He
liked Llewellyn. Really. A lot. He washed his hands
and wiped one of them over the back of his neck.
Damn.

He turned and pulled open the closet, flipped on the light, and stared inside. Everything had changed. The neat rows of khakis hung in the middle of the clothing rack, but the fashionable suits, shirts, and shoes were gone. The tote bag still stood on the floor by the back wall, but he could tell without even touching it that it had books in it and nothing else. The wig and whatever else had vanished.

Funny how that made him sad. Like maybe Llewellyn had given up some part of himself. *I wonder why?*

The whisper from his heart that said it was his fault made him want to cry.

Go back to sleep.

Quietly he pulled the closet door closed the way he'd found it. He walked toward the bathroom door and flipped off the light, but as he started to turn, he heard the cry.

"No!"

"Llewellyn!" He threw open the door and ran toward the bed, but no one was attacking.

Llewellyn thrashed his arms as his body twisted. "No. No, please. I won't d-do it anym-more. P-please."

Blaise sat on the edge of the bed and gently pressed his hands against Llewellyn's shoulders, stilling him, then ran his palm across his sweaty forehead. "It's okay, dear. You're free. You can do anything you want. Don't worry." He leaned over and kissed his cheek. "Shhh. I won't let anyone hurt you."

Llewellyn sighed and quieted. Marie jumped up on the bed from the other side, crawled onto his pillow, and wrapped herself around his head. She knew he needed comfort. She gazed at Blaise. He knew judgment when he saw it.

Blaise slipped onto the bed and pressed himself against Llewellyn's side.

Not letting anyone hurt Llewellyn. There was a promise he couldn't keep.

LLEWELLYN STARED out the windshield at the crazy-nuts traffic crowding on all sides of Blaise's little black Prius. It only took a few minutes on the 280 freeway to remind him why he liked living on the central coast. San Luis Obispo's idea of a traffic jam was too many students at a crosswalk when his car was trying to get through. He stifled a yawn. Yes, he'd slept through the night, but apparently fought his childhood demons the whole time. Demons could be exhausting.

Blaise chuckled, and Llewellyn glanced at him. Blaise said, "You look like you want to say, 'Are we there yet?'"

Llewellyn drew his brows together. "Of course n-not. I'm much too s-sophisticated, erudite, and intellectual to ask such a ch-childish question. But are we there y-yet?"

Blaise laughed, and the tension that had pussy-footed around the car for the last three-plus hours relaxed. "I love your sense of humor."

"Th-thank you. Sometimes it's hard to be f-funny. Too much w-work."

"I appreciate you sharing that."

"Does your f-family live around here?"

"Uh, yes. In Palo Alto."

Hmm. Was the tension back? "W-what does your f-father do?"

"Nothing. I mean, I don't have a father. I was raised by my mother. She's kind of a, uh, serial entrepreneur, but she can afford to be. Family money."

"Ah. N-nice to have."

"Yeah. You were raised by your mom too, right?"

"Y-yes." He took a breath. "No f-family money. Just the house and m-my education." He stared out the window and tried not to see his past.

"I don't mean to pry, but I got the feeling last night that you didn't have the happiest of childhoods."

"Y-you could say that. At least it was sh-short."

"How old were you when your mom died?"

"Fifteen. I w-was already in c-college."

"Who took care of you?"

"N-no one. I-I officially lived at school and c-claimed my f-father's family were my guardians."

"*Officially* lived at school?"

"I h-had the house my father g-gave my mother." They crawled onto the bridge into the city. "Where I l-live now."

"Did your father go along with all this? Where the fuck was he?"

"N-nowhere. He g-gave my mom two th-things she never wanted. The house and m-me."

Blaise gave a soft gasp. *Funny.* Llewellyn hardly ever talked about his family or lack thereof. But a sympathetic listener with no axe to grind seemed to trigger some desire to confess he didn't know he possessed.

"But shit, Llewellyn. You were fifteen."

"Wh-when she died, I searched out my f-father's phone number and called him. Asked if I c-could claim he was m-my guardian to stay out of the system. He answered with one word. Y-yes."

"What's his name?"

"C-can't tell you."

"Why? Is he famous?"

"N-no. Just my agreement." He turned to Blaise. "Y-your turn. W-where's your father?"

He shrugged. "Dead, I believe. He was never in the picture. I think of him as a sperm donor. My mother says he was handsome and smart. I think she chose him for that reason."

"M-maybe your father and m-mine are related."

Blaise barked a sharp laugh.

"You're c-close to your m-mother?"

Blaise glanced toward Llewellyn, then back at the road. "I guess so. She's a challenging personality, but she's mine."

"Are y-you going to stop and see her, since we're so close?"

"Oh hell no." He said it with humor but still emphatically. "Sorry. I guess I get enough of her. It's nice to be away." He nodded ahead of him. "We're almost there. Uh, do we have a plan?"

CHAPTER FIFTEEN

THE TALL, skinny house just a block from San Francisco's famous Victorian "Painted Ladies" looked stately and historic in the midday sun—and a little shabby.

Blaise said, "Looks kind of rundown for this part of town."

"Yes. I w-was just noticing that."

"That's surprising. This neighborhood's really upscale. If they can't afford to keep it up, they could get a boatload of cash for it."

Llewellyn gazed out the window over Blaise's shoulder. "Pr-probably don't w-want to s-sell it."

Blaise turned and stared at Llewellyn. "Are you thinking what I am?"

Llewellyn nodded. "Their s-sister wants to spend f-five million for a s-silly historic g-goose chase—"

"While they're trying to keep Tara."

"As G-God is their witness, they'll never b-be hungry again." Llewellyn clenched his fist and raised it toward the roof of the car.

Blaise shook his head as he laughed. "You're great."

The simple words made him suck air. If he heard that every day until he died, it wouldn't ever get boring.

Blaise didn't seem to notice Llewellyn's reaction. He stared intently toward the house, where nothing was happening. Not a curtain moving. "So what's next? We agreed we'd wait and see. We're seeing."

He'd barely gotten the words out when a gray American sedan pulled up in front of the house and double-parked. "M-must be p-police."

"Yes. Nobody else would dare pull that stunt in San Francisco." He leaned closer to the window. "That's Holiday."

"Y-yes."

A woman in a suit got out of the driver's side. "I didn't see the lady cop in San Luis, did you?"

"N-no. Probably local."

The two walked up to the front door and knocked. The door opened. It looked like a woman answered. The cops went inside, and the door closed.

Blaise slid down in his seat and rested his head back. "Guess we're waiting."

They did for about twenty minutes; then the door opened again and the two cops came out and drove away.

Blaise straightened up. For a minute they were silent, watching. "Do you think there's any way we can boldly walk up to the door and knock? I suspect they'd call the cops in about two seconds, and then Holiday would put an end to our nefarious dealings like a flash."

"They d-don't know you."

"What?"

"They probably know m-me because of Anne. But n-not you."

"Whoa. Hell of an idea. But tell me why I'm there."

"Sy-sympathy. About Anne."

He took a deep breath. "Okay. I'll do it." He glanced out the window, then grinned. He held up a finger. "I have a plan." He hopped out of the car, looked both ways, and ran across the street. Instead of turning right toward the house, he went left. *What the—oh.* On the corner he stepped into a shop. A flower shop. Llewellyn smiled. Blaise came back out a couple of minutes later carrying a bouquet and, with a wink toward Llewellyn, marched up the sidewalk to the de Vere home.

HERE GOES. Polish up the charm.

Blaise knocked on the door. Nothing happened for seconds, and then a woman—dark-haired, attractive, probably in her early forties, and overweight—opened the door. "Yes?" She didn't frown. He didn't mean to sound egotistical, but people said it was hard to frown at him.

"Ms. de Vere?"

"Yes." She looked gray and drawn, but not shocked enough to have just learned of her sister's death a few minutes before. She must have gotten notification earlier and the police were just there for questioning.

Blaise smiled slightly. "I'm so sorry to bother you in this time of grief. I'm a friend of Anne's. Maybe that's overstating the case. I only met her a short time ago, but I felt like we bonded. It was such a shock to learn of her death. I'm in San Francisco on business, so I just wanted to stop by to express my sincerest sympathy and give you these." He held out the elaborate bouquet.

"Well, aren't you kind, Mr.—"

"Arthur. Blaise Arthur. I'm guessing you're Ms. Jane de Vere."

"Yes."

"I know, uh—Miranda, is it?—is a twin."

"Yes." She glanced over her shoulder, and he held his breath. When she looked back at him, she said the magic words. "Would you like to come in?"

"I don't want to intrude. I know what a difficult time this must be."

"Unimaginable." She stepped aside. "Please."

He walked into a small but charming—or more accurately, once charming—entry.

"Come and meet my brother."

Oh yeah. He followed her into a large old-fashioned living room with a musty smell. Sitting by the bay window, facing out toward the garden view, was a man in a wheelchair.

"Roscoe."

He turned rather energetically. "Yes?"

"I want you to meet Mr. Arthur." She looked at Blaise. "Blaise, am I right?"

"Yes." He smiled and extended his hand. "I'm pleased to meet you, Mr. de Vere, despite the very sad circumstances."

"Yes." He frowned as he pumped Blaise's hand with a firm handshake.

Jane extended a hand to a chair, and Blaise sat. "Roscoe, Mr. Arthur was a friend of Anne's."

Blaise nodded. "Yes, at Middlemark University. I met her when she was trying to persuade one of the university's professors to research the possibility that your ancestor Edward was the writer of Shakespeare's works."

A nearly identical frown leaped onto both their faces.

Roscoe growled, "Are you a historian?"

"Oh no, not at all. Just a graduate student in the English department. I happened to be at a dinner where Anne met with the, uh, history department."

Jane put a hand on his forearm. "We loved Anne dearly, but she was cracked on the subject of Shakespeare."

"And ready to commit funds this family sorely needs to her ridiculous ideas." Roscoe coughed.

Blaise tried to set his face in as harmless and noncommittal an expression as possible. "She said your father wanted the research to go ahead. That he'd left the money for that purpose."

"Bull!"

Blaise must have looked startled, because Jane quickly said, "Anne was the only member of the family who was sympathetic to this frivolous project. I'm sure you understand, this kind of silliness is fine if you have money to burn, but we don't, and Roscoe's condition requires care."

"I'm so sorry."

Roscoe snarled, "And now this idiocy has gone and gotten her killed."

Jane pressed a hand to her chest. "Oh dear."

"Do you think the two things are related?" Blaise opened his eyes a bit wider in innocence.

"What else could explain it? She didn't get herself murdered in San Francisco, did she?" Roscoe actually jerked the wheels on his chair, and he half spun, his heavily muscled forearms cording. Interesting that his legs appeared just as strong. "Hell, she was in that damned historian's office. If that's not a message, I don't know what is."

"I heard that Dr. Lewis didn't want to take the case—or the money."

Roscoe snorted loudly. "That's what he says. Damned leeches preying on an addle-headed young woman."

"She seemed so bright."

"Sometimes brains are the last thing a person needs. Makes them unstable. Common sense. That's what Anne should have had." He wiped a hand across his eyes.

Jane rose. "I must put these in water." She held the bouquet out toward Roscoe. "Aren't they lovely? Mr. Arthur brought them to us."

Roscoe nodded, but his face was still set in angry, aggressive lines. "Thank you."

Blaise stood. "I should go. I don't want to intrude. Do you know when there might be a funeral?"

"N-no. The police will tell us, I suppose." Jane stared at the worn floral carpet.

"Of course. I'm so sorry." He pulled a card from his pocket and a pen. "May I give you my email? Would you let me know when it will be held in case I can come?"

"Of course."

He wrote the email address and handed it to her. "Thank you. I'm happy to have met you both. I'm sorry I didn't get to meet Miranda. This must be so terrible for her."

The muscles around Jane's mouth tightened even further. Blaise looked over just in time to see Roscoe exchange a glance with her. She gave Blaise a steady stare, like she was practicing looking forthright. "Yes. She doesn't choose to live with us, you see. I'm not even sure if she knows about Anne. I've tried to call her, but no answer. For identical twins, it's surprising that they aren't closer."

"I'd love to meet her—"

"Sorry. She's very private. If I gave you her information, she'd kill me." She swallowed. "I mean, be upset with me."

"Oh no, I totally understand. Thank you again for seeing me." He walked to the door, waved at Jane as he left, and noticed immediately that Llewellyn must be lying down in the seat because the car looked empty. He trotted across the street, then slid in the front, grinning at Llewellyn's rangy body squeezed into the seat well on the passenger side. Slowly he drove away. This time, the curtains did move.

A block up the street, Llewellyn sat partway up. "What happened?"

"Interesting. I met the sister Jane and the brother, Roscoe. Apparently Miranda doesn't live there, or that's what they claimed."

"What are they like?"

Blaise turned right around the park. "Both of them were very upset that Anne wanted to spend the money on what they deemed a frivolous, ridiculous pursuit. The house clearly needs repair, and Roscoe's in a wheelchair. Jane said he needed care and thus, it follows as the night the day, they need the money. That was the implication."

Llewellyn pointed toward the next corner. "K-keep going, if you d-don't mind. G-go by again."

"Oh, okay." He pulled up behind a line of cars waiting to turn right on the de Veres' street.

"So what was J-Jane like?"

"She seemed sympathetic, though concerned for her brother. He was royally pissed."

"I caught a g-glimpse of her. N-not too strong-looking."

"No. She's overweight and doesn't move with any speed or vigor."

"And the br-brother's in a wheelchair. S-so no suspects th-there."

"Probably so, but I will say this." The car in front of him turned, leaving him next at the stop sign. He stared to the left for an opening in the traffic flow.

"Wh-what?"

Blaise made the turn. "Sorry. Focusing. What I noticed was that Roscoe looked damned robust for a person confined to a wheelchair. And his legs appear as strong as his arms. He probably has some other kind of injury, but—"

"Look." Llewellyn slid into the seat well again.

Blaise glanced at Llewellyn, then across the street toward the de Vere house coming up on their left.

Jane de Vere stood on the top of the walkway in front of her house, wearing a light jacket. She faced back into the house, talking animatedly to her brother in his chair. She turned, walked down the stairs, and went left on the sidewalk. As she reached a half block away, Roscoe slowly stood from his chair and peered after her. He stood without a walker or even a cane. He wasn't propped against the doorframe or leaning precariously in any direction. The man looked, in a word, healthy.

Blaise rushed by the house, not glancing in. If they noticed him, at least they'd think he didn't see Roscoe. "Holy shit. I'd say that changes things. Wouldn't you?"

"Y-yes. Yes, I would."

"Should we tell Holiday?"

"H-he'd tell us t-to back off."

"Yeah." Blaise glanced at Llewellyn, who'd now settled in the shotgun seat. "Want some food before we drive home?"

"S-sure. We need a f-few more things to chew on."

TWO HOURS later, after some grilled salmon, they powered down the freeway toward home. Llewellyn leaned back in his seat, fighting his drooping eyelids. He was so grateful not to have to do the driving. But he owed it to Blaise to at least stay awake.

Just as he was getting ready to turn on some loud music, Blaise said, "So how are you feeling about the whole Edward de Vere issue?"

"Interesting."

Blaise glanced over at Llewellyn, then back at the heavy traffic pouring through Silicon Valley. "Interesting as in interested? Or interesting as in the Chinese curse, 'May you live in interesting times'?"

Llewellyn laughed. "B-both." He took a breath. "H-hard not t-to think that someone r-really believes it's true."

"You think?"

"The m-murderer probably d-didn't want her to p-pay me. If I c-couldn't prove it, she w-wouldn't have had to p-pay me. Maybe the murderer b-believed de Vere is Shakespeare."

"Yeah. I thought of that too. Of course, maybe they were just covering their bases in case it was true."

"A lot of r-risk if not needed."

"True."

They rode silently for several minutes.

Blaise said. "It's kind of exciting to think that you could have possibly proved de Vere is the one who actually wrote the greatest plays in history."

Llewellyn sucked in air to cool the fire in his belly. "Y-yes. Yes, it is. But I th-think we should get this murder solved f-first."

"First? But no one will pay you to take the de Vere case now."

"The m-money's irrelevant."

"I guess that's true. History's mysteries are your job, right?" He glanced over with a little frown. "You really haven't been all that interested in the million bucks since the beginning. That does strike awe in my pragmatic brain."

"I-I wouldn't m-mind it, but I have a nice life."

"Nice?" Blaise made a snorting sound. "As in 'She has a nice personality'? You know, the death of a blind date."

Blaise had meant it as a joke—probably. *But I've never heard such an effective condemnation of my whole life.* He made an obligatory laughing sound, then stared out the window until his eyelids drooped.

"Llewellyn."

"Wha-what?" His eyes flew open, expecting to see cats.

"Sorry to startle you. We're almost at your house."

"Oh. I-I'm so sorry. I didn't m-mean to desert you."

"Hey, you need the rest. I was happy to drive." He guided the car to the curb, put it in park, and turned to Llewellyn. "Want to plan next steps, or shall I leave you to sleep?"

Funny how he could never get enough Blaise, but getting used to him? Not a wise idea. A miniwar went into firing mode in his brain.

Behind the Prius, a car door slammed.

He heard Blaise's gasp first. His eyes were huge, and he stared in the rearview mirror. "Holy shit."

Llewellyn turned and focused on the woman walking toward them on the sidewalk—the woman who looked exactly like Anne de Vere with blue hair.

CHAPTER SIXTEEN

LLEWELLYN'S HEART slammed against his chest. "Th-that must b-be—"

"Miranda."

"Sh-she looks just like Anne."

"I guess that's the idea behind 'identical.'" Blaise grinned, which softened the snark.

"Okay." Llewellyn opened the passenger door and slid out, rising and staring at the woman across the roof of the car. "H-hello."

"Hi. You must be Llewellyn Lewis. They told me you stuttered."

"Wh-who are they?"

"Some guy at the university. Van something."

"Van Pelt?"

"Guess so." Blaise stepped out the driver's side right in front of the woman. Her eyes widened. "Holy crap, you're gorgeous. Who are you?"

He grinned. The devastating grin. "I'm Blaise Arthur. Your resemblance to your sister is positively scary."

"Yeah, especially since she's dead."

Llewellyn half wanted to smack her and half wanted to laugh.

She put her hands on her hips, which were currently clothed in a short, tight denim skirt above bright argyle thigh-high socks that in turn resolved themselves into a pair of scuffed Doc Martens. "So you're supposed to be able to tell me what the fuck happened to my sister."

Llewellyn frowned. "I h-have no idea."

"I don't mean who killed her. Hell, if you knew that, we wouldn't be standing here, right? But I want to know what led up to it, okay?"

Blaise said, "Why don't you come inside." He glanced up. "If Llewellyn doesn't mind."

He kind of did mind, but letting her in was the best way to learn whatever there was to know about this odd creature. Taking the lead, he strode up the walkway and climbed the porch. When he opened the door, of course, he was assailed by the feline attack.

"Meow."

"Merwaowr."

"Mew."

With an apologetic look, he bent down to greet his furries. Marie Antoinette was solidly pissed. She stared at him from a regal distance, then turned and flicked her tail at him as she stalked into the living room.

"I'm s-sorry."

"Hey, man, they're great. I love cats." Miranda knelt down and started petting Julius, while Emily regarded her uncertainly from a few paces away.

First appealing thing she'd said. He nodded. "M-me too."

After more extravagant appreciation of the cats, they moved into the living room.

Blaise said, "Would you like something to drink?"

Llewellyn gave him a sideways look. Proprietary bastard—but it made him weirdly happy.

Miranda plopped on the couch and propped her boot on the coffee table. "What ya got?"

"Llewellyn has exceptional craft beer. I'm not sure what else."

"Beer? I'm there."

Blaise walked toward the kitchen, and Llewellyn looked at the woman. "I g-gather you're Miranda."

"Sure. Who'd you think?"

Interesting question. "Y-your brother and s-sister have b-been trying to contact you."

"Yeah, I know. But I heard about Anne on the news, and I didn't want to hear their bullshit, so I didn't call back."

"Did you talk to the p-police?"

"Nope. They've been calling too. I'll go turn myself in."

What? He snapped a gaze at her face.

"For questioning. Jesus, you're intense."

Blaise walked in with three beer bottles and handed one to Miranda and one to Llewellyn, keeping the third. He sat next to her on the couch and across from Llewellyn in the chair. "So what do you want to know?"

"How the fuck did this happen? I mean, the most boring woman on the planet comes to the most boring university and the most boring historian on earth, and somebody murders her for it? How the fuck does that work?"

He had to admit, it was a damned good question.

Blaise cut in. "She was throwing around promises of five million dollars, which is motive for murder in a lot of people's books."

"Jesus, that stupid bitch. Who'd have thought insanity could infect half of a set of twins? I mean, our father had a screw loose, and Anne's was falling out. She thought of herself as some crusader for justice or something. I mean, who the hell cares if Shakespeare was Mickey Mouse, much less Edward de Vere?"

"A l-lot of p-people." Llewellyn took a sip of beer and glanced up at her. "Including y-you, I th-think. Y-you called and threatened m-me, didn't you?"

"What?" She looked totally—and interestingly—shocked.

Blaise also looked startled. Llewellyn had told Blaise that Anne's sister had called him, but he realized he'd never said which one. He sipped his beer and provided no information.

Miranda frowned. "Uh, jeez, I don't remember that. Why do you think it was me?"

"You said your name."

She swallowed. "Hell, maybe I was drunk." A big swig of beer seemed to support that theory. "Or maybe Jane called and used my name. She likes to play the gracious lady, but she can be damned mean when she wants something." She drank down most of the rest of the contents of her bottle in a few pulls, then set the beer on the table. "So tell me about it."

Llewellyn gave Blaise a look, but they settled down and between the two of them told her about Anne's offer, Llewellyn being attacked, and the associated robbery. Then finally Llewellyn took over and described the horror in his office.

"Shit, man, that's intense." Clouds of some dark emotion drifted across her face; then she looked up at him with laser eyes. "You didn't kill her, did you?"

His mouth opened and closed while Blaise laughed. Blaise said, "You do have a way with words. No, Dr. Lewis didn't kill your sister. After all, he was in line to make five million bucks if he could prove that de Vere was Shakespeare."

"But he didn't want to take the case, right? That's what I heard."

"Fr-from whom?" Llewellyn frowned.

"Hey, man, you can walk across that campus and that's all people are talking about. The money, the murder, and how Lewis didn't want to take it, but Van-what's-his-name made you do it."

Blaise glanced at Llewellyn. "Trust me, Dr. Lewis had the least motivation to kill your sister."

"So who had the most?"

Now there was a challenging question.

Llewellyn shook his head. "W-we don't know."

Blaise leaned forward. "I, uh, happened to be in San Francisco, so I called on your brother and sister to express my condolences. I noticed Roscoe's in a wheelchair. Do you know what his ailment is?" He sipped at his beer casually.

She gave him a sideways look with an appraising smile. "What? You think it's odd that he's in a wheel-chair but still looks healthy as a friggin' horse? Is that your issue, bucko?" She laughed.

He wrinkled his nose charmingly. "Must confess, it did cross my mind."

"Yeah, well, you're not the only one. About two years ago, Roscoe started complaining about weak-ness and not feeling well. The doctors couldn't find anything and suggested it was a stress problem. Man, he didn't wanna hear that. Shortly thereafter, he con-fined himself to a wheelchair. End of story."

"S-sounds like you d-don't believe him." Llewel-lyn watched her face as intently as he could without staring.

She shrugged. "Hey, she who's without sin and all that shit, but my father had died and Roscoe faced having to support Jane. Maybe he thought he'd get stuck with all of us. I think he didn't want to be the grown-up, so he sat down and checked out." She spread her hands. "That's my theory. That'll be a buck fifty for my doctor's fee."

Blaise said, "They'd certainly have reason to want to stop Anne from giving away the five million. Obviously they need it and felt it was theirs."

"That's crap. My father left money to each of us. Not a ton, but some. Then he earmarked the five mil for his fantasyland project and assigned Anne to take care of it. They're going to have one uphill legal bat-tle trying to crack that will. He was pretty clear about how he wanted the money used."

"But there's no one on the side of the investiga-tion anymore. Obviously you think it's foolishness and Jane and Roscoe hate it, so who's going to stop your siblings from challenging the will?"

"I guess you could say my father is. He was smarter than either of them, if slightly wacko. I'm betting he made that will airtight."

"Y-you don't s-sound upset."

She shrugged. "I never thought I had the money, so I'm not out anything."

"S-so you don't b-believe the things y-you said on the phone?"

Her eyes dropped, then flicked back up. "I don't remember making a call like that, and I can't imagine why I'd threaten you for helping my sister. Hell, no skin off my ass."

"Would your sister and brother have killed her for it?"

"Holy crap, that's to the point. Nah. You saw them. A couple losers. I read she died by strangulation. That's way too hard and too personal for them. Poison? Maybe. But they would've had to be around for that."

"So you don't think they did it?"

She had her head bent down, and she raised her eyes suddenly. "Do you?"

Blaise shrugged. "No idea. I just noticed Roscoe seemed to take her quest and the loss of the money pretty personally."

"Yeah. It would get him out from under Jane, I guess. Still, I doubt he had the balls."

Llewellyn drank the last of his beer. "S-so you and Anne weren't c-close."

A frown wrinkled her brow for just a flash; then she shook her head. "No. Sad. A lot of twins don't really like each other, but they're still inseparable. Not me and Anne. We just never got along. I think we resented each other in the womb and never got over it."

Blaise glanced past Miranda at Llewellyn, then said, "So you didn't think she was robbing the family by spending your father's money on a frivolous pursuit?"

"Nah. Like I said, it was Father's money. I thought they were both wacked, but I never expected him to give me the money."

Llewellyn spoke carefully. "Wh-what do you think will b-become of the money now that she's g-gone?"

"I'm betting my father made his wishes airtight, so maybe he appointed somebody else to take over if she dropped the ball. He was really cracked on the subject of de Vere. I doubt he'd leave it to chance."

Blaise nodded. "Interesting."

She looked at Llewellyn with narrowed eyes. "Would you still do it, even though she's dead?"

"I h-haven't th-thought."

Blaise seemed to pick up the thread. "But it seems like someone must have believed that Dr. Lewis might actually succeed in proving the Shakespeare connection. That's quite intriguing, don't you think?"

"Could be." She stared at her bottle on the table. "Yeah."

"At the same time, they must have had reason to believe that the search for de Vere's identity would not go forward if Anne wasn't here to drive it."

She made a sideways smirk. "That leaves out my greedy sibs. They know Father's will gave that money to research, not to Anne."

"Maybe they think they can break the will without her to fight for it."

"Maybe. Maybe not." Miranda stood. "Okay, so I'll leave you to it."

Blaise and Llewellyn both got up. Blaise asked, "Are you going to the police?"

"Yeah. I'll call that Holiday dude and go see him. Probably tomorrow. Call me if you think of anything. I'll be interested to see if you still want to take the case, Dr. Lewis." She walked across the room, and before they could follow, she turned and looked back. "I understand your point of view. I'd agree somebody believed this Shakespeare shit so much, they killed her." She walked out the front door.

Llewellyn plopped back in his chair and tried to close his mouth. "H-holy shit."

Blaise barked a laughed. "My sentiments exactly." He sat slowly. "What do you make of this whole thing?"

Llewellyn shook his head. "I b-barely know." Sitting back slowly, he forced the air from his lungs. "S-so much isn't w-what it seems."

A frown flickered across Blaise's face, but he said, "Yeah. I'm glad you see that too. I mean, the brother, Roscoe, obviously being able to stand, if not walk, is bizarre. And this woman. There's something—" He shrugged. "—I don't know."

"F-forced."

"What?"

"Something f-forced."

"Yeah, that's right. She seems over-the-top."

Llewellyn nodded.

"So what's next, oh master sleuth?"

"The Echev-varrias, I think."

"Oh, those donors."

"Yes. They d-didn't want me to investigate de V-vere."

"Not enough to kill Anne, surely."

"P-probably n-not. Must look into it, though." He stifled a yawn. He wouldn't mention George Stanley. That was such a long shot. But he still needed to nose around George's motivations.

Blaise rose and crossed to him, taking his hand. "Hey, it's been a bitch of a day. Time for bed."

"Y-you did m-most of the work."

"Not true." His dimples popped. "Hiding in the seat well took the flexibility of a contortionist."

Llewellyn laughed but yawned again.

"Come on." Blaise pulled him to his feet, and they met nearly eye-to-eye. Damn, he'd slept through one whole night with Blaise. He didn't want to waste another. Guys like him didn't get those kinds of chances very often.

Hand in hand, they walked to the bedroom. Inside the bedroom door, Blaise turned to him. "May I stay?"

Llewellyn let out his breath slowly. "I h-hate to get you in deeper."

"Uh, deeper was, I must confess, exactly what I had in mind." His dimples flashed, and the streak of white-hot desire that shot into Llewellyn's groin could have forged the Sword in the Stone.

He gritted his teeth. "I w-wish I didn't want you so much."

Blaise nodded, and a ripple of pain crossed his face. "I completely understand."

Llewellyn glanced into Blaise's wide eyes, then stared at his own feet. The war of suspicion and desire raged on in his gut. Why was Blaise even there? He sure didn't seem dedicated to his job. "W-why didn't you have to t-teach today?"

Blaise looked startled. "Uh, I told them I had an emergency and needed to go home."

"Why? Aren't y-you jeopardizing y-your new position?"

He frowned. "Truthfully, I wanted to help you investigate more than I wanted to work." He shrugged in that charming way. "I'm not sure I want to be a teacher, so this position may not be for me anyway." He looked up. "You really don't trust me, do you?"

"I f-find your m-motivations hard to comprehend."

"I know I must seem flighty compared to you, but what's hard to get about me?"

"S-simple. Why the f-fuck would you want me?"

Blaise cocked his head and his lips parted. "Seriously? That's your question."

"It's h-hard to b-believe."

Blaise pushed at the center of Llewellyn's chest, and he sat on the edge of the bed. Blaise knelt and started taking off Llewellyn's shoes. "If it was anyone else, I'd think you were just fishing for compliments, but I believe you're serious, so I'll answer seriously."

He set Llewellyn's tan walking shoes aside and plopped on his butt on the patterned rug. Marie crawled on his lap, and he petted her idly. "I love your curiosity, the fire that drives you to solve the unsolvable, and I envy and covet the fierce intelligence that makes it possible for you to solve those problems. I like that you're so shy and that you stutter, throwing the world off guard and making people think you're weak or vulnerable, right before you pounce on them and eat them up." He chuckled, his eyes glassy as he stared at some vision only he could see.

Llewellyn stared in disbelief. How could anyone see him that way?

Blaise ran a finger under Marie's chin, and she stretched out her neck. "I really like that you have cats and you stoop to greet them whenever you come home, and that you drink tea and craft beer, and that lurking somewhere beneath the surface is a huge mystery waiting to be solved if only someone has the will and the persistence to uncover it." He set Marie aside and reared up onto his knees in front of Llewellyn like a cobra in a basket. "And I love that beneath those hopelessly homely khakis, you have the world's greatest ass."

CHAPTER SEVENTEEN

HALF OF Llewellyn's heart didn't believe a word of what Blaise said. That half lost. He reached down and pulled both his sweater and shirt over his head in one move, then shivered as the air and Blaise's eyes touched his skin.

Blaise slid his hands up Llewellyn's legs and undid his khakis, pulling them down his legs. At least he'd worn his coolest boxer briefs, but the things were challenged by a rising erection that wanted to poke through the front and reach out to Blaise.

Blaise grinned, leaned forward, and gently kissed the intruder peeking over the top of Llewellyn's waistband. "Hi there. You look happy to see me." He continued his gentle caress as his hands ran up Llewellyn's chest. Blaise pecked against each nipple, then pressed his fingers on Llewellyn's pecs. "These are lovely. You're so surprisingly muscular, all external appearances to the contrary. Why is that?"

"Exercise. I-I run and other things."

"Maybe we can add a few 'other things' tonight." He rose up to his feet, toed off his sneakers, squatted, and pressed a soft kiss on Llewellyn's lips. "Tell me what you like. I've tried to guess and find I've got no idea."

Llewellyn looked down at his folded hands. "I-I barely know."

"Hmm. I doubt that. Tell me what you dream of." Llewellyn's expression must have looked horrified, because Blaise laughed. "Okay, too big a step. So let's play truth or dare. When we were together before, you chose bottom. Is that your preference or what you thought I'd want?"

"W-what d-do you like?"

"Nope. You first." He held Llewellyn's forearms, his body bobbing a bit in his squatting position. "But let's get more comfortable." He stood, sat on the edge of the bed beside Llewellyn, and pulled him down onto his back, with Blaise beside him resting on his forearm and gazing into Llewellyn's face. "Better. Now, back to the question. Which is your fave, bottom or top?"

Llewellyn took a deep breath. "B-bottom."

"Good." He smiled and kissed Llewellyn's nose, then ran a finger across Llewellyn's cheekbone. "Cute. Tell me all the naughty things you do to stretch."

"N-no." But he smiled so he wouldn't sound too harsh.

"Aw, come on. Dildos? Butt plugs? Anal beads?"

"Y-yes."

Blaise's laugh exploded. "Oh man, that's hot."

"It i-is?" His cheeks flamed again.

"Yeah." He framed his groin with his hands, emphasizing the bulge, then slid over and opened the bedside drawer. "You weren't kidding." He held up a large pink dildo—Llewellyn's favorite. "Impressive." He pulled out a giant tube of lube and a box of condoms. "Wow, you took me seriously. This is economy-size." He scooted back across the bedspread and reached for Llewellyn's boxer briefs.

"N-no." Llewellyn stopped Blaise's hand.

"No?"

"Y-you undress f-first." Although that was kind of dumb, because he'd seen Blaise's body. Who wouldn't suffer by comparison?

"Deal." He dropped the tube on the bed and slid off, unfastened his jeans, and slid them to the floor. His long-sleeved T-shirt came off in one move, and he reached for his briefs, then grinned. "Okay, together, one, two, three!" He pulled his own pale blue shorts to his knees, then kicked them off as his penis sprang up and slapped against his belly. There he stood in all his nude glory, and glory was no overstatement. Wide shoulders, a long torso with beautifully defined muscle, leading to strong thighs and lean legs. The grace he'd displayed on the dance floor that night in San Jose revealed itself in every curve and arc of his body as he stood, smiling at Llewellyn. "You got stuck."

"What?"

He nodded toward Llewellyn's hands, with the thumbs hooked in his briefs but stopped halfway down, hung up on a very erect cock. Llewellyn smiled. "Y-you're very distracting."

"Glad to hear it." He sat on the bed again, his erection rising between his strong thighs; then he hooked Llewellyn's shorts with a thumb and had them off in seconds.

Llewellyn's instincts won, and his hands crossed over his crotch.

Blaise mimicked him and did the same. "Here we are. Adam and Adam."

"Adam and St-Steve?"

"Right." Gazing into Llewellyn's eyes, Blaise slid a condom on himself and lubed it up.

Oh man, just the sight made Llewellyn's belly flip. Swallowing, he held out his hand, and Blaise squeezed lube into it. Eyes fixed on Blaise, Llewellyn raised his legs and shoved lube into himself, then sat back and watched Blaise's hands perform their magic on his own butt.

Blaise smiled slowly, pushed Llewellyn's shoulder until he was flat on the mattress, then rose up enough to lie on top of him. Wriggling, he fit their parts together.

Swamped. Llewellyn's nervous system overloaded with heat and pressure and tingling bursts of pleasure shooting into his groin and brain and heart.

Planting his hands above Llewellyn's shoulders, Blaise began to rock his body forward and back over Llewellyn so they rubbed together in all the best places. Fantastic friction increased the tingling until it turned to a lava flow, like fire through his veins. "Oh. Oh G-God."

"Yeah." Blaise rutted harder, raising himself higher on his arms like he was doing the cobra pose so the contact between their hips increased.

Llewellyn heard his own moans and gasps. *Too much.* He clamped his arms behind Blaise's back and locked them together, but it wasn't enough. Raising both legs, he secured them around Blaise's hips. As if he'd been waiting for that signal, Blaise pushed back until Llewellyn felt pressure at his opening.

"Look at me. Right here." Blaise gazed into Llewellyn's eyes. He wanted to close them, to hide, to do anything to break that link, but no go. Blaise held him tight, staring into his soul as he pressed inside Llewellyn's body. No resistance. Burning joy filtered into his brain as Blaise took possession. Deep. Deeper.

Everything went black—then brilliant white as the explosion that blasted through his groin filled his head. "Blaise!" Oh God, what a perfect name. What a perfect description. His body trembled and shuddered out of his control, and somewhere, a mile away, he heard Blaise yell "Oh my God!" just before his full body weight collapsed onto Llewellyn. Who knew the weight of the world could ever feel so perfect?

He never wanted to move again. Moving might interfere with the puffy clouds of bliss floating through his chest and his brain.

Blaise breathed deeply, which pressed his chest so firmly against Llewellyn it forced him to exhale. Oh man, even more than not moving, he didn't want to think, because that would drag his brain to only one possible conclusion. What just happened qualified as the best moments of Llewellyn's life. That boded damned badly for his future. He'd learned long ago that wanting anything was the surest way to misery.

"May I stay?" The soft words whispered against Llewellyn's ear.

His lips formed the reply before his brain caught up. "Y-yes." He managed to control himself before he added—"forever."

BLAISE GAZED into Llewellyn's big brown eyes. Brown. Not dark blue like biographies said about Ramon Rondell. Standing in the kitchen, they gazed eye-to-eye, making Llewellyn about six one or two, not six four as fans claimed about Rondell. No eloquent words tripped off Llewellyn's tongue. Hell, half the time he could barely get the words out. No way he faked it.

Blaise reached out and touched Llewellyn's cheek. Sadly, this man, the shy awkward one with the plain brown eyes that bored into his soul when they finally connected with his, was the guy who captivated him. Blaise didn't really give a shit about the rest. And that would go over like a flying pig with his mother.

Llewellyn smiled shyly. *Yes, it had been a pretty intense night, hadn't it?* He said, "You're th-thinking awfully h-hard."

Blaise dimpled up. "My thinking won't be the only thing that's hard if I keep looking at you much longer. We'll both have to call in sick."

Llewellyn gave him a side-eyed glance. "Kind of ch-cheesy but cute."

"Sorry." *That's what I get for not saying what I mean—that last night didn't just rock, it rocked my world. Better not.* He leaned forward and kissed Llewellyn softly on the lips. "Can I come back? After work?" He held his breath.

"Y-you really w-want to?"

"Yes, I really do." He tried to push all the feeling he could muster into those words.

"Okay." The smile Llewellyn shared lit up the dim garage.

The warmth in his chest made him half want to run and half to stay right there forever. "I'll bet we could have lunch together without anyone talking too much. Want to?" He knew his grin had to be sappy.

"Th-that w-would be nice."

"I'll meet you out front of the history building at eleven forty-five, okay?"

Llewellyn nodded with equal sappiness.

"So I'll go out the back door and cut over to where I left my car."

"Th-thank you for doing that."

Blaise shrugged. "It's better if the school doesn't get too focused on us just yet, don't you think?" To say nothing of his mother.

"I g-guess. And the p-police." He looked at his shoes.

"Yeah. When this all dies down, we can talk about the best way to be public." Llewellyn looked—what? Surprised? Shocked? No, more the first with a touch of amazement that might even be happy.

Blaise gave him another quick kiss on the nose and hurried out the back door. He'd pushed the patience of his department to the limit already, and if he wanted to keep this cushy position for a while longer, he needed to actually do some work.

After a couple of zigzags through yards, he unlocked his car on the next street and slipped inside. He glanced down at his phone—the phone he'd put on mute. Three missed calls, all from guess who. With a sigh, he hit Reply.

"Damn it, Blaise, where the hell have you been?"

"Good morning to you too. And I've been where I couldn't call you back."

"Oh, and where might that be in the middle of the night?"

Shit, he didn't want to answer. "With Llewellyn. How the hell else do you think I found the wig? It's gone, by the way. Along with all the upscale clothes he had in the closet."

"Do you think he's suspicious?" Her voice snapped. "Maybe he figures no one will believe you without the evidence. I told you that taking the wig would have been a worthwhile gamble. Damn it, Blaise. I wanted a picture of it at least, and of the clothes too."

"I didn't have my phone in the john when I snooped." A lie, but a credible one.

"Sloppy. How do you expect to get ahead in this business? I trusted you with this. Do I have to come there myself?"

"He knows what you look like, Mother." *Don't let her hear you sweat.*

"I'm good at disguise." He could hear her taking a breath to control her temper. "What's going on with the murder?"

"We met the twin sister, who's a piece of work."

"In what way? Please learn to be specific."

He hid his sigh. "As different from Anne as she can be. She's rough, cynical, and doesn't seem attached to anything or anyone. She barely seems to care that her sister is dead."

"Maybe there's a story in it?"

"Maybe. I'm staying as close to the case as I can."

"The only thing you're staying close to as far as I can tell is Llewellyn Lewis's ass."

"Thanks for your vote of confidence." Weird how he still wanted that confidence.

"Earn it. Show me something."

Shit. "I'm at my job. I have to go." With a deep breath, he didn't even wait for her to answer. He hung up.

That was a little braver than usual.

He parked, grabbed his heavy backpack he kept in the back seat, then slid out of the car and trotted into the English building to be a good teaching assistant for a change.

STOP THINKING about lunch. Llewellyn shifted in his chair at his makeshift desk in the back corner of Maria's office. Since his office was still a crime scene, he'd hauled a few bookshelves to separate a space for him. He dragged his brain away from picturing Blaise's beautiful eyes when he'd gazed at Llewellyn and said yes, he really wanted to come over. *Focus!* He stared at the picture of Alonzo Echevarria, then switched over to the bio of his wife, Carmen. *Interesting.*

Alonzo seemed to be what they claimed—a rich guy who made his money in building maintenance and happened to have a degree in history. He was a fancy janitor. All the drive and social pretensions came from Carmen. She'd pushed him onto the board of various symphonies and operas, which was hard to picture, and according to the gossip websites had ground a few people to dust in the process. In one case she'd apparently dug up a scandal about one of the other candidates for a prestigious opera board position and made sure the story got to every sensational news source online.

Wincing, Llewellyn switched over to the *Daily Phoenix* and clicked on the Digging the Dirt section. He searched for Carmen Echavarria. Sure enough, several articles turned up, one written by Octavia Otto, Ramon's nemesis. She pretty much stated that the sexy Mrs. Echevarria wanted what she wanted and didn't care who she hurt to get it.

Llewellyn sat back. What Carmen Echavarria wanted now was to contribute a boatload of money to get a building named after her husband, and by association herself. But how badly did she want it? Surely not so much she'd kill someone.

He leaned toward the screen, wanting desperately to resist the siren call. No such luck. He typed in Ramon Rondell and averted his eyes. *If I don't look, maybe the monster won't eat me.* But of course, like the proverbial helpless moth, his eyes flew toward the flame of the screen. A couple of stories he'd already seen occupied the bottom of the screen, but at the top…. *Holy shit!*

"Ramon Rondell Wears a Disguise! What Does He Look Like Under the Wig?"

What the hell? A shiver of ice crept up his spine. Okay, someone might have guessed that Ramon wore a disguise, but why the wig specifically? When had he worn it last? The club in San Jose? No. The night he went to the spa steam room. That thought produced shivers of a whole different kind. But he'd swear Blaise hadn't recognized him. He released a long breath. Maybe he shouldn't swear too solemnly.

He shook his head. *Forget it. Ramon's retired from public appearances.* Somehow that didn't feel like such a devastating thought, since Blaise seemed to like Llewellyn. Of course, he'd come on to Ramon, but he'd done a whole lot more than that to Llewellyn. A lot more. *Stop or your penis will lead you to lunch.*

He glanced at his watch. He still had an hour.

"Hey, boss." Maria peeked around the book-case. He'd spent his first hour in the office explaining the visit to San Francisco, the odd appearance of the brother standing when he had been confined to a wheelchair, and the arrival of Miranda. Maria had intelligently pointed out that many people who used wheelchairs most of the time could still stand, but she'd plunged into researching as many of the unique cast of weird ducks who'd crawled out of the wood-work recently as she could.

"F-find anything?"

A crease rode the bridge of her nose. "Yeah. It's probably nothing." She walked in and sat opposite him. "I was just digging around in some of the research that's been done on the Shakespeare issue."

"Yes?"

"Do you know some of the other people of the period who've been advanced as possible candidates to be the real Shakespeare?"

Obviously, she wanted to drag this out, so he nodded. "Marlowe, of course, B-Bacon, D-Derby, a few others."

She cocked half a smile, but her brows stayed drawn over her nose. "And do you remember the family name of the Earl of Derby?"

"Of course. St-Stanley. William Stanley."

Her dark eyes met his. "Do you think there's anything beyond coincidence in the fact that George Stanley, the Shakespearean scholar, tried to talk you out of proving that de Vere was Shakespeare?"

His mouth opened, closed, then his lips parted far enough to say, "Wow."

"Right. Probably just chance, but I saw the name Stanley and remembered what you told me about George, so I thought I'd share it."

Llewellyn sat back in his chair. "D-damn. Never thought of it."

She grinned. "Hard to consider someone who's hitting on you as a potential murderer."

He snorted. "T-true."

"You should go ask him to lunch and suck information out of him."

He felt himself blushing, both from her unique choice of verb and the confession he was about to make. "Uh, I'm h-having lunch with B-Blaise Arthur. To talk about the c-case."

Her eyes danced. "Right. I'm sure murder will be at the forefront of your thoughts."

"K-kind of." He blushed harder but chuckled.

"I think that's great, boss. In addition to all his obvious attributes, he seems like a nice guy. Where are you going to lunch?"

"D-don't know."

"Well, have fun. Maybe I'll go hang around the English department and see what comes up." She waggled her fingers.

When he walked into the outer office a few minutes later, she was already gone to lunch. *I wonder if she meant it about the English department?* Suddenly

the fact that there had been a real murder and someone
he cared about was treating the pursuit of a suspect as
a game slapped him in the face. *This could be dangerous.* He shuddered. He'd talk to Maria after lunch. She
could do research for him, but she needed to stay away
from any face-to-face confrontations, despite the fact
that George was a pretty unlikely killer.

CHAPTER EIGHTEEN

As HE locked up his office, his heart beat hard. He thought of it as the Blaise beat. Funny how he couldn't stay away from Blaise. Ordinarily he'd never reach for the sun that way lest he, like Icarus, end up with melted wings. Hell, that kind of confidence was Ramon's domain. But since Ramon had seen Blaise dancing that infamous night, Llewellyn had wanted him. Achingly. Embarrassingly. Still, he made like a mad dog and rushed down the hall and out into the midday sunshine. No Blaise yet. Dragging in a breath of fresh air, he leaned against the stone wall in front of his building, pulled out his phone from his pocket, and pretended he wasn't dying of anticipation.

He tried to settle into reading a research document he'd loaded onto his Kindle app, but he kept sneaking glances down the sidewalk toward the English building. *Should I tell Blaise about Maria and go check the English department to be sure she's not waylaying George Stanley?* Before he could decide, he saw sun glinting off Blaise's golden hair as he trotted toward Llewellyn. When Llewellyn couldn't quite control his smile, Blaise waved and smiled back. Llewellyn slipped his phone back in his pocket.

Blaise ran up, grinning. Since Llewellyn couldn't seem to lose his own grin, it was a good thing nobody was nearby to observe. Blaise said, "Hi."

"H-hello."

"My car's in the parking lot. I thought we could go someplace away from campus for lunch."

"Th-that would be n-nice."

"At least we won't be warping young minds with our evil influence."

He so wanted to reach out and take Blaise's hand, but no such luck. "I-I have something t-to tell you. M-Maria c-came up with an idea and I—"

Blaise looked up over Llewellyn's shoulder. His eyes widened and body stiffened. Before Llewellyn could turn, a familiar voice behind him said, "Blaise Arthur, you're under arrest for suspicion of the murder of Anne de Vere."

Blaise yelled, "What? What the hell?"

Llewellyn whirled on Detective Holiday. "D-don't be ridiculous!"

Two uniformed policemen rushed to Blaise and handcuffed him behind his back. As they read him his rights, he said, "I don't understand. I didn't do anything!" He looked desperate and afraid, and Llewellyn wanted to rip him from the policemen's hands and run. Everything in his gut screamed to escape.

He tried to calm his voice. "Th-there's a m-mistake. He c-couldn't have d-done this. Why d-do you th-think he d-did?"

Holiday frowned. "I'm not at liberty to say, but just so you know, he's not who he says he is. You, of all people, need to be aware of that." He walked up to where the policemen held Blaise and nodded toward a police car that was parked a few yards down by the curb. The red curb.

Blaise looked back and yelled, "I didn't do it, Llewellyn. Please believe me."

"Sh-shall I c-call a lawyer?" He clutched his hands in front of his belly that threatened to lose whatever was left of breakfast.

"No. I have one." His head disappeared into the car as the policeman pushed it down, and his body followed.

Holiday turned to Llewellyn. "We'll need you for questioning. I'll contact you in a few hours."

They drove away. Llewellyn stared after them, gradually becoming aware of a clutch of students and teachers gathered nearby, watching the proceedings. Suddenly Maria ran out of the crowd and grasped his arm. "Come on, boss. Let's get you inside, and I'll go for lunch."

He never wanted to eat again, but he followed Maria back to the office and collapsed on the couch. After she locked the door to the hall, she handed him a cup of his favorite tea, and he sucked it up like lifeblood.

She sat opposite him in a chair. "What the hell happened? Did Blaise Arthur really just get arrested for murder?"

He nodded and held his teacup in both hands.

"Man, that's wacko."

"Th-they're g-going to question m-me. So I m-might learn s-something."

"Well, that's good, anyway." She stood and walked to the phone on her desk, picked it up, and before he could say anything, she ordered pizza delivered. When she hung up, she said, "You can't go to the police department with no food in your stomach." She stared at him. "What aren't you telling me?"

He felt his brows pull down. Did he want to confide in her? *Yes.* "H-Holiday said B-Blaise isn't who he s-says he is. He s-said I n-need to know that."

"Damn, talk about being purposefully provocative. He wants to throw you off base so you'll tell him anything you know."

He wanted to believe that. Desperately. "M-maybe."

A half hour later, while he forced down a piece of pizza, he got a call from Holiday, who told him to come to the department as soon as he could. The trick would be not throwing up the pizza along the way.

LLEWELLYN SAT in the hard-backed chair and tried not to stare at the mirror that covered one wall. Knowing someone was likely behind it watching might be creepy, but not as much as staring at his own nerdy plainness. He'd been alone since he got there about fifteen minutes before.

The door opened, and Holiday walked in with a plain woman with short hair, wearing a dark blue pantsuit and carrying a file folder. Llewellyn stood.

Holiday said, "Dr. Lewis, this is CJ Muller."

"How do you do?" Llewellyn stared at his hands, then forced himself to look back.

She nodded. "Do fine, thanks. Sit."

He sat. They pulled out the chairs across from him. Muller opened the folder. "May I ask the nature of your relationship with Blaise Arthur?"

Holiday looked up. "By the way, you don't have to tell us unless you want to."

"Are y-you reading me my rights?" He managed to say it like he wasn't about to have a heart attack.

Holiday shook his head. "Not at all, Dr. Lewis. You're not under arrest. You're simply a person who has had the closest contact with our suspect."

Muller muttered, "You're not under arrest—yet."

Holiday gave her a look, then turned back with a smile. "Your relationship?"

"W-we met recently. We've b-become fr-friends."

"With benefits?" Muller practically sneered.

Asshole. He stared right at her. "Y-yes."

She looked shocked that he admitted it, and Holiday seemed ready to laugh. "The night of the murder, you've told me that Blaise Arthur was with you—all night as far as you knew at the time. We later discovered from Mr. Arthur himself that he left in the middle of the night to return to his apartment."

"Y-yes. He told me."

"Does Mr. Arthur have a key to your office?"

Llewellyn's head snapped up. "W-what? No."

Holiday and Muller glanced at each other.

Muller looked at Llewellyn. "Who did Mr. Arthur tell you he was?"

Llewellyn frowned. "H-he's a t-teaching assistant for the English d-department."

"He's never told you of other interests?" Holiday flipped a page in his notebook.

"H-he says he might not w-want to stay in English teaching, but he's y-young."

"Yes, well, so are you."

"B-Blaise had n-no reason to k-kill Anne."

Muller raised a graying eyebrow. "Are you sure of that?"

Was he? "Y-yes. H-have you investigated her b-brother and sisters? They w-were very angry sh-she was spending the m-money."

"They have alibis for the time of the murder."

He shook his head. He wanted to blurt out about the Echevarrias and George Stanley, but he couldn't bear to get them in trouble when he had no real evidence—just suspicions.

Muller looked up from her file. "You say Arthur had no reason to kill Anne de Vere. What if he wanted a really good story?"

"St-story?"

Holiday gave Muller another firm look, then turned to Llewellyn. "Dr. Lewis, are you aware that Mr. Arthur is a journalist?"

"N-n-no." Everything in his chest sank to his knees.

"Yes, for a publication called the *Daily Phoenix*."

Cold. Cold hands. Cold heart.

Muller looked up sharply. "Dr. Lewis, are you Ramon Rondell?"

His belly flipped, heart hammered against his chest, and getting breath seemed impossible.

Holiday held up a hand. "For the moment you don't need to answer that. But it appears that Mr. Arthur was assigned by his editor, who happens to be his mother, to prove that you're Ramon Rondell."

The pizza pushed against his throat for exit, and he breathed deeply. "B-but that has nothing to d-do with Anne de Vere. S-surely that's n-not reason to ch-charge him with mur-murder." Jesus, why was he defending Blaise? It seemed like Blaise had lied to him every moment they were together. His inner voice screamed *Told you so!*

Holiday sighed. "No. We have evidence that Arthur was inside your office the night Anne de Vere was killed. We've spoken to your assistant, and she's told us Mr. Arthur was never inside your private office to her knowledge."

"H-he might h-have been." *Think, damn it. Was Blaise ever in the office? Dear God, why would he be in my office at the same time as Anne de Vere?*

"If you remember such an occasion, please tell us."

Muller said, "Since you and Mr. Arthur are such good friends"—her voice reeked with suspicion—"wouldn't you assume he'd try not to let you know about his actual identity and that he was investigating you for his publication?"

"I-I don't know."

"Isn't it logical he'd try to hide it?"

"N-not enough to k-kill someone." He sounded desperate even to his own ears.

Holiday pushed back from the table. "That's all for now, Dr. Lewis. Thank you for your cooperation. If you have to leave town, please let us know."

Llewellyn stood. *Just get outside before you fall apart.*

Holiday led him to the elevator. "If you remember additional details about your interactions with Blaise Arthur, or anything else you think is pertinent, please call me." He handed Llewellyn another of his cards. Llewellyn shoved it in his pocket. *Keep it together.*

The elevator dinged, and both he and Holiday turned to face it. The doors opened.

No.

There she was. A woman he'd only seen in print and online but he'd learned to hate and fear. Octavia Otto stood in the elevator between two men in suits. She started to exit past him, looked up, and seemed to register his face. Her eyebrows rose, her mouth opened, a red flush spread across her cheeks, and she shrieked, "You bastard! You did this. If he'd never met you, he wouldn't be in this mess right now." She reached back a hand and swung it forward in a huge arc toward Llewellyn's face.

Llewellyn grabbed her wrist in midflight. *No.* "S-stop." *No one would ever slap him again.*

She wrenched her arm back, but he didn't let go.

Holiday glanced at Llewellyn with surprise in his gaze, but he reached up and took her arm from Llewellyn's grasp, gently but firmly, and held it. "Ma'am, it might be good to remember that your son wouldn't have been here at all if you hadn't sent him."

"Go to hell." She tugged back on her wrist, her teeth bared. Her companions pulled her away, and Holiday let her arm go.

He nodded toward the same room Llewellyn had been in. "Please take a seat. I'll be there shortly."

The two men half dragged Octavia Otto, or whatever her real name was, down the hall.

Holiday said, "Sorry. She's obviously upset about her son."

"Y-yes."

"I think you are too."

Llewellyn said nothing. Even Octavia Otto couldn't blame him more than he blamed himself. He stepped into the elevator. Holiday gave him a light slap on the shoulder, which was kind of nice, and he rode down to the lobby of the police station. The doors opened, and Maria rose from the chair she'd been sitting in. She smiled, but it barely covered her concern. It only took a glance to see why. Outside the doors of the police station, TV vans and a group of reporters gathered.

Maria hurried to his side and led him into an area where the reporters couldn't see him. She pointed down the hall. "There's a side entrance. I have my car there, and the police said I can use that door to get you out."

He slumped against the wall. "If I w-wasn't gay, I'd m-marry you."

She grinned. "If you weren't gay, I'd consider taking you up on it. Come on."

Against all odds, they made it out the side door, into the back of the parking lot where a bunch of police cars were gathered, and into Maria's Honda. She started it and said, "Duck down."

He complied, though it reminded him too much of being with Blaise in San Francisco. After a few minutes of intense staring through the windshield by Maria, she glanced down at him. "Coast's clear, I think."

He unfolded himself from the seat well, remembering what Blaise had said about his bravery.

"We'll have to sneak into your house. I'll bet there's press waiting."

"L-let's go to the English d-department."

"Hoo yeah. Are we taking on Stanley?"

He nodded. "Yes. And anybody else w-we can f-find."

The rode quietly for a minute; then Maria said, "I heard more about how Blaise Arthur isn't who he says he is. I figure that's pretty crappy for you. So what's our goal at the English department?"

Llewellyn took a deep breath. *Act now, process later.* "J-just because he's a lying son of a b-bitch doesn't make him guilty of m-murder." He meant the *bitch* part literally.

"Oooohkay. So we're still on the case. Cool."

"N-no. I need you to stay out of h-harm's way."

"Hey, thanks, but I'm really good at snooping, and I promise to be careful."

"Th-this isn't a g-game. Anne is really dead."

"Hey, boss, I'm taking this seriously. I feel really bad for her, not just because she's dead, but because we don't get to prove de Vere was Shakespeare, and I was looking forward to that."

"This c-could be d-dangerous, Maria."

"I know, but why's it okay for you to put your-self in danger and not me? Because I'm female? Come on."

Was that the reason? "N-no. Because you have y-your whole life ahead, and this isn't y-your fight."

"Why?"

"W-what?"

"Why isn't it my fight too? Hell, boss, I'm only a few years younger than you. You have your whole life ahead, just like me. I'm your research assistant. I have a stake in this. I want to help." She looked at him, then back at the road.

Well, hell. "I-I apologize. I w-was being dismissive."

"Nah. You just love me."

He snorted. "T-true."

She drove toward the parking lot of the English building. "Get down." He slid back into his favorite pretzel position. She murmured, "There's press in front of the department." The car turned a couple of times and then stopped. "Okay. We're in the side lot. You should be good."

He unfolded onto the seat—*do not think*—and opened the car door. Walking quickly, they crossed into the building. Inside, Maria stopped him. "What's the plan?"

"I'm g-going to see G-george."

"Okay. I'm going to go snoop in the coffee room. How long shall I give you?"

"H-half an hour, but he m-may not be there."

"I'll come out and check in a few minutes, just in case."

While Maria turned down the hall to the right, Llewellyn walked up the stairs. He stopped at a directory on the wall, then followed a line of offices down a long hall. Close to the end of the row, a small sign outside a door said Dr. George Stanley.

CHAPTER NINETEEN

LLEWELLYN TOOK a breath and stepped inside George's office. A cute young guy looked up from his desk. "Hi. Hey, you're that guy, right? The Shakespeare guy? The murder?"

Was this twink real? "I'm Dr. Llewellyn L-Lewis. Is Dr. St-Stanley in?"

"Oh yeah, sure." He bounced up from the desk and sashayed to the closed inner office door, which he opened without knocking. "Hey, George, a guy's here to see you. Uh, Lewis, right?" He grinned at Llewellyn.

George appeared in the open doorway. "Llewellyn, come in. Oh my God, I'm so glad to see you. Do you want coffee? I mean tea?" He looked at the kid. "Do we have any, Harvey? Tea?"

"Oh, nah. Too pansy-assed. Just coffee."

George gave Llewellyn an embarrassed smile. "Sorry. Come on in." Llewellyn followed George into the office, and he closed the door. "Please sit." He walked behind his desk and took the chair. "I was so shocked to hear about Anne de Vere. My God, to quote Ibsen, people don't do such things."

"Anne didn't—"

He waved a hand. "I mean, whoever killed her. Unimaginable. Things like that don't happen at Middlemark." He held the bridge of his nose. "I hear Blaise Arthur did it. My God. To think he and I were colleagues." He dropped his hand to his desk. "Shocking. Just shocking."

"I d-don't think B-Blaise had a reason."

He sprang forward in his chair. "But he was arrested!"

"I th-think they're wrong."

"But they must have had a reason to arrest him."

"You know him a little. D-do you think he c-could kill someone?"

"I don't know." He stared at his hands. "If he didn't do it, that could make it random, and that's terribly frightening now, isn't it?" He slumped. "I mean, if it's random, any of us could be next." He looked genuinely freaked, which was reassuringly interesting.

"M-may I ask you a p-personal question?"

He sucked a breath and managed to curve a quirky smile. "Yes, I did hire Harvey for his cute ass and yes, I am an idiot."

Llewellyn barked a laugh. "N-no. H-he's the idiot." He inhaled. "I w-wondered if you're related to William St-Stanley, sixth Earl of Derby?"

His eyes widened. "Wow, you guessed that. I actually only found out a short time ago. I mean, what are the chances that two people related to famous ancestors who could have been Shakespeare would wind up at the same table at dinner?"

"Yes, j-just amazing." *Amazing unless it was planned.* Llewellyn kept staring at him.

George readjusted his mouse on his desk, then frowned and glanced up. "Wait, you don't think that I was trying to talk you out of taking the de Vere case because I want Stanley to be Shakespeare, do you?"

Llewellyn shrugged. "N-not much reason to think St-Stanley was Shakespeare."

"No. As I told you, I think Shakespeare was Shakespeare, and most experts agree with me." He fiddled with the mouse again. "But I do think there's as much reason to think Stanley was Shakespeare as to believe de Vere was."

"Not really. And s-so far as I know, no one has been k-killed for believing St-Stanley was Shakespeare."

He frowned. "So you do think she was killed because of what she wanted to prove?"

"I th-think she could have been killed for f-five million d-dollars."

"Oh, right."

Llewellyn hunched his shoulders and dropped them. "B-but it was m-more likely r-random." He gazed at George.

George literally shuddered, waving his hands in front of him like he was brushing away attackers. "This is really awful. I don't know whether to hope Blaise did it or not."

"If h-he did do it, what would y-you think is the reason? I mean, y-you know him f-fairly well."

He shrugged. "Maybe she found out something about him that he wanted to hide."

"Like w-what?"

"Don't know, but the rumors around campus say he's not who we think."

Llewellyn stood. "I h-have to go."

He looked surprised. "So you just wanted to ask me that? About Stanley?"

"I w-wanted to see if you're okay."

"Oh, uh, thanks."

Llewellyn walked to the door.

George's voice sounded flat. "You're defending Arthur. You don't think I killed her, do you? Because I can prove where I was."

Llewellyn turned and gazed at George's drawn, frightened face. "N-no. No, I d-don't think you killed her." But he wished he did.

Llewellyn walked past the idiot twink and down the stairs to the building entrance. Maria stood beside the door, scrolling through her phone. She looked up and smiled. "The hounds don't seem to have tracked us down yet, so let's run."

They hurried out the door and to the car. As soon as they drove out of the lot, she said, "So?"

"So, he's s-scared to d-death and I d-don't think he d-did it. He s-says he has an alibi, anyway."

"Damn. That would have been easy. So, people are talking about Blaise being Octavia Otto's son. Apparently the press spotted her going into the police station, and she was shooting off her mouth. Did you know that?" She glanced at him.

He nodded. "Not about the p-press, but I knew about Oc-Octavia. She came to the p-police station when I was there. She b-blames me."

"You didn't tell me that before."

"I know." He sighed audibly. "She sent h-him here. He works for h-her."

"On the *Daily Phoenix*?"

He nodded.

"Did she send him to investigate the Shakespearean case?"

"I d-don't know how that's possible. He was here before Anne. Or about the s-same time."

"Maybe Otto got wind of it before Anne came here?"

"M-maybe. S-seems unlikely." He stared out the window at the trees that lined his neighborhood's streets.

"Hell, who'd ever dream someone would kill a person over the question of Shakespeare's identity?"

She pulled to the curb on the street behind his house. Should he tell her? Hell, she'd find out soon anyway. "B-Blaise was here to p-prove that I'm R-Ramon Rondell." Quiet. He looked up, and she gazed at him with an unreadable expression. "What?"

"I've wondered if there was truth to the stories."

"W-what was y-your conclusion?"

She cocked her head. "Most people think it's too ridiculous. How could shy, inarticulate Llewellyn Lewis be the gay blade, Ramon Rondell? But I decided it might well be true." She chuckled. "There's way more fire in you than most people see. You're more of a rebel. And I've read some of Rondell's pieces, and they're good. Sensational, yes, but also well researched and reasoned." She chewed her lower lip. "But it's truly crappy that Blaise came here to prove that." She looked up. "And you don't ever have to tell me if it's true. Seriously, I'd rather guess." She smiled, though it mostly reflected compassion. "Get some rest. I'll call you if I hear anything important. Will you be at school tomorrow?"

He nodded.

"Okay, see you then. Sleep, okay? Say hi to the felines for me. I'm so sorry this whole mess is happening."

"M-me too." He slid out of the car and started walking between the houses toward his place. As he cut through a neighbor's yard, he saw two strangers hanging out behind his Craftsman. He stopped and stepped closer to the nearby building. One of the men talked on his cell phone. The man nodded, looked at his companion, then seemed to click off. A moment later, they both walked around his house. Llewellyn took off like a rabbit, cut through the bushes, and made it into his back door before he was spotted. Fortunately he'd left the drapes closed. When he opened the door, the cats came running. He might be projecting, but they seemed to look surprised he was coming in the back door.

He knelt down and gave them all a pat, then stood, and they trailed him into the bedroom, meowing. "S-sorry, guys. I n-need to change before I f-feed you." With fur swirling around his feet, he walked into the bedroom and straight into the closet. *Whoa.* The simplicity of the closet contents struck him, and for an instant he felt robbed. *Take a breath.*

With a jerk, he peeled off his jacket and then his shirt and carefully hung them in a neat row, then stripped off the khakis and held them out in front of him. "When did I d-decide to sentence myself to k-khaki?" He tweaked a hanging knit. "And sw-sweater vests?" He looked down into the upturned furry faces. "Do y-you think I could do better?"

Marie sat and cocked her head at him. "Meow."

Clearly an affirmative vote.

He pulled on his sweats, slid on some flip-flops, and led the fuzz parade back to the kitchen. After he gave each critter his or her favorite food, he stared in the refrigerator. Not hungry, but one slice of pizza didn't qualify as nutrition. He pulled a can of vegetable soup from the pantry, heated it in the microwave, and set it on the small kitchen table. After grabbing a spoon as he walked by the drawer, he sat and stared at the happy cats. At least he had company.

Company. Had he gotten used to having Blaise around so quickly? Yes, Blaise was an easy addiction. He stared at the floating vegetables in the broth. A toxic addiction.

Damn. He dipped his spoon, pulled up some soup, and stuck it in his mouth. "Mmmft!" He spit it back in the bowl. "Hot." He stirred and stared at the ripples. *Hot like Blaise, and heat hurts.*

His spoon clanged against the side of the bowl, and Marie and Emily both looked up. Nothing distracted Julius when he was eating.

Llewellyn looked at the girls. "It's all your f-fault. Y-you told me it was okay t-to like him." A soft sound came out of his mouth, and he slapped a hand over it, but the words escaped. "And d-damn, I liked him s-so much."

He took a breath. *Okay, so I always knew there was no reason for him to like me. No real reason. The fact that he had a whole other agenda pretty much fits with what I suspected, so being disappointed is stupid.*

He carefully sipped the rapidly cooling soup. *Once burned, twice shy. On a lot of levels. But that doesn't mean I want him convicted of murder. Blaise didn't do it.* Llewellyn was so sure of that. *I need to prove it. Then we can be done.*

Marie raised her head a second before a knock came on his door.

All three of the felines started toward the entry.

"Don't b-bother. It's j-just the press."

The knock came again, louder and more insistently.

"D-damn." Were they allowed to do that?

Another knock and Llewellyn jumped up. Time to tell them to leave him alone. He stalked into the living room and pulled open the front door, driving the cats backward.

Oh.

The yard was full of reporters yelling, but on the porch were a man in a wheelchair and a woman. He recognized them as Roscoe and Jane de Vere. "C-come in."

He stepped away from the entrance, and Jane tipped back Roscoe's chair to get it over the flashing on the door sill, then pushed her brother inside. Quickly Llewellyn closed it behind her, shutting out a storm of questions.

Llewellyn turned, remembered that they didn't know he'd recognize them, and said, "Hello. I'm Llewellyn L-Lewis." He cocked his head as if asking who they were.

"I'm Jane de Vere, and this is my brother, Roscoe."

Llewellyn nodded. "I guessed. I'm s-so sorry f-for your loss."

"Thank you. Can we talk to you?"

He waved a hand toward the living room, and they moved in that direction, the cats following and sniffing at the wheels.

Llewellyn followed them. "C-can I get you s-something t-to drink?"

Jane nodded.

"Iced t-tea?"

"Thank you."

During his trip to the kitchen, he took a few deep breaths. They both looked very serious. Of course, they had a dead sister, but he suspected their dour expressions went beyond grief—maybe all the way to greed.

He pulled down a tray, loaded three glasses, spoons, the sugar and cream containers, and napkins on it, and carried it back to the living room.

Killing time by preparing their tea as they requested—sugar and a little milk—he tried to watch them, especially Roscoe, who scowled ferociously. When he was done, Llewellyn sat on the couch opposite Jane, who had taken the chair closest to her brother's spot. "How c-can I help y-you?"

"By telling us you've given up on this asinine obsession of Anne's!" Roscoe pushed himself several inches out of the chair with his powerful forearms.

Llewellyn raised an eyebrow.

Jane said, "Roscoe, please. Mr. Lewis—"

"Dr. Lewis." Llewellyn stared at her steadily.

"Of course, Dr. Lewis, we know that Anne offered you and the university a great deal of money to prove our father's silly thesis."

"It's n-not his thesis, Ms. de Vere. Y-your ancestor's possible identity as Shakespeare h-has been a popular c-concept for over a hundred y-years."

"I understand. Regardless, now that Anne is gone, everyone remaining in the family opposes the idea of continuing with the investigation. This is the last of the family fortune, and we desperately need it for Roscoe's care."

"I h-have no knowledge of the d-dispensation of the m-money. I h-have been t-told, however, that your f-father provided funds specific to his p-passion."

"That's all well and good while he was alive, but he had no way of knowing how our circumstances would change."

"I see. I have no specific d-designs on the m-money. It was offered in return for proving Edward de Vere was Shakespeare."

Roscoe growled, "Well, that's all over now."

"I did get the impression, however, from M-Miranda that she didn't c-care about the m-money."

Roscoe's eyebrows practically disappeared in his hair. "What?"

Jane put a hand on his arm. "You must be mistaken, Dr. Lewis. Miranda's the most vehement of all of us. She hates the idea that the money's being thrown away on a frivolous pursuit."

Interesting. "Perhaps I m-misunderstood or she d-didn't want me to know her f-feelings."

"It's possible, I suppose, but she's really very obvious." She sipped her tea. "So you won't be pursuing the research." It wasn't a question.

"I d-didn't say that. I w-won't be pursuing the m-money."

Roscoe snapped his head toward Llewellyn. "You can't do that."

"What?"

"Continue this fool's errand. It's ridiculous!"

"S-sir, I c-can research anything I d-desire." He stood. "Again, I'm very s-sorry for your terrible loss."

Jane rose, frowning. "Let's go, Roscoe."

They exited to the shouts and screams of the reporters, and Llewellyn closed the door quickly behind them. He leaned against it. Odd. Nothing about the de Veres quite added up.

His cell phone started ringing on the coffee table. Well, damn, so much for rest. He grabbed it and looked at the screen. Maria. *Wonder what she's found.* He clicked the phone.

CHAPTER TWENTY

"H-HI. WHAT'S up?" Llewellyn sat on the couch and cradled the phone against his ear.

"Hey, boss, I have someone who wants to talk to you."

"W-what?"

He heard a click. "Hi, Llewellyn."

His breath caught and his heart wanted to escape his chest and leap to wherever Blaise was. His heart had no brain. "W-where are you?"

"In my apartment. I'm out on bail. One of the stipulations was that I wouldn't call you—so I didn't."

Llewellyn couldn't think of anything to say that didn't involve yelling.

"I'm sorry, Llewellyn. I'm so very sorry. Honestly, I came here under false pretenses, but then I met you and got to know you and I really didn't want to spy on you anymore. And then the murder happened and…." He took a big, noisy breath. "I was working up the nerve to tell you who I was—am. Shit, whatever."

"S-so you w-work for your mother."

"Yes. Kind of. I mean, I was a grad student, am one. But, well, I own part of the *Daily Phoenix* and so—" Llewellyn could hear the shrug.

Oh hell. Of course. Blaise was not only radiantly gorgeous, impossibly sexy, and wildly smart. He was rich. Just one more nail in the coffin of their future. "I understand." He sighed very quietly.

"You do?" His voice dripped with suspicion.

"L-look, Blaise, I d-don't think you killed Anne, and I'll k-keep working to prove that."

"That's not what I'm asking."

"W-what are you asking?" He desperately wanted to hear this—and desperately wanted not to.

"I-I want to know if you understand that I came here on a job, but—but I didn't have sex with you as part of that job and I really, uh, like you and never wanted to lie to you. Please, please believe me."

Do I believe that? "Y-yes. I guess I believe t-that."

"Guess?" He sounded discouraged.

"You h-had a lot of chances to t-tell the truth."

"I—"

"You spied on me."

"I know. Honestly, I'm so ashamed." Llewellyn heard him swallow. "I'm so, so sorry. It's just—my mother. She's what I had, and I always tried to please her. It was like a reflex. Jesus, I even snooped in your closet." He made a little sound that might have been a sob.

Llewellyn sighed. "I suspected that."

"Then I tried to take it all back, but it was too late." He dragged in a breath. "Listen, Llewellyn, I don't know if you're Rondell. I don't want to know, and I won't let my mother investigate even one more second. I told her I wasn't doing a story about you even if she put me back in jail."

"But sh-she'll do the story."

"I said if she did, I'd never speak to her again."

"Y-you can't do that. Sh-she's your mother."

"I love her, Llewellyn, but I'm a grown-up. I can't let her run my life. I haven't got her killer instincts, and I don't want them. Please. It's you I want, not a story. There's nothing else I want."

How did he feel about this? Easy. His hands shook so hard he could barely hold the phone. His butterflies had their own butterflies. He wanted to spill his guts full of all the adoration he felt—but he still didn't really believe it. It was one thing to want to change your life from inside a prison cell. "L-let's get you out of j-jail for good first. Then w-we can talk."

"I don't want to wait! Tell me how you're feeling. Is there any chance you can forgive me?"

Llewellyn said nothing.

Blaise breathed. "I know I blew it. I'm such a rotten bastard, I should make my mother proud. But I don't want to be, and I won't give up. I'll work my ass off to prove I'm the one you should be with." Dear God, everything in Llewellyn wanted to believe him. But when he was no longer a murder suspect and had his mother promising him the moon, what would he want with a dull dud like Llewellyn?

"Solve the c-crime now. T-talk later."

"Okay." He sighed. "So tell me what you've learned."

A tidal wave of suspicion crashed over Llewellyn's head. How fast would anything he said go to Octavia Otto? Was she sitting beside him?

"W-we better stop t-talking. If Holiday f-finds out, it will g-get Maria in trouble."

"Oh, I didn't think."

The stuff he didn't think of would fill a book—and sadly not a romance novel. "It's okay. D-don't worry too m-much. We'll f-find who did it."

"Thanks, Llewellyn. That honestly makes me feel a lot better. But I have to tell you something important. I was in your office the night Anne was killed."

"W-what?"

"I was there to snoop. I got into the building with my own security card and went to your office. The door was open, and I didn't know that was unusual. A lot of professors leave their outer offices open so students can drop off assignments. Anyway, I went in and again, your inner office was unlocked. I thought *that* was unusual, but by the time I registered that thought, I actually saw her body. I thought she was asleep or sick for a minute. She didn't look dead. I ran over and felt for the pulse in her neck. That's when I saw the ligature marks. I freaked, Llewellyn. Not just because she was dead, but because I didn't want to tell you why I was in your office in the middle of the night. I wiped her neck with a tissue and ran. I didn't even realize I'd touched the desk beside her body while I was trying to find her pulse."

Llewellyn let out a long breath. He could vomit. "So t-that's what they have. Your p-prints at the scene."

"Y-yes."

"Y-you told them w-what you t-told me?"

"Yes."

"That's g-good. No m-motive and a reason to b-be there. Together they're persuasive."

"I'm so sorry." He paused, then said, "I hope you can forgive me. Please."

"We'll t-talk. Bye." Llewellyn hung up, set the phone on the coffee table carefully, and burst into tears.

Fifteen minutes later, after massive purr therapy, he sucked it up, picked up the phone, and dialed.

"Holiday."

"Detective, this is Llewellyn Lewis."

"Yes, Dr. Lewis." He sounded harried.

"You told me to call if—"

"Yes, of course. Did you remember something new?"

"No, but I w-wondered if you knew that J-Jane and Roscoe de Vere came to see me this afternoon?" He petted Marie.

"Uh, no, I didn't." That clearly piqued his interest.

"I assumed they w-were on their way t-to see you."

"I saw them today, yes."

"They w-were still very upset about the m-money. I t-told them I d-didn't care about the m-money."

"That should have made them damned happy."

"N-no. They d-didn't even w-want me to investigate the Sh-Shakespeare connection." Marie flipped over and presented her belly. Always a trap. It usually earned a bite or a scratch, but today she seemed willing to let him pet her.

"What the hell do they have to say about the subjects you investigate?"

"Exactly."

"Well, that's interesting."

Should I say it? "I've also s-seen Roscoe de Vere out of his w-wheelchair, standing."

"Yes, they told me that. He's required to try standing a few times a day to keep his circulation moving."

Damn. Blaise had probably told Holiday the same thing. Roscoe sure didn't look like he was teetering when they saw him in the doorway. Julius tried to hog his hand and got a swipe of Marie's paw in return. "They certainly have the m-most m-motive for wanting Anne g-gone."

"True, but they have excellent alibis, and there's evidence against Arthur."

"H-he told you why he was th-there, uh, I imagine. And he has n-no key to my office."

Holiday let out a long breath. "Sorry to say, that's not true. The professor that Arthur assists used to have your office. He still has keys to it in his desk. We checked them, and they all work."

"I see." He wanted to toss all the food he hadn't eaten that day. "Still n-no motive."

"I'll admit, the motives we've come up with are thin."

George Stanley's voice floated through his mind. *What if she found out something about him he didn't want people to know?*

Holiday cleared his throat. "But he could have wanted to keep her from telling you his real motives for being here."

"When all y-you have is a h-hammer, everything l-looks like a nail." He gritted his teeth and tried to sound calm.

The frown came through the phone. "Meaning?"

"If y-you're set on the idea t-that B-Blaise did it, you're not l-looking for other suspects. Ones with clear m-motives."

"I assure you, we're not leaving other suspects uninvestigated. Now, unless there's something else, I have to go."

"Of c-course."

"Thanks for letting me know about the de Veres." He hung up.

Llewellyn tossed the phone on the couch and leaned back, allowing furry creatures to occupy the available space. So many questions. Were the de Veres' alibis really airtight? How could he find out where they'd been the night of the murder and how they were proving it? Was George Stanley as clueless as he seemed? Did the Echevarrias have bigger, more murder-inspiring motives than social climbing?

No matter how he spun it, the wheel of homicide probability landed most firmly on Roscoe and Jane de Vere. Anne had been strangled, but if Roscoe was as strong as he looked and Jane helped him, they could have done it. Especially since she never would have expected it.

They had the best reason to want Anne dead. That had to be important. How could he find out their stories?

Of course, Miranda. He'd ask her.

A shadow against the windows made him look toward the curtains. Odd—it was dark outside, so the only way he'd see a shadow was if a light passed close to the side of the house. Probably the damned reporters again.

Carefully displacing the cats, he walked to the windows and pulled the curtains aside. Sure enough, a dark figure scooted rapidly to the edge of the bushes and moved to disappear behind them. As he did, the flashlight in his hand swiped a beam across his face.

Llewellyn gasped. The guy looked familiar. Like creepy familiar. He resembled that weirdo who'd asked about Jack the Ripper at the club weeks ago. Whoa, that gave him a shiver.

Quit it. I probably saw this person with the reporters hanging out around the house. Don't be melodramatic. Jesus, Blaise was accused of a murder he just didn't do—Llewellyn knew that for sure—and he was worrying about himself. How stupid.

He let the curtain drop. *Focus.* He'd call Miranda first thing in the morning.

LLEWELLYN DRAGGED himself up the sidewalk toward the history building. The number of TV vans had decreased, and only a few reporters yelled his name. *So soon they forget.* He pushed into the building lobby and stopped. *God, I'm tired.* He'd barely slept, a little bit uneasy about who'd been outside his window, but mostly worrying about Blaise and how to prove someone besides him murdered Anne. *How do the police do this every day? Deal with the horror?* The thought made him swallow hard. Of course, the police weren't in love with their suspects.

He slowly sank onto the bench by the front windows of the building lobby. Yes, he'd given up and admitted it to himself. The f-ing *L* word. Now he could brand two *L*s on his forehead, and man, did they go together. The Loser in Love. Damn, Shakespeare should write a play. But just because he'd admitted it to himself didn't mean he'd share the news with anyone else.

Just prove Blaise didn't do it and get on with your life. What exactly that life looked like was a question for another day. *After he'd seen Paree and all that.*

Footsteps clattering down the steps made him look up. Maria stopped on the next-to-last step and stared at him. "There you are. Jeez, boss, you have a very odd woman in your office. I'm not entirely sure what to do with her."

He held up a hand. "No w-worries. I'm coming. J-just thinking for a minute."

"Man, you look beat."

"I'm good. L-lead on." He pointed toward the steps, stood, and followed Marie up them.

Maria looked back over her shoulder and whispered, "She looks just like Anne, which is creepy, but she's so damned different."

"I know."

"Really weird. I put her in your office since they cleared the crime scene tape this morning. Sorry, but I wasn't quite sure what you wanted me to do with her."

"Should have c-called you."

"No, no. It's cool. I just figured it was important to make her comfortable."

"Th-thanks."

They walked into Maria's outer office, and she hurried to the teapot and poured him his drug of choice. "Go on in and put your stuff down. I'll bring this."

He hated entering his office when someone was waiting for him. It made his sanctuary feel invaded. But Maria had done the right thing. Of course, Miranda sat in his chair with her booted feet on his desk and a cup of coffee in her hands. This wasn't an invasion; it was an attack. *Get over yourself. You need this person.*

He tried to smile. "H-hello, Miranda." He tucked his briefcase with his laptop in it to the side of one of the overflowing bookcases and hung up his sweater.

"Man, Doc, this is one piece-of-shit office. I thought a big-name dude like you would have at least a view and a comfortable chair."

Since she sat in his seat, he had no choice but to take the rickety guest chair. *Serves you right for not treating your visitors better.* He perched tentatively. "I like the p-privacy."

She swung her legs off the desk, revealing a few inches of thigh in the process, and leaned forward. "Yeah, you would." She didn't, however, surrender his seat. "So what's up? Why'd you call in such a sweat?" She sipped her coffee casually.

Damn. Any normal person would have thought through how to ask these questions instead of mooning over Blaise all night. But occasionally being inarticulate cut him some slack. "Uh, I, uh—"

"Spit it out, Doc." She set down the cup, picked up his statue of J. Worthington Foulfellow and rotated it in her hands, which made him want to grab it away, but he focused.

"D-do you know where your sister and br-brother were when Anne was m-murdered?"

She raised her eyebrows. "Ooooh, you suspect the sneaky ones, huh? Nobody's going to throw you off with mere fingerprints." She laughed.

"H-how do you know about the f-fingerprints?"

"Hell, man, it's in the papers and all over. They've got Arthur's fingerprints dead to rights. But I'm with you. It's hard to believe that cute dude killed Anne."

"It's j-just that I d-don't know what the"—he made air quotes—"airtight alibi of your s-siblings is. I'm s-sure it's more than c-credible. I j-just wondered if you knew."

She cocked a grin and set down the statue. "Yeah, well, sad to tell you, man, but they were with me until really late, and then a woman who sometimes stays with Roscoe—you know, to relax him—came over." She repeated his air quotes and flashed a snarky grin. "The woman was there all night, and I guess she swore to it."

"I s-see."

"Yeah, they've got such a bad attitude, I wouldn't mind getting them tossed in jail for a while." She laughed until she snorted. "But no such luck. Have you thought that maybe Blaise Arthur didn't want anyone to know who he was? Maybe Anne found out and he killed her for it?"

"I have thought of that." But only in his nightmares.

She rose. "That it? Was that what you wanted to know?"

"Y-yes." He stared at the desk, all his insides turning to a block of ice. *Blaise didn't do it.* He couldn't have. Everything in him rejected the idea.

She took a heavy-booted step, then stopped and picked up the little statue again. "Man, I sure do love this thing. Any idea where I can get one?"

"N-no. It's very old."

"Shame." She set it down and walked to the door, then turned back. "Sorry I couldn't help more, Doc.

I'll be going back to San Francisco soon, so if I don't see you, it's been grand."

He looked up. "H-how soon are y-you leaving?"

"Day after tomorrow. I have to help the sibs make some arrangements for transporting the body back to the city after the cops get done with it."

He stood, gripping his hands together. "W-will there be a f-funeral?"

"Yeah, we'll cremate her, but I'm sure the sibs will do a service of some kind. I'll send you an invite." She grinned. "They probably won't do it since they're so pissed about you continuing with the investigation."

He met her eyes for a moment. "Th-they say y-you're also opposed to sp-spending the m-money on the Shakespeare proof."

"Oh yeah, well, they're so pissed, I just go along with them. Otherwise they'd drive me bats trying to persuade me. So you are continuing, right?"

"Yes, well, I h-haven't decided yet for certain."

A frown flashed across her face but was quickly replaced by her cynical smile. "Oh, I know you, Doc. You won't be able to stay away now that you see somebody doesn't want the investigation to go forward. That's red meat to you."

He forced a smile. "P-probably right."

"Well, thanks a million. Or should I say five million?" She laughed and walked out the door.

Llewellyn stared after her, his knees shaking so hard he had to sit or he'd fall. He couldn't take his gaze from the coffee cup littering his desk.

Like from a long distance, he heard Maria say, "Boss, are you okay?"

His head snapped up. "Yes. I need you to call Detective Holiday."

"Sure." She took a step back, then looked over her shoulder. "Hey, you didn't stutter once."

CHAPTER TWENTY-ONE

BLAISE SAT with his arms wrapped around himself on the couch in his tiny apartment. He needed the arms to keep from flying apart. His mother had broken into pieces ages ago, and each piece had a mouth. She paced from one end of the living room to the other—admittedly, a very short trip. Her two very expensive lawyers sat uncomfortably on his lumpy, overstuffed chairs he'd gotten at Goodwill with the idea they would tide him over until he could get out of this place and go home. Now, the whole "out of this place" part didn't sound so good, because it took him farther from everything he was growing to care about.

His mother returned to her litany as she paced. "It's ridiculous for the police to think that Blaise killed anyone, especially that woman. And over the disclosure of his identity? Good God, why would he even care? He was just going to expose that phony and leave anyway. Lewis would have found out soon enough." She paused in her feline pacing. "No, there are people with far better motives than Blaise."

One of the lawyers, Jared Hershey, a famous San Francisco litigator, crossed his legs to get more comfortable. No use, but he could try. "Yes, but sadly those other people don't happen to have left perfect prints in Lewis's office." He glanced at Blaise with disdain for being so careless. God, defense attorneys really did always believe their clients were guilty.

His mother folded her arms and nodded. "Yes, but have we explored the potential that the one person with complete opportunity might have actually killed her?"

Blaise frowned. "You mean Maria, the assistant?"

"Of course not, idiot. I mean Lewis, naturally."

Blaise's guts spilled on the faded rug.

She warmed to her subject. "I know they say he had the most to gain from her being alive, but what if she learned that he was Rondell?" She whirled on Blaise. "You spent time with her. What did you reveal?"

"Nothing. For God's sake, nothing. I told no one who I was or why I was here."

"But she might have divined it. Maybe she had her own suspicions? Maybe that's why she told you that if Lewis didn't take her case, she'd go to Rondell. She was testing him." She paced to the windows. "Yes, she must have revealed her knowledge and he, knowing that he'd be the last suspect, got rid of her for it." She pointed at the lawyers. "I want you to follow that line of inquiry. Llewellyn Lewis is our most likely suspect."

Blaise held up a hand and spoke very quietly. "If you follow this line of inquiry for one more minute, I'll call Holiday and confess to the crime. Is that understood? No one, and I mean no one, threatens Llewellyn Lewis. He did not kill her, and I don't want to hear a single murmur of doubt on that topic. Am I clear?"

"Don't be ridiculous, Blaise. He's just the sort of freaky weirdo the police like to pin things on."

He jumped up from the couch and shouted, "Am I clear?"

His mother stepped back, a hand to her chest.

The other lawyer, a little younger and a little gayer, nodded. "It's okay, Blaise. There's no way we can prove Lewis murdered her. Don't worry. We won't go down that path." He glanced at Blaise's mother. "Correct, Octavia?"

"Well, of course, if Blaise feels that strongly. It's only your life, darling."

He sat back down and dropped his head in his hands. It was only his life no matter which way he looked at it.

LLEWELLYN—ACCOMPANIED by Maria, who refused to be left behind—walked off the elevator at the police station, where Holiday met them.

Llewellyn nodded, trying to control his smile. "You d-did it. Thank you."

"Yes."

"Did you ask Blaise to c-come?"

"I did, although we're not usually given to so much drama in the police department."

Maria said, "Hey, Holiday, I think you owe him."

Holiday half smiled. "I think I do too, but don't tell anyone I said that. Come on."

They followed Holiday to the same room they'd been in before. Around the big table sat Jane and Roscoe de Vere, Miranda de Vere, Blaise, his mother, and two expensively dressed men in suits.

Blaise half stood from his chair when Llewellyn walked in, but Llewellyn moved to an open seat across the table, with Maria beside him. Blaise dropped back and looked sad. Jane de Vere wrung her hands, Roscoe radiated pissed-off, and Miranda appeared to be ready to prop her feet on the table at any moment.

Octavia Otto snapped, "What's this about, Holiday?"

Holiday took the chair at the head of the table. "Some new information has come to light, and I wanted to share it with all of you." He folded his hands and glanced at Llewellyn. "We know that Mr. Arthur's print was found on the desk beside where the body was discovered. He says that while he did go to the office when Ms. de Vere was there, the office was already unlocked and Ms. de Vere was already dead."

Octavia Otto snorted, and Jane de Vere wiped a tear from her cheek. Clearly Holiday was getting into the drama of the occasion.

"We know that Mr. Arthur could have gotten keys to Dr. Lewis's office from Dr. Rhule, his employer, who previously occupied the office. We also know, however, that there are a number of keys to that office extant, among them those in the top desk drawer of Dr. Van Pelt."

Miranda made a huffing sound. "Van Pelt? He's the one who wanted the money so damned bad. Hell, he'd have had her stuffed before he'd admit she was dead."

"True," Holiday agreed. "But his office is visited by many people, and we checked with him and discovered his set of keys is gone."

Octavia Otto pressed a palm to her throat. "But that's wonderful news."

The others around the table didn't look quite so enthused. Roscoe scowled. "So who have his visitors been?" He glanced around at his family. "None of us."

"In just a second." Holiday held up a finger. He nodded toward Llewellyn.

Maria pressed a hand to his arm in support. He said, "Miranda, c-can you tell me h-how you h-happened to recognize the statue of J. Worthington Foulfellow on my d-desk?"

Roscoe scowled even darker. "Who?"

Llewellyn kept staring at Miranda. Her expression went from casual to—cloudy. "I, uh, guess I remember it from when I was a kid."

"Oh, from where?"

She wrinkled her nose. "Don't remember."

"But y-you loved it so much, you wanted one of your own."

"Sure. It's really cute."

Holiday leaned forward. "Are you aware that while identical twins have the same DNA, they have unique fingerprints?"

"What?"

Holiday sat back. "We checked your fingerprints against those of your sister. The ones they took when she was teaching first grade."

Llewellyn said, "The s-same place she first saw the statue of J. W-Worthington."

Miranda stared at Llewellyn like he was a spider.

Llewellyn spoke softly. "Of course, the fingerprints of Anne w-were identical to the ones you left on the coffee cup in my office yesterday."

"No."

Holiday stood. "Anne de Vere, you're under arrest for suspicion of murder of your sister Miranda."

"No, you can't prove it."

"We just did."

It seemed oddly fitting that he began to Mirandize her.

Roscoe bellowed, "What's going on here?"

Two uniformed officers walked in and took Anne into custody. They left the room with her murmuring "no" over and over.

Jane had turned white. "I don't understand."

Roscoe yelled, "Good grief, don't you see? That's Anne, not Miranda. She killed Miranda!"

Jane slapped a hand to her mouth and sobbed.

Roscoe said, "Why the hell would she do that?"

Holiday nodded at Llewellyn. "Dr. Lewis figured it out."

"S-she desperately w-wanted me to do the research. I was disinclined to d-do it since it seemed v-very unlikely I could prove it."

Blaise's mouth opened. "And then she showed up with that manuscript copy."

"Y-yes." He gazed at Blaise. Oh man, he knew what he'd like to do with that mouth. *Focus.* "I assume s-she had the d-document created for j-just such a purpose. B-but then M-Miranda started threatening me.

Anne knew because Miranda told her. Anne thought I-I'd give up with too much p-pressure. I n-never got to tell her I was going to d-do the research. She k-killed Miranda and counted on no one checking the fingerprints before s-she could arrange a cremation. We had no reason to check them."

"But she's small. How could she strangle Miranda?" Roscoe looked in shock.

Holiday said, "Miranda may have disliked her sister, but she had no reason to think Anne would harm her. Taking her totally by surprise and using a handled wire, she was able to hold Miranda long enough to cut off her air completely. She was strong. Strong enough to knock out Dr. Lewis when she stole the copy of the manuscript."

"Why was Miranda in Dr. Lewis's office?"

"We found Miranda's phone in Anne's hotel room. There was a message from Anne, luring Miranda with promises of new evidence."

Octavia Otto scowled. "But why blame it on Blaise? What did he do to her?"

"I d-don't think she c-cared. I s-suspect she planned on one of her siblings being blamed, but when Blaise's p-print showed up, it was timely and opportune."

Holiday leaned forward. "While the idea that Blaise killed her because she found out he was investigating Dr. Lewis was thin, I think she figured with the other evidence, we'd consider it enough to take Blaise to trial."

Llewellyn felt that statement like a kick in the gut on so many levels.

Jane stared at Llewellyn. "How did you ever figure it out? We didn't even realize it was Anne, although we did wonder why she gave up her hard line on the money being spent for the research."

Llewellyn nodded. "Yes, she d-did an amazing j-job of convincing us she w-wasn't Anne. But she got v-very upset when I suggested I m-might not do the research, which Miranda would never have d-done. Then, of course, there was J. Worthington. Anne told me that one of h-her students had received the figurine from her grandmother. The p-person I thought was Miranda admired it lovingly and p-personally. It seemed unlikely, s-since they weren't close, that Miranda w-would have shared Anne's affection."

Octavia Otto stood. "Dr. Lewis, you saved my son's life. Anything I can do to repay you, I will."

Llewellyn nodded. "I appreciate t-that."

She stared at him and shook her head. "Now that I've met you, I realize there's no chance you could be Rondell anyway." She winked. "So it won't be hard to keep that promise." She turned. "Holiday, I assume the charges against Blaise will be dropped and we're free to go. I also assume that this will not be reflected in any sort of police record."

"There's some paperwork, but yes." Holiday glanced at the formidable lawyers as they all rose and left the room. Blaise looked back at Llewellyn before his mother grabbed his arm and they were gone.

Jane wiped tears from her face. "I just can't believe this all happened."

Roscoe wheeled away from the table. "So, Lewis, you're giving up this craziness, right?"

"Y-yes, and I hope there's a way to b-break the will and for you and your sister to get the money. It's v-very unlikely anyone c-can prove Edward de Vere was Shakespeare." He smiled. "Dammit."

Roscoe smiled for a second, and then the frown returned. "Of course, we'll probably have to spend all of it on lawyers for my sister." He shook his head. "I think we need to get her some treatment." Jane wheeled him out the door, still wiping her cheeks.

Maria whispered, "Hey, boss, you just did some pretty fancy talking in front of a whole room full of people."

He smiled. "M-must have been ch-channeling Ramon Rondell."

LLEWELLYN WALKED off the elevator in the lobby.

Maria pointed toward the side door where she'd picked him up on the day Blaise had been arrested. As they hurried toward the exit, Maria bounced in front of him. "You did it, boss. You're amazing. You don't just solve history's mysteries, you solve the regular kind of mystery too. That's so cool. You could hang out a new shingle, Llewellyn Lewis, PhD, Crime Solver. Can I still be your assistant?"

"You c-can be my assistant as long as y-you want, but I think we'll stick to history."

"Anything you say, boss." She pushed open the door, and Llewellyn followed. A few steps later, she stopped.

For a second the bright sun blinded him; then he looked toward the car and saw what Maria had seen. Blaise Arthur leaned against Llewellyn's Volvo.

"Hey, boss, I'll get another ride."

"N-no. Please wait f-for me."

"Okay, I'll be right inside. But call me if I need to hail a cab." She grinned and turned back into the building.

Llewellyn stared at Blaise. *Don't want to do this. Just want to go home, close the door, and hide.* He strode across the parking lot and stopped in front of the person who had literally tilted his world on its axis and eclipsed the sun so Llewellyn would always live in darkness without the Blaise of sunlight. He released a slow breath. *Things are going to get very gray.*

"Hi."

"H-hi."

"You're pretty astonishing. You know that? You saved my life."

Llewellyn shook his head. "S-someone would have realized it s-soon."

"No. Not a chance. No cop would ever have questioned that woman's identity enough to take her fingerprints. Hell, they may not even know that identical twins don't have the same prints. I didn't."

Llewellyn shrugged and stared at his shoes.

Blaise let out a long, slow exhale. "You don't want to forgive me, do you?"

He didn't look up. Too dangerous. "I can say I f-forgive you. Th-that's the easy part. But every time I remember s-some sweet m-moment with y-you, it's f-followed by an equal and opposite b-betrayal." He shrugged. "It's hard to f-forget you had s-so many chances to tell the truth."

Blaise took a turn staring at his shoes. "You're right, of course." He inhaled, long and painfully. "You don't want to see me anymore." It wasn't a question.

"There's n-no point. You live in S-San Francisco." His eyes skittered to the bushes across the lot.

"I want to stay here."

"You're a rich man with a b-big future."

"My mother's rich. Not me." It was a wail.

Llewellyn shook his head. "It w-wouldn't work."

Blaise stepped closer, and Llewellyn stepped back. Blaise said, "But you were ready to make it work before you knew." The sound of his voice had changed to discouragement and acceptance.

Good. Acceptance was a good step. "M-maybe I w-was. Before." A horn blasted from somewhere on the street, and Llewellyn looked up, noticing the limousine for the first time. "They're w-waiting for y-you." He turned and walked back into the building, where Maria stood with her nose pressed to the glass.

She looked up at him as he stepped inside with eyes full of compassion. "Boss, you don't want to do this."

He felt himself frown. She couldn't have heard the conversation from inside. "What?"

"Look, I know he did some plain awful stuff, but I see something that I've never seen before."

"What?"

"He makes you happy. Hell, I'd like to throw him under a bus, but I might never see that look of joy in your eyes that happens when you say his name. You moved heaven and earth to save him. In some cultures that makes you responsible for him."

"N-not in this one." He looked up, and no beautiful Blaise stood beside his old car anymore. No beautiful Blaise would be anywhere in his life anymore. Amazing how much that hurt. He thought in his life he'd mastered pain, sucked it in, turned it into all his complex neuroses, and never had to feel it again. *Surprise.*

Maria took his arm. "Come on, let's get you home."

"N-no. Back to w-work." The definition of his life.

CHAPTER TWENTY-TWO

WHEN THEY got to the office, Van Pelt waited impatiently outside the door. Right, because he didn't have a key—because Anne de Vere had stolen it.

He put his hands on his hips as they approached. "What the hell is going on?"

Llewellyn started to speak, but Maria answered, "Come in and have some coffee, sir. It's been a tough few hours."

After caffeine had been dispensed and the story told, Van Pelt just sat there. "This is unbelievable."

Maria nodded, having taken the stress off Llewellyn by doing most of the talking. "Yes. I don't think anyone but Dr. Lewis could ever have figured the whole thing out. Honestly, it was like the end of a mystery novel or something."

Van Pelt sighed. "So the research project is gone."

"Y-yes. I would h-have continued if the document had been real, but it seems unlikely n-now."

"So it wasn't real after all?"

"N-no. Anne m-must have gone to g-great trouble to f-fake it."

"What a shame." He must have realized what he said, because he shook himself a little. "What a shame that one woman died and another is going to prison over such a silly thing."

"Y-yes." He smiled slightly. "B-but you have the Echevarrias. They want to d-donate to the school."

His face brightened. "That's true, they do. I'll call them now." He stood, set down his coffee cup on Maria's desk, and walked to the door, then turned. "So Blaise Arthur is free. Innocent."

"Y-yes." Maybe only a little innocent.

"They said he was some kind of reporter or something, right?"

Maria burst in. "Yes, for an online magazine. His mother owns it, among other things."

"Always thought that boy was a bit flashy for an English teacher." He cocked his head. "But what was he doing here?"

"Uh, we're not sure. His media outlet is in San Francisco. Maybe they caught wind of Anne de Vere's obsession and he followed her here." Maria glanced at Llewellyn, who sipped his tea. "You remember they arrived at pretty much the same time."

"Right. Interesting. And then he goes and gets himself arrested." He shook his head. "Those damned journalists deserve to get some retribution for their strong-arm tactics. Hate to say it serves him right since he could have gone to prison for a long time,

but still—" He harrumphed. "Well, good work, Dr.
Lewis." He raised his brows. "I expect this little
crime-solving jaunt will be one more feather in your
cap as a solver of mysteries." A smile spread slowly across his face like light was dawning. "Yes, yes,
I'll bet it does enhance the reputation—of all of us."
Chuckling, he walked out the door.

DEAR GOD, can this day be over?

Llewellyn opened the door to his home and knelt
automatically to greet the fuzzies. As Marie Antoinette pushed against his hand, he felt a shiver up his
back and looked over his shoulder. *Nobody. Nothing.*
The day had freaked him out. *Killing your own twin.*
Truly horrible. So much sadness for so many reasons.

"Merwaowr."

"Mew."

"Meeow."

"Okay, you g-get a whole evening of undivid-
ed attention. I'm s-sorry I've been gone so much."
He scooped up Marie in his arms, snuggled her, and
kicked the door closed with his foot. "Come on.
F-food time."

In the kitchen, he set Marie on the chair and
pulled out all their favorites, including Marie's chick-
en and Emily's tuna. Julius ate anything. Carefully, he
spooned the chicken in Marie's bowl, since she had to
be served first.

Odd. Is there something wrong with the chicken?
He sniffed closer. Kind of an acrid smell. He heard
Marie growling at the same moment he realized the
smell was coming from behind him—and then was
pressed over his nose and mouth.

He gagged and thrashed backward with his right arm while grasping for the knives on the counter with his left, but the cloth suffocating him didn't release.

For a second he wondered if Anne had escaped— before everything went black.

BLAISE DROVE toward Llewellyn's house, his brain seething. *He has to listen to me. This is stupid.*

He'd left his mother gaping after him in her car as he announced he wasn't going back to San Francisco and he didn't care if she cut him off from everything. He was staying in San Luis Obispo until Llewellyn agreed to at least give their relationship a chance. Hopefully that meant Blaise would be staying in San Luis forever.

An old black pickup truck raced by Blaise as he neared Llewellyn's house. Not the usual type of vehicle for that gentrified neighborhood. He pulled up in front.

What the fuck?

The door stood agape, and Marie peered from the top step of the porch.

Without even turning off the car, he leaped out, ran across the lawn, grabbed Marie—she must have known it was a crisis because she let him do it—stuck his head in the house, and screamed, "Llewellyn!"

Nothing.

"Llewellyn!"

He tossed Marie ignominiously into the entry, slammed the front door, and was back in the car in seconds. *What the hell?* His foot stomped the accelerator so hard, the car actually leaped forward, laid rubber, and took off like a careening banshee. *The truck. The truck.*

Please, please let the light at the intersection be red. Please. He had a bad-assed feeling about that truck.

The light in front of him as he powered down the street shone brilliant green, but he saw the black truck turning left. *Yes. Do I dare call? Hell, yes.* Pressing his Siri button, he said, "Call Detective Holiday."

"Calling Detective Holiday." It started to ring.

"Holiday." He sounded grumpy.

"Holiday, this is Blaise Arthur. I just arrived at Dr. Lewis's house to see a black pickup truck racing away. Llewellyn's door was standing open, and he's not there. I'm afraid something's happened."

"Like what?"

"He's been kidnapped. Abducted."

"How do you know that? Maybe he went for milk and those damned felines decided to visit the neighbors."

"I don't know how I know. I just know." Blaise's foot pressed the accelerator.

"Are you sure you're not addicted to law enforcement? Because I know a good police academy you can apply to."

"Dammit, Holiday, this isn't a joke."

"Okay, where are you?"

"I'm chasing the black truck."

"What the hell? You are not."

"Yes, I am. Wait." The truck stopped at the next light. Blaise sped up to get behind it, cutting off a Mercedes that tried to get into the lane. He got a huge honk for his trouble.

Holiday growled, "What was that?"

"Doesn't matter. Pay attention. Write this down." He recited the license number.

"You're serious about this."

"As a heart attack, man. Do something."

"Do not hang up. I want to know what's going on."

"Get some cops out here fast." He read the street names at the intersection. "But we're moving fast, so tell them to hurry. I don't think he knows I'm following him."

"Okay, stay back. I'll have a squad car there in a few minutes."

"Where 'there' is changes pretty fast."

The truck signaled a right turn. A large gas sign stood at the corner.

"Wait. I think he's pulling into a goddamn gas station. What kind of idiot kidnaps someone without enough gas in their fucking vehicle?"

"Stay away, Blaise. Just drive by and let us take care of this."

"Yeah, right." Holiday probably caught the sarcasm. Blaise drove by the station and turned right. There was another entrance from the perpendicular street, and he took it, ending up on the side of the station where the restrooms were located. He pulled over and stopped in a couple of spaces probably designated for those who needed the john. Quickly he searched his glove compartment and found a flashlight, the closest thing to a weapon he could find. He tucked it in his waistband and slid out of the car.

Walking softly, he moved up the side of the building and started to peek around just as a cute, dark-haired guy came around the corner, moving fast. Something about his wild, weird eyes and furtive expression suggested he might be the guy Blaise was looking for. For a second, Blaise froze.

The guy said "Excuse me" as they nearly collided, and then he trotted toward the men's room. *Seriously, the guy got the runs in the middle of his crime?*

Wait. I've seen him before. Where? Blaise kept walking like he had business there, and he did. Finding Llewellyn.

The desires to both hurry and not look suspicious warred in him. Trying to appear natural, he walked over to the pumps where the black pickup was connected to a gas hose. For a second Blaise looked at the pump next to it, like he was trying to figure it out; then he turned and stared into the truck's windows. The badly applied dark tint blocked out most visibility, but he pressed close and peered into the tiny back seat. His heart leaped in his throat. Llewellyn lay folded like a broken doll, unconscious.

Blaise's hands gripped into fists. *If the bastard hurt him, he's dead.*

Blaise tried the door handle on the driver's side. Locked. He circled the truck and tried the other side, but he wasn't surprised to find it shut tight. *Shit.* His stomach ground into a huge knot of anger, pain, and fear.

A small trash can full of dirty windshield wipes stood beside the gas pump. Blaise slipped around the front of the truck and grabbed it.

As he raised it over his head, a woman in a minivan beside the truck yelled, "What the hell do you think you're doing?"

Think fast. "There's a guy in there. He looks really sick or maybe even dead, and the driver of the truck is in the head." He nodded toward the window. "Look for yourself."

She ran to the windows on the other side of the truck as Blaise smashed the trash can into the driver's side window as hard as he could. The damned thing cracked but didn't break.

The woman yelled, "Oh my God. We've got to get him out of there."

Blaise called back, "Find me something sharp and metal." He smashed against the window again. *Damned safety glass.*

The woman ran for the building where they sold a few snacks and soft drinks. Not much hope. No mechanics in there. Blaise smashed the window again. Llewellyn hadn't even moved, and Blaise didn't want to think what that meant.

The cracks in the window looked like a spiderweb, and pieces of glass fell out of the pattern, but the window didn't collapse enough to let him reach inside. He pulled out the flashlight for one more huge smash, and the window finally gave way enough to leave a hole.

Thank God. Carefully he reached inside and flipped the lock. In a flash he pulled open the door. "Llewellyn. Can you hear me?" He folded back the seat and crawled toward Llewellyn's so still body.

"Hey! What the hell do you think you're doing? That's my truck. Get the hell away from there."

Blaise looked up as sirens filled the air. Running toward him was the black-haired guy. *Oh my God, I saw him at that gay club in San Jose.*

The sirens got closer but weren't there yet. The guy ran toward him, and Blaise didn't even decide. He took two steps forward and slammed his fist, complete with flashlight, into the man's belly and, as the dude folded over, hit him again in the jaw.

"Ooof, ow."

Blaise bared his teeth and shook his hand. Damn, that hurt. He hadn't hit a lot of people in his life.

The woman from the minivan ran past Blaise to the other side of the car with another woman who was apparently the cashier. They tore open the door. "Hey, mister, are you okay?" As they crawled into the back seat, Blaise started toward them.

An arm circled his neck and the edge of a blade pressed against his throat. "Don't move or I'll kill you."

Blaise hissed, "Have you lost your mind?"

"I'm serious."

"The cops are almost here. If I were you, I'd be running for the hills."

Blaise could feel the indecision pumping through the man's body.

"Seriously, right now you're just an attempted kidnapper. Kill me and you'll fry."

A police car swung into the gas station just as Blaise kicked backward and connected his leg with the guy's balls.

"Ow!" The dude freaked, dropped the knife, and ran like a rabbit. A couple of seconds later, two big cops took off behind him, weapons drawn.

Blaise took a breath and piled into the truck. Llewellyn's eyelids were fluttering as the women dribbled water against his lips. Blaise knelt in the seat well in front of Llewellyn. He whispered, "Hey, smart guy. Time to wake up and let me take care of you. Come on." He leaned forward and gently kissed Llewellyn's lips.

Minivan Woman cooed, "Oh, is he your boyfriend?"

"Yes, ma'am, starting this very minute."

For a second the whole world was all about staring into Llewellyn's eyes as they blinked open. Instantly, before he had a chance to think or worry or doubt or take it all back, he smiled radiantly up at Blaise. "Hi."

Blaise kissed him again gently. "Hi."

"Am I in heaven?"

"Yes." He grinned.

He blinked some more. "Then why do I feel like I'm going to throw up? That's not very heavenly."

"You were drugged. Ether, I think." Blaise cocked his head. "Hey, you didn't stutter." He pressed a hand against Llewellyn's cheek and felt the soft skin and light stubble.

"No stuttering in h-heaven." He closed his eyes and pressed his face against Blaise's hand.

Minivan Woman shoved her head in the door, "Hey, mister, you should have seen what your boyfriend did for you. I mean, he punched out a guy with a knife! Talk about brave."

Llewellyn frowned. "Knife?" Suddenly his eyes widened. "Boyfriend? W-what happened?"

An oh-so-familiar voice said, "That's what I'd like to know." Detective Holiday stuck his head beside Minivan Woman into the back seat.

Blaise pressed his forehead against Llewellyn's. "All shall be made known."

AFTER THE EMTs arrived, looked Llewellyn over, and pronounced him not much the worse for wear, he once again found himself in the police station. This time Blaise was beside him, not across the table.

Holiday shook his head. "This dude was really willing to perpetrate kidnapping and assault to get you to prove Jack the Ripper was a member of the royal family of England?"

Blaise snorted. "You actually used 'perpetrate' in a sentence."

Holiday raised an eyebrow.

Blaise seemed to swallow his snark. "I wouldn't be surprised if the guy had designs on parts of Llewellyn other than his brain, but his main motive appears to be historical."

"Jesus." Holiday shook his head. "I never knew I had to keep such a close eye on members of the history department. All of our recent crimes seem to center there."

Llewellyn looked up. "We're s-scary."

"Yeah. I can't let you loose without supervision." Holiday barked a laugh.

Blaise sat forward on his chair and leaned on the table toward Holiday. "Yes, as to that, Detective, I think you should require that Dr. Lewis be held under close watch for, you know, the rest of his life."

Llewellyn's head snapped up, and his heart fell out onto the table.

Holiday visibly forced the corners of his mouth down. "Yes, I see what you mean. He needs a solid member of the—uh—" He waved a hand.

Blaise formed the words with exaggerated care. "Eng-lish—"

"Right, English department. Because after all, everyone knows that English teachers live very sedate lives."

Llewellyn barely wanted to hope. Yes, Blaise had saved him from God knew what fate. Yes, he'd been wildly brave and chased after an armed psycho to rescue Llewellyn. But maybe it was just tit for tat. Llewellyn had saved him. Now they were even. "B-but you're not an English t-teacher."

Blaise took both Llewellyn's hands in his. "But I will be, starting next semester. Dr. Rhule assured me if I wanted it, I can have the TA position and finish my doctorate. You can help me." His eyes dropped. "Of course, I won't be able to afford a place to live, and I will require cats, so you'd have to take me in." His eyes snapped up, and he flashed that irrepressible Blaise smile. "But you require constant supervision from an English instructor as terms of your release, so hey, I'll be serving a purpose."

Breathing. Breathing would be good. Llewellyn tried to suck air into lungs compressed by a band of fear around his chest. Fear this might all be a dream. "Y-you'll get tired of me."

"Jesus, are you kidding? Since I've known you, my life's been in jeopardy twice! Boring you aren't."

Llewellyn shook his head. "Usually I just d-drink tea and p-et cats."

"And that's what I want to do with you. Please, Llewellyn, let me be a part of your life."

Llewellyn glanced up. Somehow Holiday had slipped out of the room. "Your mother—"

"Is figuring out how to come to terms with the new reality. Don't worry. She'll reconcile. She loves me."

Llewellyn sighed. "Who wouldn't?"

Blaise leaned in and stared into Llewellyn's downcast face. "I'm sure there are lots of people who wouldn't—but oh God, I hope you're not one of them."

"N-no."

"No you're not one of them, or no you don't love me?"

Llewellyn let out a long column of air. "I've loved you, I think, since the first moment I laid eyes on you."

Blaise cocked his head. "And when was that exactly?"

Llewellyn started to laugh. "I'll never t-tell."

Together they laughed all the way out the door—to the future.

CHAPTER TWENTY-THREE

Three months later

LLEWELLYN STARED out the big Tuscan-style window into the expanse of vineyards beyond, his fingers entwined with Blaise's on the patio table. He slowly released a breath in pure contentment.

The handsome waiter/sommelier at their favorite small winery in Paso Robles brought them their loved chicken, brie, and apple sandwiches and a crisp, cool glass of sauvignon blanc for each of them. The guy flashed a set of perfect teeth. "Enjoy." With a little swing of his hips, he walked away.

Blaise chuckled.

Llewellyn looked at him. "What?"

"That crease between your eyebrows?"

Llewellyn pressed a finger to the spot. Sure enough. "What about it?"

"That wouldn't have anything to do with the flashing teeth of El Cutie Pie-o, would it?"

Llewellyn snorted. "No." Then grinned. "Well, maybe. I do notice that he s-seems to have about six extra teeth when you're around."

"And I happen to believe that he reserves those teeth for you."

"Nonsense. Why would—" He stopped and said, "You're p-probably right. I'm irresistible."

Blaise extended his glass, and Llewellyn clinked it. Blaise said, "So true. And I totally agree. A fact I plan to prove when we get home." He leaned forward and stared at Llewellyn expectantly.

Whew. PDA. He loved it, and it still made him blush. Llewellyn moved closer and pressed his lips against Blaise's. Since there were two other couples on the patio enjoying their wine, this was a big step, but one it thrilled him to take. Blaise not only made Llewellyn love him, he made Llewellyn love himself, a much harder job.

Blaise slowly opened his eyes as he pulled away from the gentle kiss. "Sweeter than wine." He sipped from his glass. "I have to admit, this is good too."

"Nobody beats Bo's wine."

A low voice from behind Llewellyn said, "Would y'all say that into the microphone, please?"

He looked over his shoulder and smiled at Bo Marchand, the owner of the winery, who not only created treats for the palate, he was a treat for the eyes. A little taller than Blaise's six two, he had wavy brown hair, pale green eyes, and dimples you could lose a finger in. His voice dripped Southern honey, and his manner redefined charm. The dimples weren't on display, however. In fact, he looked stressed. Llewellyn nodded. "Hi, B-Bo. We're enjoying y-your cuisine."

He stepped to the table. "May I join you for a moment?" His Southern drawl made *join* sound like *jaine*.

Blaise smiled. "Of course."

Bo pulled another chair to the table and sat across from them. "You two look so happy, I should bottle it. I'd make a pure bushel of money."

Blaise grinned. "We're celebrating our three-month anniversary."

"Well, it's not diamonds yet, darlin', but quite an accomplishment."

"Yes, since I've been on the job, Llewellyn hasn't received a single death threat." Blaise took a swallow of wine.

Llewellyn snorted wine up his nose and coughed. "My h-hero."

Bo laughed. They'd told him how they met on one of their visits to the winery.

Blaise gave Bo an appraising glance. "Besides, we hope you're already making several bushels of money without our joy juice to bottle."

Bo shrugged and rotated the small vase of flowers in the center of the table. "There's a lot of competition in winemaking."

Blaise glanced at Llewellyn with a little frown. Llewellyn shared it. "There's n-no one as good as y-you, Bo."

"Take our word for that. We've tried all the wine in the central valley." Blaise laughed.

"Thank you, darlin's. I'll try to remember." He finally flashed the dimples. "Let me get you both a glass of something new I've just added to the list this week. To celebrate your amazing longevity in love."

"W-we'll never refuse a t-taste of your wine."

He stood. "I'll get it."

As Bo walked inside, Blaise said, "Excuse me, love. Men's room. I'll be right back." He followed Bo through the door into the tasting room.

Llewellyn sat back, gazing at his glass. It might be empty, but his heart and his life were full. Though a little piece of his brain kept waiting for Blaise to get restless and bored, he was, if anything, even more settled into their quiet life of writing and petting cats than Llewellyn was. Blaise still held out for coffee, however. He seemed to enjoy his job, worked hard on his dissertation, and filled their days with laughter and nights with delicious sex. Even his mother seemed to be coming around. She could hardly believe her son was so settled. That was probably because she was such a restless woman. But she'd been flat-out scared by Blaise's swipe against prison, so she gave him space to be happy his own way. Llewellyn actually liked her better than he thought he could.

The door to the tasting room opened, and Blaise backed out holding two flutes of a lightly pink sparkling wine, pretty as flowers. He walked over, being careful not to spill, and placed a flute at his place, then swept a bow and handed Llewellyn his glass.

"Thank you." He smiled up into Blaise's eyes. "So Bo is m-making bubbly?"

Blaise seemed to sparkle like the wine. His eyes danced, and the corners of his mouth kept curving up before he controlled them. "Yes. He says it's pink but it's still very dry. Look at that amazing color." He held his flute up to the light and nodded toward Llewellyn's glass. "Check it out."

"Oh, okay." Partly to humor his love, who seemed to want him to do this, he picked up the slim flute and held it toward the fading sunlight. Pretty. A very pale pink. Wonderful bubbles rising from the bottom and—

He gasped.

Blaise's smile finally burst forth with full force.

Llewellyn brought the glass closer to his eyes so he could clearly see the shining platinum circle set with some sparkling diamonds inside the flute.

In the fight to hold in tears, he lost. In fact, they slid out of his eyes and down his cheeks until they dripped from his chin, no doubt looking silly, but he couldn't stop. "R-really?"

"Please say yes. Please." Blaise slid out of his chair, took the wineglass from Llewellyn, and sank to one knee. "Llewellyn Lewis, the kindest, smartest, most amazing man I know, will you marry me? It can be tomorrow or a year from now, whatever you say. Just as long as you say yes."

"You honestly w-want to marry me?"

"More than anything."

Llewellyn stared down into the face of beautiful Blaise. *Believe. Just believe.* "Yes. Yes, I will."

Blaise stood and held the glass to Llewellyn's lips. "Drink carefully."

He did. It was probably delicious. He barely noticed.

Blaise drank the rest and dropped the ring into his palm. He took Llewellyn's hand and slid the ring on his finger. It fit perfectly. "Marry me, darling, and

we'll spend our life unraveling the mysteries of love."
He wrapped his arms around Llewellyn and kissed
him while the other guests and every person in the
winery applauded.

Keep reading and see what happens next in

THE CASE OF THE VORACIOUS VINTNER

The Middlemark Mysteries: Book Two

By Tara Lain

Where Bo Marchand comes from, gay men are just confirmed bachelors who never found the right girl. But now Bo's a successful winemaker on the central coast of California, supporting his whole damned Georgia family, and all he really wants is the beautiful, slightly mysterious Jeremy Aames.

Jeremy's vineyard is under threat from Ernest Ottersen, the voracious winemaker who seems to know all Jeremy's blending secrets and manages to grab all his customers. Bo tries to help Jeremy and even provides a phony alibi for Jeremy when Ottersen turns up dead in Jeremy's tasting room. But it's clear Jeremy isn't who he claims, and Bo must decide if it's worth tossing over his established life for a man who doesn't seem to trust anyone. When Jeremy gets kidnapped, some conservative winemakers turn out to be kinky sex fiends, and the list of potential murderers keeps dwindling down to Jeremy, Bo has to choose between hopping on his white horse or climbing back into his peach-pie-lined closet.

Coming soon to
www. dreamspinnerpress.com

CHAPTER ONE

How can I love my life's work so much and hate it at the same time?

Bo Marchand sipped the delicious wine provided by their host for the evening, Jeremy Aames, owner of Hill Top Wineries and the newcomer to the valley. *Jeremy. Don't sigh too loudly, asshole.*

Bo glanced quickly around the big restaurant and wine tasting area packed with the members of the Central Coast Vintners Association, but no sign of Jeremy. Probably good since the glorious Jeremy made Bo drool, and that was damned bad for his illustrious image with his fellow winemakers. He'd worked hard to be a leader in his industry despite his youth. No giving that away, darling. He'd paid too high a price.

He made one more survey of the room from his seemingly relaxed position near the wall. No Jeremy, but quite another target for his attention. Standing next to the wine tasting bar, deep in conversation with two men Bo didn't know and had never seen before, stood Ernest Ottersen, the central coast's new golden boy—or he would have been if his hair wasn't black as midnight. Same color as his heart, most people said. Bo took a sip of his excellent glass of cabernet franc and forced his eyes away from the snake.

Genevieve Renders separated herself from the boisterous crowd and sashayed to the corner where Bo had sequestered himself, all the better to gaze at the object of his affection without interference—if he could find him.

"Why are you being so antisocial? Come drink with us. The guys need your opinions."

He pushed away from the wall. "Sorry, darlin', I didn't mean to be an outsider. After that spread Jeremy provided, I'm just full as a tick and needed a little lay-by."

She snorted. "Where do you get those expressions?"

"Deep in the heart of Georgia, darlin', you know that."

"California's gain, dear, our gain." She took his arm and pulled him to the largest group of arguers, made up of her husband, Randy—a name which suited him; Ezra Hamilton, the deacon of the local born-again church and mighty proud to be it; his wife, Marybeth, maybe not quite as reborn as Ezra; and Fernando Puente, owner of one of the largest wineries in the Paso Robles area—and don't you forget it.

Randy stuck out an arm and gathered Bo in closer. "Here's the man. You gotta help us out here, Bo. Ezra and Ferdinand"—whom Randy insisted on calling Fernando—"has been saying that Ottersen's bound to win top prizes for central coast wines this year. Hell, he's aced half the contracts with Napa since he opened." His words sounded slightly slurred. For a vintner, he couldn't hold his alcohol, but at the same time, Ottersen made people so mad they could chew barbed wire and spit out a fence, so drinking too much went with the territory.

Bo smiled tightly. "I know no more than any of y'all and have just as much to lose. Sorry." That wasn't entirely true, since Bo's growing methods separated him from the pack somewhat, but still. Ottersen threatened them all. Especially Jeremy Aames, it seemed.

Bo took a quick glance around, trying to spot Jeremy. Since he had two or three inches of height on even the tallest guys in the room, it gave him a decent vantage point, but no luck.

Fernando sneered, and his dark eyes snapped. "Ottersen wouldn't win any prizes if Lucky was still in business."

Two of the women shook their heads sadly. "Such a terrible thing, the fire."

A devastating fire in the winery and fields of Lucky Larrabe had driven the popular vintner from business six months before.

Ezra said stiffly, "I notice Ottersen is talking to strangers. He must be getting the message that none of the other vintners like him."

Fernando nodded. "I wonder who those men are? This event is only supposed to be for our association of growers."

Genevieve said, "Yes, but we can invite guests. I assume he invited them."

Bo noticed movement near the far wall, glanced up, and had to control the slam of his heart as Jeremy Aames walked out of the kitchen with that easy grin of his, talking to the young guy who seemed to be his assistant.

Marybeth followed Bo's eyes. "Not sure what Jeremy has to smile about. Hell, Ottersen's taking the biggest toll on his profits."

Bo's lips turned up on their own. "Jeremy always smiles."

A waiter hurried out of the kitchen to grab Jeremy's arm, and he rushed back through the door with the assistant in tow.

Ezra raised an eyebrow. "All those gay boys smile a lot."

Bo glared at him, but not much got in the way of Ezra's righteousness.

Marybeth slapped his shoulder. "Ezra, when will you learn to be PC?"

"Never. PC's for Democrats." He raised his wine glass and drained it.

Bo wouldn't have minded giving Ezra a fist to the jaw but had no right. He'd never declared himself out of the closet, partly because it might really give his mother the heart attack she was always claiming was imminent, to say nothing of the collapse of the social standing of his sisters. He kept saying when he had a relationship, he'd come out, and the devil take the hindmost, but not coming out meant it was doubly hard to meet someone, since gay men assumed he was straight. It also meant women still thought he was fair game—with a lot of encouragement from his mother. Vicious damned cycle for a twenty-six-year-old man, but where he came from, gay men were still "confirmed bachelors." California might vote blue, but under his family's influence, his blood couldn't even get from red to a tinge of purple.

Ezra glared at the spot where Jeremy had disappeared into the kitchen. "Ottersen'll wipe that smile off Aames's face soon. Apparently he's already reverse-engineered Aames's latest vintage and snapped up a big contract that cute-face Jeremy was counting on from Shields brokerage."

Bo frowned. "He just unveiled that blend. No one could have reverse-engineered it that fast."

"Yeah, well, those are the facts." Ezra's smile was nasty.

Bo's hand clenched into a fist, but Gen squeezed his arm, a little too close to her chest. "How's the family, dear?"

He dragged his eyes away from Ezra before he laid him out. Ezra was an asshole, but he had a lot of power among the other vintners. No use getting Jeremy in more hot water. He forced a smile. "Well, thank you." He gently extricated his limb on the excuse of checking his watch and sipping his wine.

"Your mother's health?"

He wanted to say way *Better than she thinks it is*, but that wasn't fair. "Mama's doing well, thank you, Gen. She's considering a trip to somewhere cool for the hottest part of the summer this year. Our central coast heat does take its toll."

"New England? Maine's lovely in the summer. That would give her a number of months to plan."

She gazed at him with far more interest than a married woman ought, but sauce for the goose and all that. Randy was a terrible philanderer.

"I'll pass along your recommendation, thank you." He stepped back. "Excuse me, please. I'm seeking a rest stop."

She flashed teeth. "You're so cute."

Ezra grabbed Bo's arm. "You're still heading the dry farming committee, right?"

"Yes." He glanced at Ezra's firm grip, but the man didn't take hints easily.

"You've got to keep Ottersen and his cronies off that committee. He doesn't need any additional advantages."

Bo shrugged himself free. "I can't do that, Ezra. If he applies for an open seat and is voted in, I can't keep him off." Bo smiled. "But we don't happen to have an opening at the present moment in time."

"Excellent." Ezra smiled big and nasty.

"Excuse me." Bo walked away from the group and threaded his way through the crowd, trying to look focused on his goal since he knew most everyone in the room and they all had something to say to him. The pats and fist bumps followed him, but he kept smiling graciously and staring towards the men's room like he was in danger of bladder failure.

The organ under stress at that moment was higher in Bo's chest. *One look. A smile.* He walked down the hall toward the kitchen and peeked in the door. Controlled chaos reigned inside. Cooks and waiters loaded hors d'oeuvre plates to carry out to the picky guests. Jeremy Aames had only come to the valley a little over a year before, when he bought one of the smaller wineries from a retiring old-timer. Jeremy had made a name for himself not only by enhancing some of the winery's blends right away, but by adding a very creative kitchen that gave his tasting room enough cachet to compete with full-scale restaurants, at least for lunch.

Since Bo's winery was the only other in the area that served serious food, people had assumed they'd be vicious competitors, but so far Jeremy had coexisted with Bo quite comfortably, recommending Bo's Marchand Wines as liberally as he promoted his own brand. As a result, Bo returned the favor, and they sent business back and forth so patrons never got bored.

Bo glanced around the kitchen. Jeremy's cute young assistant directed waiters around like a five-foot-six-inch general, but Bo didn't see Jeremy. Bo sometimes wondered if the assistant was more than an assistant. That thought made his stomach clench. He stretched his neck to the side so he could peer into the corner of the kitchen. *Come on, just one glance.*

"Bo, is there something you need?"

The lilting voice came from behind Bo, and he froze and then turned slowly. "Uh, hello there." *Dear god of wine, what a beauty.* Jeremy would have been handsome no matter what—his beautiful bone structure and wide blue eyes assured that. But for some reason Bo had never heard, Jeremy had chosen to grow his dark blond hair past his shoulders, where it hung in a thick curtain that made you want to sink your fingers into it. Like Brad Pitt in *Legends of the Fall*, the hair took a great-looking man and made him a myth.

A grin spread itself across Jeremy's sweet face like maple syrup on pancakes. "Hi." For an instant they just stared at each other, Jeremy looking up since, like most people, he was a few inches shorter than Bo. Then Jeremy took a breath. "Can I be of help?"

Don't sound like an idiot. "Just spying. Looking for insider tips." Bo was told that his dimples were an unfair advantage, so he used them.

Jeremy laughed, just a *ha* or two. "I'm sure there's not one thing I can teach you, Mr. Marchand."

Oh, he's so wrong.

Jeremy's pretty face sobered. "But I sure understand. These days we all need every competitive advantage we can get."

Bo frowned. "Ottersen's takin' a toll on your business, I hear."

Jeremy nodded. "He's copied every vintage and bought up vineyards near me so his blends taste as much like mine as possible. I figure I'm his next target."

"Damn the bastard!"

Jeremy glanced up, startled. "Thank you." He shook his head. "I'm told he's installing a kitchen."

Bo nodded. "I've heard tell."

Jeremy smiled, but it still looked sad. "I'm glad your dry farming protects you. He can't duplicate your unique flavors."

"At least not this year." Bo stared at the polished concrete floors. "Maybe we can do something to stop him, or at least slow him down."

"Really?" Jeremy looked skeptical. "He seems to have an awful big bankroll or backers with deep pockets."

"Yes, but if we put our heads together, we just might find a plan." The more the idea wormed into Bo's brain, the better it sounded.

"Uh, are you talking about all the other owners, or, uh, just you and me?" He glanced up quickly, then away.

"Trying to get this whole herd of cats movin' in the same direction would be harder than pickin' fleas off a sheepdog. I think a smaller ship can turn more quickly, if you'll forgive the mixing of metaphors."

Jeremy stared at Bo for a long count, then started to laugh. "When would you like to plan trying to get this canine in the water?"

"I could give you my phone number. We could text."

Jeremy held out his hand and wiggled his fingers. "Gimme."

Bo tried to not look as excited as he was as he handed over his phone and watched Jeremy type in numbers. Jeremy handed it back. "Text me yours, okay?"

Since no words were coming out of his dry throat, Bo nodded as he took the phone and glanced at the number.

A crash sounded from inside the kitchen. Jeremy looked over his shoulder, wide-eyed. "I better get in there before they burn down the place." He glanced back at Bo. "Can't wait to hear from you." He cleared his throat. "Uh, about your ideas for countering Ottersen."

Bo watched him disappear through the swinging door.

Oh my heavens, did I just find a way to spend time with Jeremy Aames?

TARA LAIN writes the Beautiful Boys of Romance in LGBT romance novels that star her unique, charismatic heroes. Her best-selling novels have garnered awards for Best Series, Best Contemporary Romance, Best Erotic Romance, Best Ménage, Best LGBT Romance, and Best Gay Characters, and more. Readers often call her books "sweet," even with all that hawt sex, because Tara believes in love and her books deliver on happily-ever-after. In her other job, Tara owns an advertising and public relations firm. Her love of creating book titles comes from years of manifesting ad headlines for everything from analytical instruments to semiconductors. She does workshops on both author promotion and writing craft. She lives with her soulmate husband and her soulmate dog (who's a little jealous of all those cat pictures Tara posts on FB) in Laguna Niguel, California, near the seaside towns where she sets a lot of her books. Passionate about diversity, justice, and new experiences, Tara says that on her tombstone, it will say "Yes!"

Email: tara@taralain.com

Website: www.taralain.com

Blog: www.taralain.com/blog

Goodreads: www.goodreads.com/author/show/4541791.Tara_Lain

Pinterest: pinterest.com/taralain

Twitter: @taralain

Facebook: www.facebook.com/taralain

Barnes & Noble: www.barnesandnoble.com/s/Tara-Lain?keyword=Tara+Lain&store=book

Amazon: www.amazon.com/Tara-Lain/e/B004U1W5QC/ref=ntt_athr_dp_pel_1

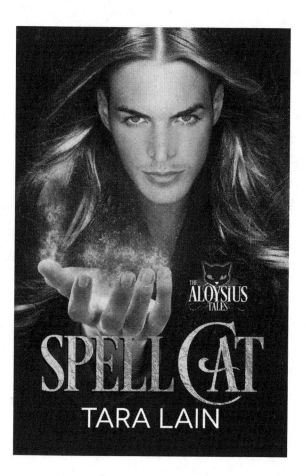

THE
ALOYSIUS
TALES

SPELL CAT

TARA LAIN

An Aloysius Tale

When Killian Barth, history professor, meets Blaine Genneau, quantum physicist, they ignite their own big bang. But Killian can't pursue a physics professor—or a human. As the most powerful male witch in ten generations, Killian must bolster his dying race by reproducing—despite the fact that he's gay.

Even a fling with Blaine is out of the question, because Killian has been told sex with humans drains his power. But if that's true, why can young human Jimmy Janx dissolve spoons with the power of his mind? If Killian can sort through the lies he's been fed, he'll still face his biggest obstacle—convincing rational scientist Blaine to believe in magic.

With his ancient and powerful cat familiar, Aloysius, on his shoulder, Killian brings the lightning against deceit and greed to save Blaine from danger and prove love is the greatest power of them all.

www. dreamspinnerpress.com

DREAMSPUN DESIRES

Tara Lain

TAYLOR MAID

He'll marry the maid to get $50 million but a secret could queer the deal.

He'll marry the maid to get $50 million but a secret could queer the deal.

Taylor Fitzgerald needs a last-minute bride.

On the eve of his twenty-fifth birthday, the billionaire's son discovers that despite being gay, he must marry a woman before midnight or lose a fifty-million-dollar inheritance. So he hightails it to Las Vegas… where he meets the beautiful maid Ally May.

There's just one rather significant problem: Ally is actually Alessandro Macias, son of a tough Brazilian hotel magnate. But if Ally keeps pretending to be a girl for a little while longer, is there a chance they might discover this marriage is tailor-made?

www. dreamspinnerpress.com

TARA LAIN
RETURN
OF THE *Chauffeur's* SON

Luca McGrath may be returning to Napa Valley, California, as a promising chef with dreams of starting his own restaurant and winery, but his heart still lives with the bad-boy son of a billionaire, James Armstrong. Luca spent his childhood playing games with the golden boy of California society, so blinded by James he barely noticed the dark, quiet lure of his conservative older brother, Dylan Armstrong.

But now Luca's home, and his own powers of attraction are enough to make James question his dedicated heterosexuality and his promised marriage to a wealthy and powerful businesswoman. The obvious attraction between Luca and James spurs Dylan into action—but he's fighting a huge secret. While Luca dreamed of James, Dylan dreamed of Luca. When Luca gets caught in the struggle between the brothers and gets accused of culinary espionage he's ready to chuck the fairy tale—unable to even imagine Dylan's power to make his dreams come true.

www. dreamspinnerpress.com

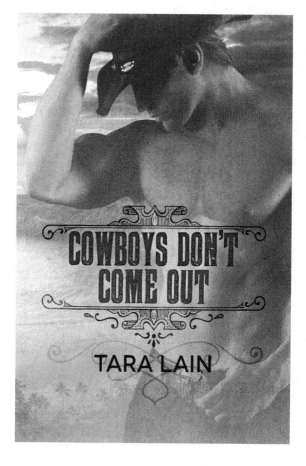

COWBOYS DON'T COME OUT

TARA LAIN

The First Cowboys Don't Story

Rand McIntyre settles for good enough. He loves his small California ranch, raising horses, and teaching riding to the kids he adores—but having kids of his own and someone to love means coming out, and that would jeopardize everything he's built. Then, despite his terror of flying, he goes on a holiday to Hana, Hawaii, with his parents and meets the dark and mysterious Kai Kealoha, a genuine Hawaiian cowboy. Rand takes to Kai's kid brother and sister as much as he drools over Kai, but the guy sports more prickles than a horned toad and more secrets than the exotic land he comes from.

Kai's earned his privacy and lives to protect his "kids." He ought to stay away from the big, handsome cowboy for everyone's sake—but since the guy's just a haole on a short vacation, how much damage can he do? When all of Kai's worst fears and Rand's darkest nightmares come true at once, there's not much chance for two cowboys who can't—or won't—come out.

www. dreamspinnerpress.com

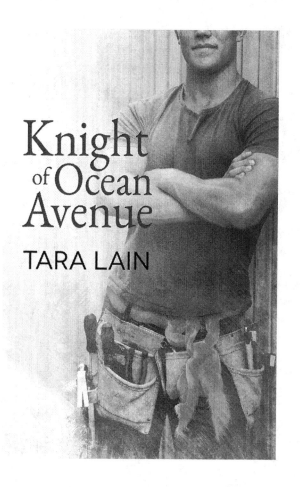

Knight
of Ocean
Avenue

TARA LAIN

Love in Laguna Novel

How can you be twenty-five and not know you're gay? Billy Ballew runs from that question. A high school dropout, barely able to read until he taught himself, Billy's life is driven by his need to help support his parents as a construction worker, put his sisters through college, coach his Little League team, and not think about being a three-time loser in the engagement department. Being terrified of taking tests keeps Billy from getting the contractor's license he so desires, and fear of his mother's judgment blinds Billy to what could make him truly happy.

Then, in preparation for his sister's big wedding, Billy meets Shaz—Chase Phillips—a rising-star celebrity stylist who defines the word gay. To Shaz, Billy embodies everything he's ever wanted—stalwart, honest, brave—but even if Billy turns out to be gay, he could never endure the censure he'd get for being with a queen like Shaz. How can two men with so little in common find a way to be together? Can the Stylist of the Year end up with the Knight of Ocean Avenue?

www. dreamspinnerpress.com

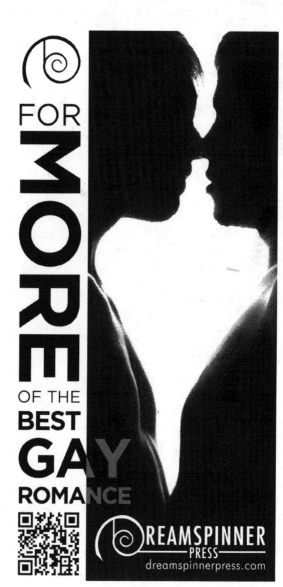